THE FIRE OF WAR

"Lay it down close to us," the lieutenant radioed from the ground. "The Cong are practically on top of us."

"We might scorch you," Steve Randall called back from the cockpit of his F-4.

"Never mind!" The reply was emphatic.

It was going to be close. Steve had to ride the fine line on this one. Cold rivulets of perspiration ran down his legs. His hands grew sweaty in his gloves. He knew the consequences. So did the young lieutenant on the ground. So did his grunts. They were watching him now—waiting for their deliverance from the sky—or their annihilation.

He lined up on the trees. One hundred meters back? Seventy-five? Fifty? He had to judge for the spread. Napalm was unpredictable. How close?

HELLBOUND

By Richard Parque

ZEBRA BOOKS
KENSINGTON PUBLISHING CORP.

ZEBRA BOOKS

are published by

Kensington Publishing Corp.
475 Park Avenue South
New York, NY 10016

First printing: May 1985

Printed in the United States of America

*For my sweet Vietnam, Vo Thi Lan, my wife, whose
faith and inspiration have made this work possible.*

Part I

The Child Warrior

"Again, I must do it again."

Chapter One

*1 January 1968. Binh Hoa Province, Republic of
South Vietnam.*

Long, pencil streams of sunlight shot through the
jungle canopy washing the foliage below in a
cathedral-like glow. Dust particles danced in the hot,
filtered rays, and the air was fetid with the smell of
rot. Nothing stirred. Not a breath of fresh air. The
oppressive Southeast Asia jungle.

The young girl, Nguyen Thi Xinh, cradled the
Chinese 7.62-mm in her arms and sighted on a point
just beyond the clearing where the Americans had to
cross. She smoothed her long, raven black hair
straight down her back and tied it out of the way with
a scarf, peasant fashion. Her small hand slid down
along the forward-curving magazine then retreated
to the wooden pistol grip just behind the trigger
assembly. Her index finger came forward and gently
slipped around the trigger. She felt at home with the
Type 56-1 assault rifle. She liked the feel of it, the
fold-up metal stock, the comfortable forearm and

grip, its dependable operation and fast, accurate action. The nuts, bolts and springs were faithful old friends and she took pride in tearing down the rifle and putting it back together in less than three minutes. It was a good weapon and she felt secure with it now, as she waited for the first soldier to show himself.

The pretty Vietcong guerrilla leader squinted through the cover, across the clearing to the stream where long gray shadows were already streaking its banks. She could easily have been mistaken for a Saigonese school girl if it hadn't been for the soldierly discipline of her actions and for the strong will conveyed in her steady gaze. For one so young, she was very poised. But then, her job required unusual qualifications, and the VC and the jungle were demanding taskmasters that had matured her beyond her years.

The sun began to settle behind the tree line.

"Nguoi My se den lien bay gio." The Americans will be coming soon, she whispered to herself.

They always came at the same time in the evening, big and clumsy in their bulky gear, sounding like a herd of water buffalo. She pushed her jade bracelet high up on her forearm to prevent it from clinking against the rifle's metal parts.

Xinh's small, firm body was comfortable on the hard ground. Months in the jungle had enured her to physical hardship. Her bouts with malaria were decreasing, and she could go for hours lying in the same position without discomfort. Her soft hand again moved across the 7.62's magazine and she felt comforted. Only lingering questions made her nervous, although sometimes she thought her heart would beat so loudly it would give away her position. She could hear it now, hammering away as if it were going to leap from her chest.

The tropical air had the taste of dead plants and stagnant water, but she breathed deeply anyway, trying to still her screaming nerves. The odor of decay was everywhere.

Xinh once more analyzed the trap she had set for the Americans. She had remembered to keep it uncomplicated just as they had taught her. "Make the trap easy to fall into," Tang had said. "It is when you try to be too sophisticated that you run into trouble." Her training had been thorough.

Let the point soldiers cross the stream and move well into the clearing. Hit hard and fast, split the patrol, and destroy communications. Cut off the Americans before they can retreat to the stream bank for cover. Methodically encircle the patrol, pick the men off one by one. Kill everyone and withdraw before the fast-reacting howitzers and deadly AH-1 Cobras can find us. A swift victory.

Xinh adjusted her bracelet again. For a moment she fondly caressed the delicate blue-green stone that softly contrasted with her bronze skin—darker than that of most Vietnamese women, closer in tone to a Cambodian's. She remembered the day Duc had given her the bracelet as an engagement gift. Better days. Then she had been happy and unconfused, and life had had purpose and meaning. Then there were no Americans and Steve didn't exist.

11

The shadows had lengthened across the clearing and reached beyond to the tree line. Two of her guerrillas exchanged positions and crawled deeper into the undergrowth. Xinh looked to her left and saw Tan vigorously sniffing the air. She smiled.

"Why do you do that?" she asked him.

"I can smell the Americans when they get near," he replied.

"How so?"

"They smell pretty, like women. I can smell one at three hundred meters—sometimes farther."

"Mmmmmmmmmm," Xinh nodded. The sweet odor of after-shave lotion and perfumed toilet soap had alerted her many times to the presence of GIs. They all smelled like Steve. She sniffed hard at the air but all she got back was the heavy stench of hot, stale jungle. Still, the heat was beginning to let up as cool air drifted down from the Cambodian hill country.

An American soldier broke from the trees and walked to the streambank. The point man was tall and heavyset, with a thick neck. Xinh watched carefully as he hesitated, his eyes busily searching the edges of the clearing. Suddenly, he pointed his rifle at Xinh and she froze solid. He dropped the M-16 to the ready position, jogged through the stream, and then climbed the slope into the clearing. Xinh noticed that he wore the standard olive-drab combat dress and flak jacket. Slung around his body was a belt of 7.62-mm ammunition for his squad's M-60 light machine gun. His web gear contained two canteens of water plus other items familiar to her from picking over dead bodies: first-aid packet, 5.56-mm ammo

12

clips, grenades, etc. A bottle of insect repellent was strapped to his camouflaged helmet. He carried a pack.

"Crazy Americans," she said to herself, "burdened down with all that equipment. So immobile and slow to react."

The next soldier emerged from the wet undergrowth and worked his way through the stream, rifle also at the ready. He followed the point man into the open.

After a few dozen meters the rest of the patrol began filtering out of the tree line and crossing the stream. Xinh waited anxiously for the lieutenant to appear. The point was getting dangerously close, and she knew that she would have to take the soldier soon if the lieutenant didn't show.

Suddenly Xinh's body jerked involuntarily. The sight of the lieutenant had shot an extra load of adrenaline into her veins. She clenched her teeth and her eyes narrowed as she raised the rear sight of the 56 until it formed a crucifix on the man's chest. Again, she must do it again. Oh, Steve, I'm sorry. She pressed the stock to her cheek, squeezed the trigger, and the hot steel came alive, trembling and pounding against her shoulder. She clutched the pistol grip with all her strength, forcing the bucking stock farther into her shoulder. Her left hand steadied the piece on the crumpling target. The assault rifle roared again and kicked in her hands like a writhing snake. The gun's explosions banged at her brain, but she heard its determined barking only as a background to the cacophony of war sounds rising around her. Shouts and cries floated above the steady stuttering of automatic weapons and shots. A pall of blue-gray smoke was quickly filling the clearing. Xinh continued pouring rounds into the jerking man on the ground. A few U.S. troops began returning fire. A bullet smashed into a tree. She shifted the sights to a tall corporal and watched the heavy slugs tear into the radio on his back, ripping chunks of green metal away from the frame.

She slammed another clip into the assault rifle. Rounds tore up the earth, stitching a line of flying dirt across the falling soldiers. Through the smoke she could still see the stream, but she could no longer hear its quiet poetry. The water was crimson.

She shouted an order and a black pajamaed man rose and resting on one knee, lifted a Russian RPG launcher to his shoulder. Xinh shoved a load into the weapon. She tapped the man on the head and pointed to four soldiers at the rear of the column. They had gotten up and were running forward while the other men laid down a base of fire.

The guerrilla took careful aim. *Whoosh*! The self-propelled projectile left the steel tube and spun through the air on a flat trajectory.

Some of the Americans saw the RPG arch out of the trees and shouted a warning. But it was too late for the young Pfc. The heavy rocket grenade caught him, on the dead run, in the center of his chest, and imbedded itself up to its fins. It didn't explode.

Xinh cursed. "It did not detonate." She picked up another round. "Try again, comrade." She rammed the rocket home.

The launcher spit fire and the second projectile sped through the air. *Ka-Whoom*! One American was lifted from the ground and smashed against a tree. Another was decapitated by a hot shard. Two more sprawled on the ground, their limbs twisted grotesquely. Dirt and debris rained down through the thick smoke.

"*Tot qua*!" "Good shooting!" the guerrillas around her shouted.

Xinh singled out some men and sent them around the flanks of the U.S. troops to cut off any retreat. "Hurry, my friends. Take the RPG with you." She smacked the man kneeling beside her. "Go, slow-witted one."

An M-60 began coughing from the streambed. Xinh squinted, trying to locate the machine gun through the drifting blue smoke. "Where is it?"

"Near the bamboo, comrade," someone said.

"Right or left?"

"Right."

"Concentrate your fire in there. Shut it up."

But the steady stuttering wouldn't be stilled. Bullets raked the trees. The guerrillas wriggled into the dirt.

"He is too low. We can't get a line of fire into him. He is down between the rocks in the bank."

"Keep firing at him," Xinh said. "Keep him worried." She crawled up to the edge of the clearing, took a bearing on the gun, and slid like a knife into the tall grass, leaving her rifle on the ground.

She crawled fast, legs spread wide like a frog, pushing hard against the ground. Her hands grabbed

15

tufts of grass which she pulled as she simultaneously pushed with her feet.

In a short time she came to the dead point man. She stripped two grenades from his web gear and crawled around him in line with the pounding of the machine gun.

If they see me I am dead. There is no way I can get out of the clearing alive. She changed directions and came around ninety degrees, thirty yards below the gun. She rolled down the bank into the water.

Hugging the bank, she rounded a bend in the stream. The gunner and his rifleman were concentrating on the tree line in front of them. They didn't see Xinh crawling up on their flank.

A burst of fire splattered into the bank, inches above her head. Fifty yards away, a GI was standing in the open, a bucking M-16 in his hands. His lips were drawn back over his teeth.

Suddenly three puffs of smoke rose from his chest, and his body jerked violently. His fingers spread stiffly, dropping the M-16 to the ground as he pitched backward, dead.

Xinh looked over at the machine gunners.

"Jeez! How did she get down here! Get her Kutcher!"

The rifleman was spinning around at the same time Xinh flipped the grenade.

"Oh, no!" Kutcher fired blindly.

She threw herself back around the corner and pressed hard into a shallow depression in the bank.

"You bitch!"

Whoom! The grenade blew the M-60 ten feet into

the air. The two soldiers flopped around on the stones, moaning. A red tributary ran from them into the stream.

Xinh didn't run. She clung to the bank, waiting. When the Americans came for the wounded, she let them collect the bleeding men. Then she pitched the last grenade.

She ran for all she was worth, sprinting hard down the streambed. She heard the second explosion, followed by more screams of pain. A few shots were fired at her just as she disappeared into the tree line.

"Xinh! Xinh! Xinh!" The guerrillas shouted, applauding her fearless attack. "*Tot! Tot! Tot!*"

As Xinh took up her position again, a young girl handed her the Chinese 56, admiration in her eyes. "I kept it for you while you bravely attacked the American dogs."

Xinh smiled affectionately. "Thank you, sister Cuc."

The girl stretched out next to Xinh and opened up with her AK-47. A thump gunner started forward. A long burst drove him back.

"There are many dead American bodies," the girl said. "We have accomplished our mission and Comrade Tang will be pleased."

The 56 played a tune with the AK.

"Yes, Cuc, Comrade Tang will be well pleased." Xinh's full lips turned down in a sneer at the mention of the name.

"Should we not withdraw now, sister Xinh? We have annihilated the Americans. Is it not best to go before reinforcements arrive?"

"We will kill them all." Xinh's eyes were cold and blank.

"Yes, comrade."

The thump gunner was coming forward again.

"Stupid boy," Cuc said, leveling the AK on him. "Watch this."

Just as the soldier raised the weapon to his shoulder, a single bullet hit him in the face. Xinh turned away in disgust. Cuc put another round in the same place.

There was little fire coming from the American patrol. Xinh raised up and looked across the clearing. Many bodies lay, twisted and facedown, in the stream and on the banks. She could hear AKs stinging the rear of the patrol. No one would escape.

"How many casualties do we have?" she shouted to her people.

"No casualties!" someone replied.

She nodded. We were fortunate today. Yes, Tang will be pleased. But does it matter anymore? She looked for another target. There were no more.

The poisonous effluvium of the hot, rotting jungle mingled with the thick spreading fumes of exploded ammunition. Cries of the dying and wounded hung in the air. Xinh stood on shaky, cramped legs, her blood still wildly racing. She felt sick to her stomach as she studied the devastating effects of her ambush. She shook off an impulse to vomit and waved her people into the clearing. The bodies were stripped of grenades, weapons, and ammo. Those not yet dead were killed.

It was finished. The VC were already beginning to filter back into the bush. But she hesitated for a few seconds, staring at the torn, limp forms sprawled in the rain-drenched grass around her. *Whatever happened to the rag doll grandmother gave me? The one with stuffing coming out and a missing arm.*

"Forgive me, Steve," she said quietly to herself. Then she melted away with her guerrillas, as silently as she had arrived.

Chapter Two

Xinh carefully opened the heavy security-file drawer. Her well-manicured red nails quickly traveled over the folders, slowed at the Rs, then abruptly stopped at the name of Randall, Captain Stephen A. She pulled the folder, gently closed the drawer, and quietly walked back to her desk and sat down.

The office was empty except for another Vietnamese girl at the far end of the room, eating her lunch of rice and salty pork. Behind the girl was a large window through which Xinh could see two U.S. F-4 Phantoms accelerating down the runway, loaded with napalm and rockets. She watched the two ships flash by, wing tip to wing tip, engines wide open. Suddenly they pulled up, in unison, noses pointed high into the Indochina sky. Poetry in motion. They wheeled around to the west, toward the Delta, long trails of black smoke tracing their turn, the thunder from their engines still vibrating through the building. Breathe deeply, oh, mighty Manchu. Xinh watched the jets fade away into gray specks, then disappear from view.

She hadn't caught the tail numbers but she had noticed the double green stripes on the tail fins, indicating that the aircraft were from his squadron. Her eyes fell to the folder again. For a long time she was silent. How her world had changed. Everything had been so simple. The Communists, the Vietcong, the Americans. All neatly pigeonholed in the recesses of her mind. She could feel something vital leaking out of her . . . slowly . . . almost imperceptibly. Her full lips tightened and she clenched her teeth.

There were no answers. Only more questions. She soothed her temples with her fingertips, eyes riveted on the words—CLASSIFIED INFORMATION—SECRET—stamped in bold red letters across the top of the cover. The longer she stared at the letters the more blurred they became until all she could see was a broad, undulating red line fading in and out of focus. She rubbed her temples again, attempting to push the memory from her mind, but the images persisted. In the distance she could hear the shots again. They grew in intensity. Then the cries. The red letters on the folder became a blood-choked stream. The clearing, filled with smoke . . . the smells . . . falling bodies. The shots grew louder. Deep-throated automatic weapons chattered. All building to a crescendo. . . . She started to scream.

"Are you all right, Xinh," the girl asked in Vietnamese, using wooden chopsticks to push another lump of rice and salty pork into her open mouth. Some rice dropped onto a folder.

Xinh wiped the rice away and slipped the file into her top drawer. "Oh, yes. No trouble. Just a small headache."

"I thought I heard you cry out. Are you sure you're all right?" the girl asked again.

22

"Yes, yes. I'm fine. Nothing to trouble yourself about." Their eyes met in unspoken understanding.

"Please, have a bowl of rice with me," the girl said, anxious to help Xinh.

Xinh got up from her chair and walked over to the girl's desk. She was filling an extra bowl with steaming rice from a small pot. She unplugged the electric rice cooker and handed Xinh a pair of chopsticks, adding slices of pork and a helping of bean sprouts to the white mound.

"*Nuoc mam?*" she asked Xinh, offering her a saucer of the fish sauce.

"Thank you little sister," Xinh said to the younger girl in polite Vietnamese. "You are very kind to me."

Xinh picked up a piece of the salty pork and some bean sprouts with her chopsticks, dipped the morsel into the *nuoc mam*, and scooped it into her mouth with a ball of rice. The girl poured her a cup of green tea. The hot food felt good in her belly, warming her insides. She unclenched her hands.

"I need to talk to someone," Xinh said.

"Yes," replied the girl, pushing more rice into her mouth and looking straight at Xinh.

Xinh brushed her long hair off her shoulders and then daintily sipped the bitter green tea from the handleless cup. "You know don't you?"

The two Vietcong girls looked steadily into each other's eyes. Neither spoke. Both squatted on the floor, two farm girls taking a break in the rice fields, their pretty *ao dais* spread around their feet.

"Well, don't you?" Xinh repeated, a bite in her voice.

"Yes, I know, elder sister."

"I'm a tormented woman."

"And your duties? What will become of your duties?" the girl asked.

"I don't know, I just don't know. I have bad dreams now. It has never bothered me before."

"They kill us . . . destroy our way of life. If we don't stop them? . . ." The girl's voice trailed off, unwilling to pursue the alternative. "You have been fighting many years, sacrificing much for what we have believed in." She was angry. Her voice rose. "We have no choice but to keep fighting them for however long it takes. We have no choice," she repeated, almost shouting. "You're a good soldier, Xinh. You have come a long way and the Communists have important plans for you. You will be placed in a high post in the new government when we win. Wait and see. You can't give all that up. We need you. You must continue to lead us."

Xinh's eyes had not left the girl and now, for the first time, she addressed her by name rather then as *em*, little sister, to express the gravity of what she was about to say.

"Thanh," she began, "you and I have been very close. We come from the same village. Our parents' parents played together under the tamarind trees as children beside the river Phu Cuong. I think of you as my own sister. I trust you with my very life and you have shown your concern and love for me beyond what I deserve. You have followed me into battle with much courage and loyally obeyed my orders."

"Yes," said Thanh. "I have. I have great confidence in you."

"But I am no longer the person I was when we both

24

began, full of hope in a new life for our people. We are very young, Thanh. There is much that we don't understand. We follow orders. We do what we're told without really thinking."

Xinh reached out and wiped away the tears from Thanh's face with her fingertips.

"Yes, we are very young. There is much for us to learn," Thanh said. "But Vietnam is all we know. What else can we do?"

"I wish I knew, Thanh. I wish I knew."

Xinh got up and went to the window. Her arms hung at her sides, tiny fists clenching and unclenching, expressing her anxiety. She stood, gazing out over the runways of the sprawling Binh Hoa Air Base. Waves of heat rose from the tarmac, distorting the images of the F-4s and F-5s parked in their revetments and along the apron. They appeared to be ghostlike birds shrouded in costumes of green, brown, and silver. Instruments of war, thought Xinh, were all alike. Regardless of their shape, size, or color, they all had the same purpose—to cause suffering.

"We've watched our people suffer. First from government exploitation, demands, and regulations. Then came the troops. Vietnamese like us from the south, from our own province. Remember when it first began, Thanh?"

"I remember." She was eating again.

"Threatening, warning. Enforcing silly rules and laws. ID cards, curfew, rice rations. Accusations. Dragging our friends and families off for questioning. Being beaten. Tortured. Some taken to prison. Then came the Americans with their napalm and artillery. Innocents dying. The Ben Cat massacre. Hamlets being torched indiscriminately. Free-fire zones. Our families uprooted from their centuries old ancestral ground to be relocated in 'secured' areas where nothing grew and they were 'protected' by barbed wire but not allowed beyond the perimeter. Their 'protectors,' in machine-gun towers, were always a reminder of their 'freedom.'"

Her eyes narrowed and her small nostrils flared slightly as she recalled the bitter memory of being raped in her own home by ARVN soldiers. She had been working in the fields with Duc, her mother and sisters. The troops had walked down the paddy dike and stopped in front of them. One of the soldiers had stepped out from the others, waded into the paddy, and dragged her out by the hair. "Vietcong," he said. "VC." She was taken to her home and lashed to a post. The house was searched and ransacked. She was questioned, accused, beaten, then brutally violated. She was only thirteen years old.

Xinh unclenched her fists, her body went limp, and she began shaking uncontrollably. Her little frame vibrated with deep convulsive sobs of shame and remorse as the memory poured from her soul. Oh, God, how she had hated them. How she wanted to kill them all. Becoming a Vietcong had been easy. Revenge had been sweet.

It was some time before Xinh calmed down. She returned to her desk and dried her tears. She sighed deeply and opened her top drawer, pulling out Captain Randall's file again. She knew what was in it. She had read it several times before: his special reconnaissance training with advanced avionics systems, the secret raids into Cambodia and Laos, secret messages to Washington verifying his double Mig kill, the "smart-bomb" incident, and all the rest.

She flipped open the cover and studied his picture. Blond hair, ruddy complexion, handsome, a wry smile on his lips—confident. She liked that. Confidence. He was quietly confident with not a trace of arrogance in him. He was gentle too—in a manly way—and not at all like Vietnamese men. In fact, she had had to get used to his affections. She hadn't been comfortable with so much attention, especially the tender kind he gave her. She hadn't known how to handle it.

She turned the page: PHYSICAL STATS. Height—5' 11", Weight—185 lbs., Hair—blond, Eyes—blue. . . . Mentally, she compared these with her own 5' 0", 98 lbs., black hair, black eyes. Identifying Marks—½" crescent scar on left cheek, birthmark on right buttock. . . . She smiled at that. She turned more pages, glancing through the material, stopping at the photos here and there.

She looked at her watch. The staff would soon be returning from lunch. Even though she had a secret clearance and her work as records' supervisor for the wing required frequent use of classified information, she still didn't want to arouse any unnecessary suspicion. Colonel Brooks was always on the alert for employees who pulled information without a "need to know." Brooks had a great deal of confidence in her and she didn't want to jeopardize his trust.

She replaced the folder in the steel file case and

27

inserted the heavy security bar, locking all the drawers. She walked back to her desk, put her work away, and tidied up. Then she walked over to Thanh and said, "Cover for me." The girl nodded.

Xinh glanced at her watch again and then headed for Operations.

Chapter Three

Steve gently pushed the stick forward and applied a little rudder with his left foot. The F-4 fell off into a wide turn.

"Rivet Fire, this is Scorpion leader on station with two Phantoms. Do you read?"

"Roger, Scorpion lead. Have you in sight. Boy are we glad to see you guys."

"Rivet Fire, Scorpion lead. What is your target?"

"VC in company strength along tree line three hundred meters north of river. Lay your napalm east to west."

"Uh, roger, Rivet Fire. Can you give us some smoke?"

"Negative. We're pinned down. Can you make one pass to line up?"

Steve hesitated for a few moments. Making a pass was dangerous but if he didn't line up he might burn his own people. He needed to know their exact position.

"How close are they, Rivet Fire?"

"I can smell their *nuoc mam*. If you don't get down here *now*, you're going to have to lay the jelly on top of us." The young lieutenant was trying to keep his voice calm, but Steve could detect signs of panic.

"O.K. We're rolling in."

Sweat-lined, hopeful faces turned up from fighting holes to watch Steve and his wingman pitch off. Some of the VC had already penetrated the lieutenant's perimeter and were threatening encirclement. He said a quiet prayer.

Steve flattened out about a hundred feet off the deck. He was hot, his wingman tucked in tight. "Tell me how far I pass to your front," he instructed the lieutenant.

"We're taking fire off to the left," the RO, John Diluca, shouted in the back seat. Steve turned his head in time to see the countryside light up like a Christmas tree. The muzzle flashes continued to erupt all along the tree line.

"What the hell do they have down there?" his wingman, Chuck Hensley, asked.

"Twenty millimeter, looks like," Steve answered.

The two F-4s screamed across the battle lines going supersonic. Having crossed, Steve lit his afterburner, pulled the stick into his seat, and the big jet leaped into the vertical. He rolled out over the top, afterburner still cooking, and caught a glimpse of Hensley pulling in behind him.

"Damn good wingman," he said to himself.

"Scorpion lead, Rivet Fire. Your pass was one hundred meters to our front."

"Roger, Rivet Fire."

"Lay it down close to us."

"We might scorch you a bit," Steve said apprehensively.

"Never mind!" The reply was emphatic.

The two aircraft commanders prepared for their bomb run. Steve gave Chuck final instructions.

"Follow me in at about a ten-second interval. I'll lay in the gas first. Check out the damage."

"Rog."

It was going to be close. He had to ride the fine line on this one, Steve thought to himself. Cold rivulets of perspiration ran down his legs. His hands grew sweaty in his gloves. He knew the consequences. So did the young lieutenant on the ground. So did his grunts. They were watching him now, waiting for their deliverance from the sky or their annihilation—at least the ones up front. He drew on all his resources, his training, his experience. Was it enough? Could he make it? Split-second timing. The line-up. Release. He rolled out.

Over he went, the horizon suddenly pitching into the vertical. Round and round went the brown-green earth below him. His g suit inflated, pressing the perspiration from his tissues. His body heaved and strained against the seat harness. Down he went, working the stick and pedals, bringing his weapon around to deliver the DuPont.

He began talking himself in. "Steady, Steve boy. You've got a lot of guys down there who are going to be awfully upset if you don't put your load in the right place." He lined up on the trees. One hundred meters back? Seventy-five? Fifty? He had to judge the

31

spread. The stuff was unpredictable. How close? Close enough to cook the VC but not his boys.

"You're looking good! Looking good!" the ground controller yelled to him. "Put it down—down close!"

At the last moment Steve let his reflexes take over. The tree line lit up again. He dropped his airspeed, brought the nose around. Just a bit longer . . . just a bit . . . just . . . *Now*! He punched off the napalm tanks, pushed the throttle forward and lit his **AB**, cranking around in a climbing turn. He rolled the ship ninety degrees and watched over his shoulder as the jellied gasoline exploded in a long, wide fiery path along the tree line, consuming everything in its way. It jumped and swayed, rolled and leaped. A bubbling two-thousand-degree Fahrenheit river of hell.

"Right on! Right on! That stopped them." The lieutenant was going crazy. Steve could see him in his mind's eye, jumping up and down, flushing like a toilet. "Can you put another right in the same spot, Scorpion?"

"Roger, Rivet Fire. Happy to oblige. Scorpion two on his way."

Steve watched Hensley pull into the tree line and unload. Another flash and roll of liquid fire, another swath of devastation.

Steve came over the top, and rolled out for his rocket run, following close behind Hensley. The VC were visible now, running to and fro, some on fire, blindly searching for deliverance from the destruction following them. Steve pressed in, armed his rockets. The panel light came on and he fired. The white plumes of smoke arched out, reaching for the Vietcong. The rockets ripped into the fleeing enemy, scattering bodies over the landscape.

Chuck was now high in position for his second run. He rolled over and in a few seconds was again accelerating along the tree line, firing his rockets and further decimating the Cong.

By the time Steve came in for his final run there wasn't much left. Bodies were scattered over several acres of rice paddy and the tree line was on fire. Weapons, equipment, and body parts were strewn all over—on paddy dikes, in trees. Dense black smoke roiled up from the burning napalm and drifted over the battleground in a pall of ruin and death. It seemed impossible that anyone could have survived the holocaust, but Steve could see dazed VC, some with patches of burning, sticky napalm clinging to their flesh, being helped away by their comrades.

"Damn war," he said, firing his remaining ordnance into the survivors. "Stupid war."

The lieutenant and his beleaguered infantrymen slowly rose from their fighting holes like men returning from the grave. They observed their vanquished foe spread over a quarter-mile of smoldering ruin, picked up their weapons, and gave a thankful wave to the disappearing Phantoms. "Damn war," said the lieutenant. "Stupid war."

He dropped his torn, bloody pants and scratched vigorously at his crotch. "Where to now?"

* * *

Steve increased his altitude and then throttled back. He looked back over his port wing to see Chuck slide into position. Large, billowy masses of cumulus were building to the east, dwarfing Hensley's ship, its brown and green battle camouflage a stark contrast to the cottony white purity of the clouds. The thunderheads, loaded with life-giving water, continued their journey west over the South China Sea. Everyday at this time the clouds made this trip to deposit their precious sustenance across the land, bringing forth new hope and continuing the cycle of life.

Steve closed his eyes. How different was the load he carried. He could almost smell the carnage. His job. What he was paid to do. His career. His place for the moment. He opened his eyes and skimmed the tops of the clouds, floating on the sea of air, free and dauntless. He was high technology, a cyborg. He was the dream and design of men. He was a messenger—a messenger heralding man's invincibility and progress, power and superiority. He brought the message that man was master of all. Vietnam . . . a proving ground. He pushed over through the clouds and watched the altimeter unwind. He checked the Phantom's gauges and glanced over at Hensley still flying tight formation on his left wing.

Below and behind him, the Mekong River slowly snaked through the flat, verdant delta on its journey to the sea. Steve could see the far-off hills that marked Cambodia and Laos through which the Mekong twisted. Millions depended on the Mekong. Without it there would be no rice . . . no life . . . no hope. It brought the possibility of tomorrow, but there would be no tomorrows for those he had left on its banks this morning.

"*Binh Hoa*, Scorpion one and two on final approach."

"Roger, Scorpion. You're cleared to land."

Chapter Four

Xinh was an enigma, shrouded in mystery. Steve knew nothing of her private life, her family, friends, personal activities. He knew she came from humble beginnings—somewhere in Binh Duong province—he seemed to recall. She never talked about her home, in fact he had no knowledge of where she lived or what she did when not with him.

From the very beginning she had insisted that they meet privately, never on the base or in public. At a friend's home she would cook him her good food and then they would take short walks along the river. Later in the evening she would serve him tea and ask him questions about America and his life there. She was intently interested in his descriptions of American customs, his family, and his boyhood days. She was particularly curious about American women, their upbringing, their dealings with men, and how they managed a home. And when Steve explained that in many American marriages the husband and wife shared household and family duties, and made decisions together, she reacted strongly and said that men had no business meddling in women's affairs and disrupting the natural order of things; women were much better prepared emotionally and in other ways to raise a family.

Working for the Americans, Xinh had weekends and holidays off. But he seldom saw her on these days. "I visit relatives," was Xinh's simple explanation. "Vietnamese family very close. Must honor relatives. Visit uncles, aunts, cousins, grandmother. Bring food and money, help on farm," she would say in her terse, broken English. She was strangely silent about her parents, brothers, and sisters. And then there were the evenings. Xinh frequently had to break an evening date because, as she put it, "Something happen, cannot meet you tonight, we talk tomorrow maybe."

There were times when she wouldn't show up for work at all, once for a week. "Very sick. I very sick. Cannot come work," she had explained. She sometimes looked exhausted when she returned from these absences.

But lately Steve had noticed that she was troubled . . . anxious. Something was bothering her. She would often cry unexpectedly, frightening him. He would take her into his arms and try to comfort her. But this seemed only to increase her anxiety. Her small body would tremble aginst his chest and she would mumble incoherently in Vietnamese. Her tears sometimes soaked through his uniform to his skin as she clung to him in despair, softly whimpering. Eventually Steve's patient talk, his reassurances, would slowly bring relief. He would stroke her silky hair, put his lips close to her ear and speak softly in simple Vietnamese: *"Any yeu em nhieu lam, cung oi.*

38

Em dem den cho anh nhieu hanh phuc." After a while she would turn up her tear-streaked face to him and a trace of a smile could be seen at the corners of her pretty lips. He continued to encourage her, nuzzling her hair with his nose and making funny faces at her which always made her laugh.

Xinh was Steve's fascination and great delight. Her lovely Asian face, her high cheekbones, petite nose, and full lips haunted him. He was enamored of her light copper-toned skin, smooth to his touch, and her jet black hair which shone like seal skin as it fell to her pretty bottom, flowing over her lovely *ao dai*— the pink one with the delicate bamboo print was his favorite. Her body exuded a natural, heady perfume that transformed him into a rutting bull elk.

But to Steve, Xinh's most striking feature was her eyes. He was hypnotized by their beauty. They were very wide and sensuous and, of course, framed by the Eastern lid. They tapered slightly and had a lovely slant downward, toward the middle of her small nose. She reminded him of an aristocratic house cat with her quiet independence, feline motions, and soft loveliness.

Xinh was a cornucopia of femininity and gentleness; a woman of keen perception and excellent judgment, generous and full of hot enthusiasm of youth. Yet she was shy. Nonetheless, now and then Steve noticed signs of cocky boldness and of strong leadership qualities in her. He wondered if there wasn't another Xinh somewhere beneath that beautiful exterior.

And he was right. Living inside the girl he knew was another Xinh, a cunning jungle killer. That part

39

of her had surfaced the night the Vietcong had entered Dau Tieng village and held a meeting with the young people. After listening to Tang's forceful and moving speech, she and Duc had felt that it was their duty to join the Communists. They had volunteered.

Xinh then disappeared into the jungles of Tay Ninh and Binh Duong to fight with the VC. She was given a Russian Kalashnikov AK-47, shown how to load and fire it, and told to kill Americans. She was only sixteen years old. She dedicated her life to liberating the south.

Though born of tough peasant stock and raised in the country, she was well educated and much more sophisticated than her comrades. Fox-smart, shy on the outside but tough and stubborn on the inside, she displayed the proud demeanor and defiant spirit of a seasoned, hard-core Vietcong guerrilla fighter.

From the moment Xinh joined the VC forces she demonstrated an unusual aptitude for jungle fighting and an outstanding loyalty to the Communists' cause. She aggressively pursued her duties and acquired a reputation for courage and for enduring hardship. Being an alert and intelligent girl, she learned fast and soon became an experienced jungle warfare tactician, skilled in the art of ambush, maneuver, and evasion. It wasn't long before her superiors noticed her unusual leadership qualities. She was singled out for special training and sent to Hanoi, where she spent four intensive months learning about support weapons, their use and deployment. Upon completing her training, she was sent back to Binh Duong and given her own weapons unit to command. She immediately distinguished herself by making several successful raids on ARVN posts and U.S. installations, and she succeeded in thoroughly terrorizing government-controlled civilian populaces. Her reputation quickly spread, earning her the epithet, "Dragon Girl of Binh Duong."

By the time she was eighteen years old, she had spent two long, hard years in the jungle redoubts of War Zone C, demonstrating her capability as a seasoned jungle fighter and an effective military leader. She was given full command of a VC artillery unit—to U.S. Intelligence Binh Duong 404—operating in the expansive piedmont area between Binh Hoa and the Cambodian frontier. The region, a notorious sanctuary for communist troops, was the scene of many large-scale U.S. and ARVN "search and destroy" operations, and it bordered on the main North Vietnamese Army and Vietcong supply depots in Cambodia.

Xinh's weapons inventory included: 122-mm and 107-mm rockets, 81-mm mortars manufactured in North Vietnam and a copy of the U.S. 81-mm M-1 mortar, Chinese 75-mm recoiless rifles, and exact copies of the obsolete U.S. M-20. The 75s were popular with her guerrillas because they combined fire power with light weight. Xinh's troops also carried Soviet supplied RPG-7 portable rocket launchers, the B-40, a shoulder-fired antitank weapon effective to five hundred meters. She had one hundred twelve men and twenty women under her command, a truly extraordinary achievement for such a young girl.

41

Xinh's favorite weapon was the individual heavy rocket, either the 122-mm or the lighter but just as devastating, 107-mm rocket. The 122-mm rocket weighed fifty-one kilograms (one hundred twelve pounds) of which an extraordinary nineteen kilograms (forty-two pounds) was warhead. It had a range of sixteen kilometers (ten miles) and was launched from a light, simple firing stand easy to carry and set up.

Xinh's "uniform" was composed of a jungle shirt made from camouflaged U.S. parachute nylon, black pajama bottoms, and sandals whose soles and straps were made from U.S. Army truck tires and inner tubes. The U.S. Army web belt she buckled around her waist held cartridges, grenades (made by the VC in jungle factories), and a water canteen (U.S. stamped on its cover). A hammock, a mosquito net, and a two-day ration of cooked rice were slung over one shoulder, and her Chinese Type 56-1 or Russian AK-47 hung over the other. Her long hair she sometimes tied Vietnamese peasant style at the back of her head. At other times she let it hang straight down her back. Occasionally she wore it in a single, long rope braid.

At first Xinh lived in the dense jungles of Tay Ninh and Binh Duong with her guerrillas. They were frequently short of food and medical supplies. Many were sick with malaria and dysentery. The unit was always on the move, digging tunnels, living off the land, and generally attempting to conceal their whereabouts from the enemy. Through terror tactics they persuaded the villagers loyal to the government to support them with rice and to hide them when necessary. More than once a village chief was murdered and VC agents were put in charge, especially when cooperation was not good. Most of the time she and her guerrillas lived in jungle hideouts, venturing forth to attack only when the odds for success were greatly in their favor. Later, Tang arranged for her to work at the Binh Hoa airbase—her present assignment—as an undercover agent while retaining command of her unit. Her operations were switched to the area within a forty-mile radius of the base and they now included the rocketing of Saigon.

For two, long harsh years she had been giving her best. She was tired.

And then she had met Steve. He had searched her troubled eyes and sensed her piercing loneliness and anguished spirit. Their relationship evolved slowly: a brief encounter in OPS, his visits to her section in personnel, lingering conversations, little attentions and small gifts. Her trust and confidence grew. In the end he had toppled her world, stripped her of defenses, broken her cover. From the ruins rose the solid foundation of her Asian womanhood. It had been lying dormant, a volcano covered and sleeping. He had opened a small window to her past. She had peeked in. Frightened, she'd crawled inside and pulled her heart after her, to begin the long process of healing.

And then like soft rain, her time came. She blossomed like a spring flower, nourished by Steve's love. She grew strong in the light of his affection, taking all that he could give, grateful and giving more in return. Like an insatiable sponge, dry and empty from the long years of childhood neglect and desolation, she absorbed his love. She sank roots in the fertile soil of his understanding and attention. She drank the sweet waters of his love and dedicated her life, her very soul to him.

Chapter Five

The MP curiously eyed Xinh's security badge, quickly checking her photo and noting the red stripe that gave her secret clearance. He dutifully nodded as she passed into the operations building, admiring her flowing walk set off by the delicate *ao dai* which clung tightly to her waist and upper body. Two provocative splits along the sides revealed the white silk beneath that hid Xinh's shapely legs from the MP's ravenous eyes. Mentally exploring her charms, the MP continued to follow her with his eyes while she walked down the long corridor and disappeared into the Mission Operations Center.

Inside the busy OPS Center, the insistent clacking of typewriters, noisy conversations, the constant motion of personnel, and shouted orders gave the appearance of great confusion and disarray. But in reality everyone was performing a specific duty for a well-coordinated operation that planned, scheduled, and controlled the days' strikes. The large wall map of Vietnam was flanked by smaller regional area maps and by mission plot charts. A variety of colored pins and magnetic symbols were spread over these, their significance understood only by the trained eye. Computers hummed and display terminals glowed, feeding data into the center. Information was translated, converted, then transmitted to aircraft commanders for vectoring targets.

Xinh went directly to a young Vietnamese girl seated at a computer terminal.

"*Kim oi.*" Kim dear, she began, in country dialect, "Can you help me?"

"*Chao chi Xinh.*" Hello sister Xinh, she answered. "What can I do for you?"

"Is Captain Randall flying today?" Xinh asked.

"Look for yourself," Kim said, pointing to the big mission-control board.

Xinh's eyes quickly scanned the board. Lopez, Smith, Jackson, Wendall, Scarletti . . . Randall . . . Yes, he was up. As she had thought, the two F-4s she had watched take off earlier were Steve and his wingman.

Xinh turned back to the girl. Kim smiled and punched instruction codes into the terminal, her fingers moving swiftly over the keyboard. Immediately the read-out came up on the CRT:

R22 S43 2 F-4E CAPT RANDALL LT HENSLEY VEC MEKONG N15Z 22-1 CS SCORPION ETA 1043 ZULU FB RIVET FIRE

"Looks like he should be returning soon," Kim said, smiling again, this time with a twinkle in her eyes.

"Will you spend Tet in Da Nang with your family,

Kim?'' Xinh sat down on the desk next to the CRT.

Kim looked up. "Mother and Father expect me." Her Da Nangese flowed like warm honey from her flower-petal lips. We plan to make moon cakes this New Year instead of buying them."

Xinh looked longingly out the window. "Grandmother used to make me a moon cake every New Year when I was a child."

"I never got one. We were too poor."

"We were poor too, but Grandmother always made me one."

"You were fortunate," Kim said.

"I suppose." Xinh absent-mindedly watched the flickering green glow from the CRT screen.

"Will you stay in Binh Hoa?" Kim asked. She toyed with the keys.

"I would like to visit Grandmother."

"Why don't you?"

"She lives in Tay Ninh," Xinh answered.

"Oh, Tay Ninh. That's far."

"Near the Cambodian frontier."

"Cambodia is far," Kim said.

The CRT flickered. It was quiet.

"Maybe if you go she will have a moon cake for you," Kim said.

"She makes moon cake for me every Tet whether I come to see her or not."

"Does she give you lucky money too?" Kim asked.

"Sometimes, if she has any. She's poor."

"I'm too old for lucky money." Kim said.

"You're not too old for lucky money." Xinh still looked out the window.

"Yes, I am. I'm twenty."

"I still get lucky money." Xinh smoothed her *ao dai*.

"You're younger."

"I suppose I should get envelopes for the children."

"I have extra if you want some." Kim opened her desk drawer and handed a few of the festive red lucky money envelopes to Xinh.

"No, thank you." She handed them back. "I think I'll order my own this year."

"The ones with good-fortune poems?" Kim asked.

"Yes." Xinh turned from the window and looked into Kim's lonely eyes. "It's a long war."

"Yes . . . it's a long war."

Shimmering waves of heat rose from the hot tarmac, creating ghostly mirages on the runways. Xinh cupped one hand over her eyebrows and shaded her eyes from the penetrating brilliance of the tropical sun. She searched the horizon for returning aircraft, noticing that the rounded masses of cumulus clouds had taken on enormous proportions and were now an awesome display of power and great force. The regular afternoon thundershower would soon be unleashed, bringing refreshing moisture and cooling breezes. Even now the prelude, dancing thunderbolts, could be seen in the distance. Vehement and sudden discharges of electrical energy accompanied by sharp, loud claps of thunder erupted from the darkening sky.

Two Phantoms streaked overhead, then cranked around in a tight turn, fully displaying their power and fury. Turning onto the last leg Randall pitched off, dropped his landing gear, and banked around the low hills. He slipped over the rice paddies, flaps lowered, at two hundred knots and lined up on the wide runway. Letting the nose fall off a little, he gave some right rudder, easing off on the throttle with his left hand. Then he brought the stick back and flared the ship. The two main wheels hit the runway simultaneously, giving off a trail of gray smoke as tires burned into the tarmac. He chopped the power and the F-4's nose instantly dropped onto the runway, settling on the front gear.

Xinh stood behind the parking area, her *ao dai* billowing in the wind as her eyes followed the F-4 roaring past her, its drag chute blossoming out behind. Steve turned off the runway at the far end and disappeared behind a line of sandbagged revetments.

"Waiting for someone, sister Xinh?"

Xinh's catlike reflexes, conditioned to a fine edge in the jungle, sensed danger as she wheeled around to face this sudden intrusion on her privacy. Without thinking she had assumed a defensive posture—the classical kung-fu position, body crouched, arms extended, hands flexed—to repel an expected attack.

"Ah, very quick. I see you remember your lessons well," said the intruder.

"Yes, I remember well. I have had occasion to use your training often enough as you well know, comrade Tang," Xinh said, relaxing her tensed frame and standing normally, the picture of perfect femininity once again. "Please forgive me. You surprised me. I hope I didn't offend my honorable teacher. I beg your humble pardon." She folded her arms and bowed her head in respect to her Vietcong superior, being careful not to be too obvious.

"No matter. I just hope your judgment concerning your relations with Americans is as good as your quick reaction to surprise," Tang replied.

"I see that my behavior is not approved of," she said.

"Not entirely. I will be frank. You have been seen on occasion with an American Air Force Captain by the name of Randall. Even though you have gone to great lengths to conceal your rendezvous with him, you have been noticed."

"Captain Randall has just returned from a mission and I am waiting for him."

"I know. I have been informed of your inquiries at the OPS Center."

Kim! Xinh's eyes narrowed. A rancid taste climbed in her throat.

Tang continued. "You will turn the occasion to the advantage of the National Liberation Front. Encourage his friendship to the extent you feel necessary to gain information that would be of value to us." He drew a pack of cigarettes from his shirt pocket.

"Yes." Xinh could say no more.

"When your friendship with the American first came to our attention, you were suspect—naturally." He grinned fiendishly. "At this point we still don't know what your intentions are. However, the situation needs no further investigation as long as you are willing to cooperate." He pulled a menthol tip from the package and stuck it between his thick lips. "Understood?" he asked, lighting up and eying her suspiciously through his glasses.

"Yes," Xinh said again, eyes diverted to the ground. Sly devil, she thought to herself. If there was anything she had learned about the Communists, it was that they were masters at controlling people through fear.

"As I said, you will go to whatever lengths necessary in your relationship with Randall to obtain the information we ask you to get from him. Is that perfectly understood?" He exhaled a thick cloud of smoke into Xinh's face. The smile was frozen on his face.

"Yes, perfectly." She forced herself not to wince from the stinging smoke. She returned his smile.

"You will be hearing from me."

With that, Tang gaily changed the subject to family and friends, and the planned Tet New Year celebrations.

The sound of idling engines and the heavy smell of jet exhaust broke off the conversation. Tang excused himself, exhibiting the feigned sincerity Xinh was accustomed to when dealing with her VC superiors, and headed back to his squadron of South Vietnamese Air Force F-5s on the west side of the field.

The vertical stabilizer from Steve's ship, looking like the tall dorsal fin of a giant shark, moved above and behind the row of parked aircraft then merged with its fuselage as Steve turned the corner and came into full view of Xinh's expectant eyes. The huge, gaping red mouth and sharp white teeth painted on the Phantom's nose gave the F-4 an ominous look which caused Xinh, who was a Buddhist and quite superstitious, to widen her eyes and take a few

51

apprehensive steps backward.

"May bay do, no co the nuot song toi!" Damned thing looks like it could eat me alive! she said. Her expression remained unchanged, somewhere between controlled fright and curiosity, and she seemed momentarily frozen to the tarmac, unable to move, eyes fixed on the forty-five-thousand-pound monster crawling straight toward her looking for its den.

"Miss, you're going to have to move out of the parking area," the burly crew chief said. Strong arms gently pulled her out of the way and escorted her beyond the concrete blast shield. The noise was deafening and she had to hold her hands to her ears.

Steve inched the jet forward with another blast of engine thrust, intently watching the crew chief's arm signals directing him into the revetment.

"Come on, junior, bring my baby to bed," the sergeant mumbled to himself, talking Steve in. "You're not driving a motor scooter, sonny; that's my ship you're bringing home. I just loaned it to you for a few hours."

The barrel-chested veteran of three wars continued to pull the Phantom in. Abruptly he crossed his hairy, tatooed arms over his head and Steve cut the engines. The RPMs instantly dropped and the high-pitched whine of the turbines slowly fell off to a low moan. End of mission. Wheels were chocked, and the crew ladder was brought up and hooked to the fuselage the moment the canopy began lifting.

Xinh's eager eyes watched closely. She took a few steps forward, away from the barrier, but was reluctant to come any closer to the frightening weapon. She was still staring at the shark mouth. The ground crew quickly began rearming the aircraft; empty rocket pods were filled and the Vulcan gun checked. Napalm was wheeled into position along with racks of two-hundred-fifty- and five-hundred-pound frag bombs. These would wait until the command came down as to what kind of load would be required for the next mission.

Steve unbuckled his harness from the armored seat. Xinh's Oriental curiosity kept her attention on every detail. She didn't miss a lick. He took off his oxygen mask and flight helmet together and rested them on the windscreen. He unplugged himself from the radio and LSS, and stepped onto the top rung of the ladder. He adjusted the .38 on his hip, grabbed his helmet off the canopy and descended the ladder, gripping his map case and metal clipboard in his free hand.

"Good mission Captain?"

"Yeah, Kelly," he said to the crew chief, landing on the tarmac. "Good mission. We busted 'em up good."

"Real good, sir?"

"Roger, Sarge. Real good."

The two walked around the Phantom together.

"I think I took some hits."

"Right, Captain. In the aft fuselage . . . 'twentys' it looks like," Kelly said pointing to the ragged-edged holes in the bottom of the tail section. "Next time take better care of my baby," he added with a tobacco-stained grin.

"We sure had the right ordnance for this one, Sarge," Diluca shouted, exiting the Phantom from the back seat.

"Really buggered them, eh, Lieutenant?" Kelly said.

"Yeah, really. Must be a hundred VC fried back there."

"More like a hundred and fifty," Steve said in a low voice.

He could still see flaming torches—men—stumbling and falling into each other. Napalm. Rockets. Oh well, someone had to do it. But like the sticky napalm, the picture adhered to his mind. He looked at Kelly beaming at Diluca's animated description of the death scene. Asses, he thought to himself. What do they know? No depth.

"Stupid war. Messy, stupid war," he said quietly.

"What's that, Steve?" Diluca asked.

"Nothing. Nothing at all."

"Say, Captain, that sweet piece of chicken over there has been waiting a long time for you, sir," Kelly said, pointing to Xinh who still clung to the protection of the barrrier. If you ask me, sir, there's something strange about that girl. She's been out here before watching you land and take off. But this is the first time she's stayed until you parked. You know her?"

"Right, Kelly. I know her." He looked across the wing at Xinh, then quickly glanced back at Kelly.

"Well, like I said, if you ask me there's something peculiar about her. A good looker, but I'd be careful, Captain. I don't trust any of these Vietnamese. Even the red stripers. They're all the same to me. I treat them all like Vietcong. You never know. If you ask me, I'd say get them off the base, even the ones like her, the red stripers."

54

Only a few patches of blue remained in the sky. The air had turned dank and the masses of billowing white clouds were now black with the heaviness of rain, a confused heaving swarm. Xinh smoothed her hair back over her shoulders and moved out in the open where Steve could see her better, her back rod straight, and chin held up proudly. Her heart fluttered in anticipation.

Steve picked up his gear, hoisted it over his shoulder, and walked over to where Xinh was waiting.

"Hello, little one. How are you?" He would have preferred to take her in his arms and give her a big kiss.

"*Da manh, cam on anh oi. Con anh cung manh cho?*" I'm fine, my darling, how are you? she answered. Her voice was a musical scale of flutelike tones, rising and falling in a beautiful melody of communication. He loved to listen to her speak Vietnamese. She moved up close to him, so close that he could smell her intoxicating pure, natural fragrance that never failed to excite him. Her long sloe eyes looked shyly up at him and her hand imperceptibly felt for his. She fitted her small palm into his hand and squeezed his fingers.

"I very happy see you." There was a sparkle in her eyes.

"I've missed you, Xinh. I always miss you when I don't see you for a few days. Why do you stay away from me so long? You know I miss you." He ran his fingers through his hair.

"*Da, cung oi.*" Yes, darling. "I sorry. I try not stay away no more too long. You need me, yes?"

"Yes, little one. I need you."

"You can meet me tomorrow night after work."

"Tomorrow night? Where? Same place?"

"No. I meet you My Canh, restaurant boat on river."

"Sure, Xinh. That's fine with me. The My Canh restaurant. Nice place. But what changed your mind?"

"I tell you later." She squeezed his fingers again.

"O.K." He knew better than to continue to question her.

"Everything fine now." She breathed a deep sigh.

"I'm glad, Xinh. I'm really glad." He led Xinh toward the waiting jeep.

"You have good mission?"

"I suppose."

"You kill Vietcong today." She looked away with half-closed eyes.

"Yes, I did. How did you know?"

"I tell from your eyes when you leave airplane. I say, he kill today. His eyes cry."

"It was a mess, Xinh. A real mess this time. But it's my job. It's what I'm paid to do."

The ambivalent feelings welled up inside her again, churning her insides. She should hate him for what he had done. And she did in one sense. But she had an advantage over him. He didn't know that she was one of those he left on the Mekong today.

"Will you wait for me, Xinh," he asked, climbing into the jeep that would take him and Diluca to debriefing.

"No. I go back work now."

"See you tomorrow night then."

"Yes. Tomorrow night."

She stood on tiptoe waving good-bye, *ao dai* curling in the wind around her trim legs. Suddenly she was cold. A clap of thunder and the rain broke. Somewhere along the Mekong a charred boy cried for his mother; a GI reached into the gurgling little stream running through the pretty clearing and pulled out his buddy's boot. It still had a foot in it.

Chapter Six

Click . . . Click . . . Click . . . The trigger action echoed in the dimly lit, hollow room. The overhead fan slowly rotated, casting flickering images on the yellowing ceiling and the peeling, musty-smelling walls. A single, lonely dresser stood in one corner. On top was a miniature Buddhist shrine with burning incense sticks and an offering of fruit and rice. A small, unpainted table sat near the uncurtained, open window. On the table was a rice cooker, a cracked porcelain teapot with cups, a glass full of chopsticks, two rice bowls, a bottle of fish sauce, a jar of hot peppers, and a dish of black bean paste. A fly circled over a bowl of partially eaten sour fish soup. Near the small sink a lone, handmade chair rested against the wall. Beside the chair, on the floor, were stacked a Vietnamese-English dictionary, some Vietnamese and French classical novels, an English and French grammar book, and a U.S. Army manual on squad tactics. Two clips of .45 ammunition lay on the floor next to the books. French doors opened onto an ornamented, wrought-iron terrace overlooking a narrow side street filled with noisy, smoking Japanese motorcycles, man-powered cyclos, hawking vendors, and busy pedestrians. There was nothing on the terrace.

Inside, a large wooden, carved bed occupied one wall. A cord with a single, low-watt light bulb hung from the ceiling over the bed, the only source of illumination for the small room. At the head of the bed hung a fading photograph of an old man and a woman dressed in peasant clothing. The heavy scent of *nuoc mam*, mingled with incense, filled the room.

Xinh finished cleaning the U.S.-made .45 automatic. Click . . . Click . . . She tested the action for the final time and wiped the excess oil from the barrel with a clean cloth. She got up from the bed and carefully hid the pistol under her underwear in the top drawer of the dresser. Then she returned to the bed and lay on her back counting the revolutions of the fan while it made circling paths of shadows on the ceiling above her. She turned her head and looked out the open French doors into the night. Flares illuminated the skyline on the outskirts of town as the "widow-makers" began their evening drops that would continue until dawn. The roar of a howitzer could be heard in the distance, probably searching for the exact coordinates called out by a reconn patrol. The sights and sounds of war. Will it ever end, she wondered.

As long as she could remember there had been war. That was all there was. War. Only eighteen and she was an old woman. What had happened to her youth? Gone. Would she ever find it again? Bring it back? She longed to live like other young women. She wanted to laugh, have fun, go to parties with people her own age, enjoy her youth. What was it like to be young?

She propped her head up with a pillow and watched Mr. Phi embrace his young wife in their room across the street. She had a big belly and in a few months was expecting their first child. How she envied the girl. She had a husband, and a baby was developing inside of her . . . a precious baby. Something of permanent value. The girl's life was just beginning. Her entire future lay before her. There was love in her life, someone cared. She could talk to her husband, share his experiences. She had someone to understand her. Oh, yes. Someone who understood and cared, who would help her in time of need and take away the loneliness.

A light tap . . . tap on the door.

"*Ai do?*" Who's there?

"*Em.*" Little sister.

The door opened and little Thanh walked in. An invitation was unnecessary. She folded her arms in front and bowed at the waist, her long hair falling forward across her small breasts. She quietly closed the door behind her and walked to the bed where Xinh remained, looking out the French doors. There was a long silence; then Xinh spoke.

"What happened to our youth, Thanh? Were we ever young?"

Thanh's eyes, long and pretty like Xinh's, slowly closed. A sigh escaped her small lips.

"I . . . I don't know, Xinh. Do you feel old too . . . like me, sister?"

"Old? Do I feel old? Thanh, I feel ancient. I have nothing in common with girls my own age. Yes, I feel old. Very old."

"I know. I can't talk with young people anymore. They seem so . . . so . . . inexperienced. Idealistic."

"Idealistic?" Xinh asked.

"Yes. Idealistic. Like we used to be. Remember, Xinh, how we used to talk about how it was going to be. I mean before we joined the NLF. Do you remember, sister. It was fun to dream and talk wasn't it?" There was a pause. Xinh didn't answer.

"Dreams. We did dream. We talked a lot. Do you remember the tamarind trees? The ones we played under, where we talked about our dreams? Remember, sister Xinh?" Xinh remained silent, looking into the night.

"The tamarind trees—and the river Phu Cuong. How big it was when we were children. Duc would make us those little bamboo boats we floated in the river and yours, Xinh, would always go out too far and Duc would have to swim out and catch it for you. Oh . . . Duc. Gone now. Bamboo boats gone. Tamarind trees . . . the river . . . the pretty green river. All gone.

"What happened to our youth?" Xinh said again, sadly. Another howitzer barked in the night and the parachute flares drifted down and people died and children cried.

"We were going to be married," Xinh said, slowly turning the solid ring of jade on her wrist.

"You and Duc?"

"Yes. By the river . . . under the tamarind trees." She turned the engagement stone some more, lost in memory.

"I remember. By now you would have had a big

belly," Thanh said with a sad smile. "Your own child."

"My own child," Xinh said weakly. She turned her head from the open doors and rolled over facing Thanh.

The two pretty Asian girls looked at each other momentarily, reaching out for strength and hope. Their eyes spoke of the grief and suffering of others like themselves who cried out for solace. But there was no one to comfort them. They found consolation only in each other. And like so many of the war's young people, Xinh and Thanh acutely felt a sense of loss. A loss that was irreplaceable. Youth. It was gone. Very young they had become old. The responsibility and problems of age came early. And they dutifully accepted. No questions. No refusals. Overnight they were thrust into the arena of the survival of the fittest. Children like Xinh and Thanh survived only by their wits. There were no parents to run to when their world fell apart. There was no comforting home filled with loving and supporting family. No place to hide except within themselves or among those who were as unfortunate as they. The howitzers barked again.

Xinh got up from the bed and walked out to the terrace. She breathed in the humid night air. She and Thanh stood silently, holding hands in the manner of Vietnamese women, comforting each other and gazing out over the rooftops and hills beyond. Ghostly images played on the landscape, a surrealistic display in the dreamy half light created by the drifting flares. A helicopter gunship sped through the night, banked over the jungle canopy, pivoted in a hover, and fired a salvo of rockets into the tree line. Somewhere a baby wailed.

It was nearing curfew, and the street below was fast becoming deserted. Only a few stalls remained open. People scurried home to board themselves up for the night. A last motorcycle puttered by, leaving a gray trail of smoke. The well-heeled Korean man next door staggered along the walk, his nightly whore walking dutifully behind him. The air stank of urine and exhaust fumes and rotting garbage.

"Xin loi chi, Xinh." Excuse me sister Xinh. The voice of authority shattered the moment. Tang stood in the open doorway.

"May I come in?" he asked.

"Moi ong vo vao choi." Please come in, Xinh said, turning around to face him.

"Chung toi doi ong." We have been expecting you.

Tang quickly entered, followed by a nervous little rat-faced man. Without pausing, he moved to the table and began clearing it. He was an efficient man and wasted little time.

"I think it would be best to get to work immediately. We mustn't stay long. Don't want to attract suspicion," Tang said. Thanh poured tea for the four of them. The rat-faced man refused his.

Tang pulled a well-creased, stained map from his pocket and spread it flat on the table.

"The attack is scheduled for 01:30 hours, the first day of Tet. You must have your rocket and mortar teams in position here, Xinh," he said, stabbing the map with a bony finger, "by 01:00."

The four VC bent over the map, studying it closely,

Xinh tracing the approach path with her fingernail. The rat-faced man greedily eyed her smooth, beautiful complexion. Thanh looked at him in disgust. He diverted his eyes back to the map.

Xinh rubbed her forehead in thought. "It will take me two weeks to plan the approach and identify areas for concealment of the weapons."

"Make it one week. We can't afford two," Tang ordered.

"Yes," Xinh said obediently. "With the help of villagers, the ammunition and weapons will be stockpiled underground in the tunnels and hidden in trees in preparation for the offensive," she continued. "On Tet minus one, my people will filter into the staging area. Thanh, you will be responsible for deployment of the 81-mm mortars. I will take the 122-mm and 107-mm rocket sections and supporting equipment myself," she said.

"Will we uncover the ammo and weapons along the route and carry it by relay teams to the fire base as we've done before?" Thanh asked.

"Yes," Tang said, answering for Xinh. "But I want you to exercise caution by carefully marking the withdrawal route and by identifying several alternates."

"*Dung roi.*" Of course, Xinh said.

"Should we use the small carts and bicycles to help carry the load?" Thanh wanted to know.

"No," the rat-faced man injected. "Too difficult to negotiate along the jungle paths. The risk of detection is also higher. If we had more time— maybe. Everything will have to be carried by hand."

Thanh was about to argue with Rat-face, but Xinh

65

cut her off with a stern look. Rat-face lustfully eyed Thanh.

"Xinh, I want you to personally take charge of selecting and preparing the fire base. This is a major responsibility and much too important a task to delegate to someone else," Tang said.

"Yes, I understand."

"When you arrive at the fire base on the night of the attack, rapidly deploy your artillery. Quickly direct several synchronized salvos in rapid succession at the appointed time. Be sure your rocket launches are coordinated effectively with Thanh's mortar barrages. When the attack is concluded have your guerrillas quickly dismantle their equipment and withdraw to the staging area where they will rebury and conceal the weapons."

"What then? Shall we follow the usual procedure of hiding in the surrounding jungle or among the villagers until we can safely regroup?" Xinh asked.

"Yes. But be prepared for a second and third attack on my orders; I may also need you down on the perimeter."

"I won't be taking the RPG-7s or '75s'. We won't have much use for them," Xinh said.

"That's right," Tang said. "The extra weight could slow you up."

"Since we'll be traveling under cover of darkness we'll have to use the tiny homemade kerosene bottle lamps. Round up as many as possible from the villagers, Thanh," Xinh said. "I figure that we can move the unit to within one to three miles of the target without serious risk of discovery if we approach from the north."

"Fewer reconn patrols because of the river terrain," Thanh put in.

"Yes, and growth is denser on the north side," Ratface added.

"We'll have to use sampans for the crossings," Xinh said.

"I can arrange that," Thanh replied.

"Good. We can cover the fifteen miles from staging to fire base, complete the mission, and return to the unit's sanctuary within twenty-four hours," Xinh concluded. She paused, thinking, rubbing her forehead again. Rat-face still had his eyes glued on Thanh.

"Patrolling aircraft and flare drops will be our biggest problem. We'll have to stick to the denser trails," she continued. "As I said, I don't believe we'll have trouble with ground patrols, not approaching from the north, but I think I should be in position the night before the attack, just to be safe."

"Negative," Tang said. "Too big a chance of being discovered. The final approach can only be made on the night of the attack."

"It's going to be staggering work carrying the heavy base plates, firing tubes, launchers, and rounds down the jungle trails to position them in time for the attack. Miles have to be covered and the patrols evaded. All in darkness," Xinh said, arguing for more time.

"You've done it before."

"But not on such a large scale."

"No. It will all be done in one night."

Tang began folding the map. "One more thing," he said. "I want you to play one of your little tricks on the Americans."

"Which one?"

"The sandbags."

"The sandbags?" Rat-face asked.

"Yes, sandbags," Thanh answered sarcastically. "You must have heard of Xinh's sandbag technology."

"No, I haven't," he said stupidly, giving her a lecherous look.

"One section of heavy rockets is set in position a considerable distance from the main batteries. They are concealed and aimed at the target," Thanh explained. "Slowly draining sandbags are hung from the rockets in such a way that when the bags are emptied the loss of weight releases the triggering mechanism and the rockets fire."

"This confuses the enemy and makes them think we have more forces in the area than we really have," Xinh said. "They also think we are still in the vicinity when in reality we have left the area some time before and are uneffected by the predictable counterattack."

"In addition to supporting the main battery by inflicting damage on the target, the sandbag technology acts as an effective diversion, allowing our people to escape the accurate and rapid artillery response from the enemy," Tang added. Rat-face wasn't listening. He was too busy watching Thanh refill the tea cups. "Also, numerous booby traps have been set among the launchers and in the general area to inflict further casualties if they're discovered."

"Mmmmmmmm . . . clever," Rat-face said, still

studying Thanh.

"One last thing," Tang said to Xinh, placing the bulky map inside his shirt, next to his skin. "My sappers need to know the exact location of the two objectives we discussed yesterday. I trust you can obtain this information from your 'friend'?" His eyes bored into hers.

"Of course, sir," she answered with assurance.

"Good-bye then. Sleep well," he said.

Thanh held the door open, and Tang quickly slipped out onto the staircase landing. Rat-face gave a final hungry backward glance at Thanh, then to Xinh. "I will look forward to our next meeting," he said.

"Good-bye," Thanh said, putting a bite into her words.

Rat-face just leered at her.

"That man disgusts me," Thanh said, contorting her face and closing the door. "He's dangerous. I don't trust him—not a bit."

"I don't like him either. But we have no choice. He's Tang's right-hand man and we have to work with him."

"I still don't like it. Be careful, Xinh—very careful."

"Thanh, I want you to get Minh and Dong. I want to brief them right away. Don't mention anything to them."

"Yes, sister."

Thirty minutes later Thanh escorted Minh and Dong, two of Xinh's section leaders, into the room.

"We have heard the rumors of a big attack," Minh

said eagerly.

"Yes, a Tet offensive throughout the south," Dong added.

"Is it true? Are we to play a big role?"

"The rumors are correct. We have one of the main objectives."

"What is it?"

"Bien Hoa."

Chapter Seven

"This whole business stinks, Xinh. How did you ever get mixed up with an American anyway?"

"Don't give me any trouble, Thanh," Xinh said. She hurried down the gangway.

"He's the enemy."

"Enemy?" She stopped and looked back at Thanh.

"Technically he is the enemy, regardless of how you feel about him," Thanh said, exasperated but maintaining a respectful tone.

"We've been over this before, Thanh."

They entered the busy floating restaurant and chose a table in a quiet corner overlooking the river. A half moon was rising and its incandescence sparkled off the smooth waters, illuminating the surrounding rice paddies in a dancing display of water diamonds. For a while the two of them sat without talking, enjoying the beauty of the Vietnamese night.

"I know this is not the time to talk about it," Thanh said, breaking the silence, and looking cautiously around, "but how do you plan to get the information?"

"I'll ask him."

"Just like that? Ask him?"

"Yes. Just like that."

"But won't he become suspicious?"

"No. He won't suspect a thing. Just leave it to me."

"Tang is expecting the information to be accurate. It's critical you know."

"Thanh, I know precisely what Tang requires. I haven't worked with him this long without learning how he thinks."

"Well, I'm just nervous I suppose. Our attack on the air base will signal the beginning of the Tet offensive throughout the south. It's our hope for the national uprising we've been expecting for so long."

"I know. We've all been jittery these last weeks. The tunneling has required more of my time than expected and I've been surviving on very little sleep. Tang has needed me more and more to direct the digging to the targets I've identified. It's been slow going. Maps and layouts have been hard to obtain. What wasn't on the charts I had to get from the base files or from just being nosy."

"But we still don't know the location of the bomb dumps and underground jet-fuel storage tanks— prime targets, along with the aircraft."

"Steve," Xinh said with a long sigh, looking out the window. It was the only way.

She wanted to walk away from this. It was foolish. But she knew that she had to follow Tang's orders. For weeks she had been putting him off, making excuses. Everyday since the planning meeting in her room he had pressured her for the vital information. He had first grown tired of her apologies, then angry, and finally openly hostile and threatening. "It's a pity you never understood, Xinh. Such a pity." He did not speak of it again.

"Here he comes," Thanh said, looking uneasily at Xinh. "He's awfully good-looking—even for one of the enemy—I have to admit."

Xinh turned toward the bar and saw Steve following behind the maître d', tall above the Vietnamese, his blond hair contrasting with their dark heads, his walk firm and confident.

Suddenly her attention shifted. Her alert eyes had picked up the nervous motions of a mousy little man darting between the tables adjacent to Steve's path.

"Cac co manh gioi Khong?" How are you, ladies? Steve asked as he slipped into the booth and sat down beside Xinh.

"Manh gioi, cam on ong." Fine thank you, the girls said smiling, Xinh keeping a watchful eye on the other tables. She felt in her leather handbag for the .45. Thanh looked around the room, then back at Xinh.

"Would you care for a cocktail before dinner, sir?" the maître d' asked.

"Martini, dry." Knowing that Xinh and Thanh never drank, abstinence being the rule among Vietnamese women, Steve nevertheless nodded their way. They politely declined.

Thanh had become wriggly, a reaction she frequently had when nervous. Sensing danger, her little nose and toes twitched, and she jiggled from side to side on her small bottom. Xinh nudged her in the waist with her elbow. This succeeded only in quieting Thanh's nose.

A well-proportioned, exotic-looking waitress (all Vietnamese women were well-proportioned and exotic to Steve) brought Steve's martini. He quickly looked her over and paid for the drink. Xinh pinched him.

The girl, Xinh's cousin and also a Vietcong, lingered at the table for a few moments whispering to the girls in rapid Vietnamese. She put her back to Steve. Thanh got up and followed the girl through the curtained doorway. Steve's eyes widened but he said nothing.

The band started into a Vietnamese ballad, slow and romantic, a tale narrative of a country peasant, sentimental and brooding. The long-haired singer in Western dress and heavy makeup seemed out of place as she sang of the long suffering of the people and the never-ending tragedy of war. Steve wanted to wash her face and change her clothes. The popular music of Vietnam was hypnotic. He loved it. Moody and expressive, it had a delicate sensibility and an emotional idealism that spoke for the common person. The schoolgirl in love with a young soldier. The hope of the newborn. The end of war.

"I'd love to dance with you, Xinh."

"Yes. I dance if you like."

Steve held her boneless little hand as he threaded his way through the tables. Xinh's eyes busily searched the room like a lizard's. The mousy man had disappeared. She didn't know whether to be relieved or more anxious.

"You dance pretty well for a country girl," Steve said.

"Thank you. But I no stay country all time. I go

74

capital too."

"Oh, yeah. I'd forgotten you'd lived in Saigon. No country girl all time," Steve said with a grin.

"Country girl, *chut chut*—city girl, *chut chut*," she said, smiling back at him.

Steve was in heaven, totally absorbed by Xinh's exotic beauty and charm. He was blind to everything around him. All his senses were focused on her. He had no past or future. Everything was now. He was enthralled by the delicacy of her movements as they danced to the rhythm of the sensitive music. Her femininity was overwhelming and he reveled in the closeness of her flesh. The soft parts of her sleek, well-conditioned body, easily detectable through her thin *ao dai*, excited Steve to near flash point. He indulged his bodily appetites. It was the first time he had had the good fortune to hold Xinh so close in public. He wanted the feeling to linger forever, the dance to never end.

"Xinh, this is the first time we've ever danced together. The first time you have ever let me meet you in public. I'm so glad you asked me to come tonight."

"I think it time now."

"Now's the time?"

"Yes. Okay now."

"But why now? Why not before?"

"Vietnamese girl very slow. Move slow with man. Not charming to go fast."

"Charming. That's a big word for you, but an appropriate one."

She ignored that. "I love you very much. You are my '*cung oi*'. I love only you. No other man will ever be in my life. I want you enjoy me now. No want you have to wait." She looked up at him with her beautiful long eyes and he almost melted into the dance floor. "No ask too many questions. Just trust me, Steve *oi*. Whatever happen, you trust Xinh. She die for you."

His legs were shaky and he thought he might have to sit down. He floated over the dance floor.

"I still young girl, only eighteen. Need you teach me. You teach me, Steve?"

"Y-Yes, Xinh, I teach you." Her honesty and charm was nearly too much for him. He really had to sit down. She was unbelievably beautiful. He could never get used to her uniqueness. It penetrated the very core of his being. It was maddening.

"I know you think maybe I too young. That maybe I only child."

"Not really, Xinh," he said.

It was true that her knowledge—except for Vietnam, the war, and her own experience—was very limited, but she had demonstrated a great deal of common sense and an ability to learn very quickly. He had detected in her a talent to discern inner qualities and relationships, and she always seemed to exercise good judgment. She was quick, alert, intelligent, and always made him feel that he was in the presence of one who had seen and experienced much more than he.

"You are not a child," he assured her.

The singer lamented the last refrain. Steve held Xinh closer, and she momentarily relaxed her alert senses to dream the dreams of a girl in love. She saw herself living with Steve in a large villa on a green hillside overlooking the sea. She tried hard to imagine the serenity and peace that she wanted so much, but in the background she still heard the far-off sounds of artillery, the screaming of jets, and the crack of her Chinese assault rifle. However, she tasted enough of the dream to satisfy the little girl still in her and she snuggled closer to her man.

The song ended. Steve took her by the hand and led her back to their table. Xinh's senses returned to full alert. Her eyes flashed around the room again, looking for anything out of the ordinary that would signal danger. They slid into the booth and Xinh quickly hefted her handbag. The familiar heaviness told her what she wanted to know. Thanh hadn't returned.

"Xinh, can I ask you a question?"

"Ask."

"Where are your mother and father?"

"Dead."

"Oh. You never told me. How?"

"War."

"You have brothers? Sisters?"

"All dead."

"How many?"

"Seven."

"All dead?"

"All dead."

"The war too?"

"Yes. The war too."

"I'm sorry, Xinh."

She smiled at him. She blinked a few times and drew in a long breath. Her eyes made another pass around the room. She noticed Thanh motioning to her from the curtained doorway near the bar. She excused herself.

"Where are you going?" Steve asked.

"*Ve-Sinh.*" Restroom. She smiled. "Xinh no be long."

She quickly made her way around the tables and entered the partially lighted room. Thanh pulled the curtain tightly closed behind her.

"What is it?" Xinh asked.

Thanh pointed to Xinh's cousin, Mai.

"Xinh, they're going to try to kill you tonight," Mai said. She placed the cocktail tray she was carrying on a table. The room seemed to grow darker.

"What? What are you talking about?" Xinh's eyebrows arched. Her red lips pursed.

"It's true—tonight. Right here in the restaurant."

The black ceiling fan directly over their heads lazily rotated.

"Here? In the restaurant?"

"That's right. Tonight at eleven o'clock."

Xinh looked at Thanh and then back at her cousin. "Are you sure?" Her lips tightened into a fine line.

"There's no question. A special agent, Kim's brother—"

"Kim's brother!"

"Correct. He's been given the assignment. Do you know him?" She handed Xinh a glass of coconut milk from the tray.

"No. I've never seen him. But, Kim . . ."

"I know." Mai fumbled with a glass on the cocktail tray.

"Eleven o'clock?" Xinh asked, taking a drink of the sweet juice.

"Precisely at eleven."

The candles on the Buddha shrine flickered weakly.

"How's he going to do it?"

"That I don't know."

Thanh went to the curtain and carefully parted it, studying the diners. "A gun or plastic."

"What?" Xinh said, turning toward Thanh.

"A gun or plastic—that's what he'll use—Kim's brother."

"A gun, yes. But not plastic," Mai said.

"No. Thanh's right. It could be plastic. Easy plant. Effective. He would be gone before it does its work."

"He'd have to blow up the whole restaurant!" Mai said.

"Right." Xinh walked to the curtain and peeked out. "He'd do it."

"What are you going to do, Xinh?"

The fan gave off a monotonous hum.

"Do you know what he looks like? Can you recognize him when he comes in?"

"I'll know him."

"Signal me, show me some sign when he gets here. When you've got my attention, walk to his table and take his order. Got it?"

"Got it, Xinh. But why don't you just leave now—before he gets here?"

"The doors are guarded outside," Thanh said. "She'll be picked up before she's gone ten feet."

"Just remember to give me a sign when he comes in. Thanh and I will take it from there." She patted Mai's hand. "Thank you, sister."

"Be careful, Xinh."

"I will." She handed her glass to Mai.

Mai picked up the tray and arranged the glasses. She walked through the curtain into the dining room without looking back.

There was a long silence.

"Thanh, if I don't make it . . ."

She took Thanh's hand in her own and pressed it to her cheek. The fan droned. From the dining room muted conversation filtered through the heavy curtains.

"Protect Steve. Get him outside as fast as you can," she said. "And Thanh . . ." She paused.

"Yes, sister."

"Don't let him know . . . I mean . . . ever."

Chapter Eight

The two girls walked back to the table together. Steve was still seated where they had left him. He was working on his second martini and was enjoying himself immensely, watching the busy restaurant activity. As the girls approached the table he quietly studied them. The perfect picture of Vietnamese youth and loveliness, he thought to himself. Long, ebony hair fell over their high cheekbones perfectly framing their soft, bronze faces and beautifully slanted eyes. His eyes followed their hair downward to their slim shoulders where it stopped briefly to form a soft curve and then cascade down their backs. Xinh's hair was longer than Thanh's, ending at the middle of her pretty bottom. Both girls wore identical *ao dais*, blue with lavender flower prints, and set off, of course, with perfect translucent green jade bracelets and earrings. Additionally, Xinh wore her treasured heirloom, a blue-green jade ring—a large stone ensconced on delicately handcrafted gold filigree. Thanh's *ao dai* was simply accented by the lovely gold necklace encircling her neck just below the high mandarin collar.

These were not wealthy girls. They came from very modest beginnings. But like all Vietnamese women, they scrimped and saved to accumulate enough money to buy the best gold, jade, and *ao dais* that they could possibly afford. The jewels were passed on to their children so that, eventually, in some families a small fortune had been amassed in jewelry. But no one ever thought of converting the jewels to cash, except in extreme emergencies. It was important, at least, to appear prosperous though one might be down to his last bowl of rice.

"You two always look so pretty, but especially so this evening," Steve said sincerely.

"*Cam on.*" Thank you, they said, bowing their heads to him in unison.

"How about some dinner?" he asked. They both nodded.

"The food very good this restaurant," Xinh said. "I think you like. You let Thanh and Xinh order. O.K.?"

"Good idea."

There was still plenty of time for dinner. The assassin wasn't scheduled to arrive until 11:00 and it was now only 9:00, giving them two hours before they would go into action.

But Xinh was worried over what to do with Steve. She didn't want him to be hurt and the risk of that happening was high. It would be best to get him out of the restaurant before the hit, but that would be impossible without further endangering his life.

"You like fish," she said, turning to Steve and picking up the menu.

"Sure do," he said, taking a sip of his martini.

"I want crab," Thanh said timidly.

"Oh, Thanh. Don't be difficult. You like steamed fish," Xinh said to her in Vietnamese.

"But I want crab tonight."

"*Con ca.*" Fish, Xinh affirmed.

"*Con cua.*" Crab, Thanh repeated sheepishly. She whispered something in Xinh's ear.

The two young women made an interesting sight to Steve as they argued over the choices. Their two heads, pressed together, were wedged inside the large, oversized menu, and they jabbered rapidly to each other in fluid, musical tones. He smiled to himself and took another pull at the martini.

After a few more minutes of debate Xinh was ready to announce the dinner selections to Steve. She took this task very seriously, she felt it was her responsibility to see that Steve was well fed. This might be his last meal—hers as well. So with a great deal of enthusiasm and animation, Xinh explained what they were having.

"First, we order big steam fish. Big one!" She spread her hands wide indicating its size. "Fish cooked with little bit peanut oil and leeks. Very tasty. You like."

"Will it come with the head?" Steve was curious to know.

"Oh, yes. But I promise head to Thanh. You cannot have."

"Fine. That's fine with me," he quickly answered. "Yes, that's just fine with me. O.K."

"Then we eat *cha gio.*"

"*Cha gio*? What's that?"

"Spring roll. Have crab, pork, bean thread rolled

83

in *banh trang*."

"*Banh trang*?"

"Rice paper."

"Oh."

"Everything fried in very hot oil. We wrap in vegetable leaves and dip in bean sauce. You like. Very good."

Xinh went on to meticulously describe the remainder of the menu, ten dishes all together, a veritable feast of Vietnamese delicacies. She took the same care in treating details when she conveyed the order to their waiter, telling him to make a special effort to see that their dinner was given the best consideration by the cooks. After several minutes of close consultation between herself and the waiter, Xinh appeared satisfied that the man had fully understood the innovations and special touches that she expected. At the last minute Thanh sulkily mentioned the crab again and Xinh finally relented bringing the number of courses to eleven.

The band swung into a tango and little Thanh began swaying her body to the Latin beat, oblivious of Steve's watchful eyes.

"Thanh, would you like to dance?" Steve asked her.

Thanh didn't understand at first, not being as conversant in English as Xinh. She looked at him for a moment then at Xinh.

"Would you like to dance?" he repeated, this time more slowly.

She suddenly became quite embarrassed, realizing what he had asked, and abruptly stopped keeping time to the music. She grew silent and just stared at the dinner plate in front of her. No way was she going to dance with this foreign dog. The nerve of him asking her to dance. It was one thing for Xinh to be cozy with an enemy pilot, but it was an entirely different matter for her. Still, he was handsome, and awfully polite. Maybe just one dance. She would make it short. She would have to ask Xinh's permission.

"*Toi co the nhan khong?*" Can I accept? she asked.

"*Di nhien, neu em thich.*" Of course, if you like. "*Toi ngac nhien thay em muon nhay voi anh ay.*" Frankly, I'm surprised that you would want to dance with him.

"*Toi rat thich thu.*" It will be an interesting experience.

At first Thanh was stiff and nervous. But as the chemistry of her young body became active, she loosened up and started to enjoy herself. No American had touched her before and in her youthful curiosity she began to experiment with Steve. She moved her hand delicately over his shoulder feeling the heavy muscles. She subtly allowed him to pull her in closer, so she could explore his large chest. She looked closely at the hair on his arm and studied his heavy bone structure. He's much different from Vietnamese men she decided. I think he's nice.

It's one thing to pick off these big Americans along jungle trails and in rice paddies, but it's an entirely different matter to be dancing with one and having dinner with him, she argued. In the former situation Thanh's feelings were cold, calculating, and hostile. In the latter, she noticed that she had become sensitive and responsive, and was enjoying it. I don't want to feel this way. But I'm a young, healthy girl and need the attention of a man. And Steve is a special person, I'm beginning to discover. Yes, I like this foreign invader. She stole a glance at his face from under his chin. Maybe he has a friend for me. She snuggled in a little closer, hoping that he wouldn't notice. Her little body quietly vibrated.

The music ended and they walked back to the table. Xinh noticed that Thanh was flushed and looked a bit lusty when she sat down. She smiled to herself and reached over to whisper in Thanh's ear.

"It appears that the enemy has conquered you."

"Well, he didn't contaminate me, if that's what you mean."

"Did you enjoy it?"

"Yes. I will admit that I enjoyed it."

"Would you dance with him again if he asked you?" Xinh asked, still smiling.

"Yes I would," Thanh said without hesitating, then quickly added, "Maybe he has a friend for me?"

"Oh, oh. My goodness, I certainly didn't expect this from you."

"Well, if you can do it so can I," Thanh whispered seriously.

The waiter interrupted them. Their food had arrived, carried by two serving attendants. A large, revolving tray was placed in the center of the dining table by one server. The other placed the special sauces, spices, and condiments on the tray and gave it a twirl to make room for the first three courses: Bi Bun, rice noodles covered by a layer of sliced roast pork, crushed peanuts, and vegetables, and served

86

with fish sauce; the whole, steamed fish, marinated in a hot oil, garlic and leek sauce; and *chao tom*, spiced shrimp grilled on sugar cane slices and served with Vietnamese vegetables, rice paper, and shrimp sauce. The head waiter arranged the food attractively on the circular tray and handed each of them a pair of beautifully carved pearly white chopsticks. He then filled their water glasses and placed a small, hand-painted rice bowl in front of each diner. Xinh stopped him from pouring tea into the tiny handle-less cups, reserving that ceremony for herself. She also did the serving of the steaming white rice heaped in a large ornate pot which the waiter passed to her. Xinh carefully ladled out portions of rice into each bowl with a wide, wooden spatula, serving Steve first, then Thanh, and finally herself. She followed the same pattern with the tea, all the time smiling demurely at Steve. Thanh sat patiently, her hands folded in her lap.

"You may go now," she said to the waiter in Vietnamese. "We eat now," she said to Steve. The two girls waited for him to begin before they picked up their first morsel of food.

As the meal progressed Steve did most of the talking, Xinh paying strict attention to his conversation and occasionally asking him a question. Periodically she would select a rather tasty-looking piece of pork or fish and place it in his rice bowl. Thanh, feeling closer to Steve now, chose one of the larger, more appetizing shrimp and placed it on Xinh's rice who in turn transferred it to Steve.

And so the next hours passed delightfully for Steve who thoroughly enjoyed being attended by two

Vietcong girls. They were good listeners and served him attentively. He danced with both of them again and toasted their beauty and long life. All the while Xinh kept a watchful eye on the door. Mai hovered nearby.

Just as the dish of *chao gio* was being placed on the table, Mai suddenly appeared before their table and gestured with her eyes toward the door. Kim's brother had come in. Xinh looked at Thanh who nodded in understanding. Steve was helping himself to the *chao gio*. There was no time to get him out. The VC agent would only stay a moment, long enough to set the bomb and hastily depart. Every second counted now.

Mai quickly walked to the thug's table and took his order. Xinh called over the waiter and asked for the bill.

"Aren't we going to finish the last course," Steve asked.

"It almost 11:00. We must leave now to hear Khanh Linh. She sing at Vinh Son bar. Must hurry or we miss her. O.K., Steve *oi*?"

"O.K. Whatever you say. You seem to be running the show tonight. Besides, I don't think I could get another thing down."

"*No qua*, full, yes?" Thanh smiled, patting her tummy.

Steve payed the bill and the three of them got up just as Mai left the agent's table. She glanced at Xinh from across the room. Xinh led the way, weaving her way through the tables, past the bandstand, Thanh and Steve following close behind. She stopped at the executioner's table, pulse racing.

"Excuse me, sir," she began in Vietnamese, "but aren't you Mr. De, Giao Vo Hai's cousin? I believe I met you at her wedding last year. She married Nguyen Van Tuan, you know."

"No. You must be mistaken."

"But I'm sure it was you. I remember because you were sitting next to my uncle and aunt. They seemed very fond of you. You remember don't you, Thanh?"

"Yes. He talked with your uncle and aunt most of the time. I don't think we could be wrong, sir."

"Are you sure you weren't at the wedding?" Xinh asked again.

"Yes, I'm sure," the agent said uncomfortably.

"Maybe it wasn't the wedding," Xinh said thoughtfully. "It might have been somewhere else. You look very familiar. Doesn't he look familiar, Thanh?"

"Yes, very familiar."

The wary assassin, himself experienced in matters of subterfuge, started to fidget and show signs of suspicion. He began casting sharp glances at Xinh and Thanh, then across at Steve. The two girls quickly caught his rapid eye movements and the sudden tapping of his fingers on the tabletop. They realized that he was going to make his move. Xinh quickly looked across at Thanh. She was coiled like a cobra. Her muscles were tensed, catlike, rippling under her thin skin. Steve, totally ignorant of what was developing, was completely taken by surprise by what happened next.

The assassin, now satisfied that his intentions had been discovered, suddenly jerked his leather jacket back and reached into his belt. Thanh quickly pulled

Steve out of the line of fire and threw herself in front of him as the blunt nose of the Smith and Wesson pulled free. Xinh, who had plunged her hand deep into her shoulder bag at the instant the man had committed himself, threw herself over the table and chairs, into the man's chest. She jammed the bag into his face and pulled the trigger as the two of them crashed into the customers seated at the next table. The explosion of the .45 was deafening in the confined room. At point-blank range the heavy slug tore off half the agent's head, scattering his cranium over the diners. His fingers reflexively contracting, he discharged his own gun into his groin; then his sphincter muscle let go and he emptied his bowels on the floor.

Xinh crawled out from under the overturned table, brushing noodle soup and brains from her gown. She and Thanh feverishly began searching around the floor. They pushed the agent over and found what they were looking for beneath his jacket, taped to his body. Plastic explosive—enough to kill most of the people in the restaurant. The crowd, already unnerved by the sudden violence, came completely apart when they saw the dreaded "plastic." They charged for the door in total panic, screaming and trampling and fighting with each other to save themselves. Some shattered windows and leaped into the river. Others clawed their way into corners or fought their way behind the bar, seeking protection.

Steve stood in the middle of this frantic mass of humanity, stunned by Xinh's attack, and handcuffed by his own ignorance. He just stood where he was, not really afraid, but very much confused at the terrible violence that had taken place right in front of him. His mind was trying to fit the pieces together but they wouldn't go into place. What was going on? Xinh and Thanh, two quiet and gentle girls suddenly taking command of a dangerous situation and demonstrating deadly skill in a violent attack— this baffled him. It was incongruous. Had he misjudged Xinh? Who was she?

It wasn't until he saw Xinh bend over the body, expertly remove the two electrical leads from the plastic, and defuse the bomb from the timing mechanism that he began to understand that he was in the presence of an extraordinary girl, one who was even more of a mystery to him than before.

Thanh began rushing among the people shouting, "*Min da bi go chot,*" The bomb has been defused, the danger is past. At first, the people wouldn't believe her, but gradually their panic subsided and they began to calm down. Those hurt in the overpowering flight were tended to. People even returned to the scene and curiously poked at the explosive, examining it to be sure it was inert. The Vietnamese now took to wild incessant chattering, trying to figure out what had happened. They gathered around the corpse and asked questions of each other. The police arrived and pushed their way through the crowd at the same time Xinh was rolling the body over on its back. Steve stood transfixed, wondering with the crowd what she was going to do next. She placed her two small strong hands on the V of the man's collar and pulled down with all her might, tearing away the shirt. The people let out a gasp and fell backward, repelled by the large Oriental eye tattooed on the man's chest.

"Dao Dua!" they all moaned. *"Dao Dua!"* They took to low whispers and pressed together in small groups. *"Dao Dua, Dao Dua. Ong la Dao Dua."* He's a Dao Dua.

The Vietnamese surrounded Xinh, patting her, touching her. A reporter from the *Saigon News* who had been eating dinner in the restaurant forced his way up front and began asking Xinh questions. Outside, a mousy, rat-faced man peered through the window.

But the police were less enthusiastic about Xinh's heroic actions. They parted the crowd and escorted her to a waiting car. As the car roared away, Steve saw her small face pressed against the glass, her sad eyes saying good-bye.

Chapter Nine

As Steve was pondering what to do next, Thanh was hailing a cab.

"Di di." Quick, hurry, she said. "We follow Xinh. Help her."

"But how?"

Thanh shoved him into the cab and she jumped in beside him. She gave instructions to the driver to take them to the police station and then turned her full attention on Steve.

"Xinh big trouble."

"I know. She blew that guy's head off in there," he said, looking out the rear window at the huge crowd gathering around the restaurant. He pulled out his handkerchief and wiped his perspiring face.

"Khong! Khong!" No! No! In her haste to express herself, Thanh started talking in very rapid Vietnamese, forgetting that Steve wasn't completely fluent in the language.

"Hold on, kid. Wait a minute," he said, grabbing her by the shoulders. "Slow down. I don't understand what you're saying."

She quieted down, then started in again, slowly.

"Xinh in trouble."

"Yes, we've already established that."

"No. You no understand. She trouble because gun."

"Right. She shot that bloody fool."

"O.K. shoot bloody fool. Xinh no go jail shoot bloody fool. He have bomb. Go jail because gun."

"What? What are you talking about?"

Thanh stopped and took a big breath, wishing she had more English words.

"Xinh no can have gun. Vietnamese law say only army can have gun. Xinh no army. Understand?"

"Uh, huh. Civilians can't carry guns. Of course. But where did she get the gun?"

"No matter," Thanh said passing it off.

"So she's going to jail for possessing a gun, not for shooting the Dao Dua—strange."

"Dao Dua have bomb. O.K. shoot. No O.K. have gun. Understand?"

"No, I don't understand. But go on. What can we do?"

"You do. No we."

"I do?"

"Yes. You tell police Xinh shoot Dao Dua your gun. You give Xinh gun. Your gun. No Xinh gun."

The taxi squealed to a halt outside the police station. Thanh kicked the door open and pulled Steve out. He had to hold her back so he could pay the driver. She kept pulling at his shirt trying to hurry him, *"Di di."*

She ran up the stairs and burst into the station house, Steve close behind. Inside, the police officers were emptying the contents of Xinh's handbag onto a table and examining her gun. One man in particular was angrily questioning her. She looked confused, unable to respond to the policeman's attack. He kept pointing at the gun. Xinh remained silent.

"It's mine! That's my gun," Steve shouted, striding confidently up to the police. "She got it from me. I gave it to her."

The policeman looked Steve over, carefully noting the captain's bars, pilot's wings, and air medals pinned to his uniform.

"Your gun, sir?" he said, dropping the tone of his voice.

"Yes, that's right. My gun. She often works late at the base and there have been attacks, as you well know. VC and otherwise. I gave her my gun for protection."

"But sir, you must know that it's against our laws for a civilian to have a gun," he said in excellent English.

"It's a damn good thing she had it tonight or you would have had a lot of dead people on your hands," Steve said politely.

"Well, there's no doubt she did prevent a disaster and— But there's still the matter of the gun. The law clearly—"

"I'll take full responsibility for the gun. It's only right that you punish me since it's mine and I gave it to her. May I suggest an official report to my commanding officer?"

The two men continued to argue over the gun. The longer they argued the more obstinate the policeman became, demanding that Xinh must be punished for carrying a gun. The shooting of the Dao Dua was never mentioned.

Thanh, who had remained quietly in the background, grew impatient. She could see that Steve was totally ignorant of Vietnamese political ways. She came up behind Steve and tugged at his shirt, drawing him aside.

"He want money."

"What?"

"Give him money. He let Xinh go. He understand not Xinh gun. Ready let her go. Want money now. You give him money, he give you Xinh."

"How much?"

The next day Steve took Thanh back to the police station—this time with 40,000 piasters.

"Shall I come with you?"

"No. Better I go. Easier for policeman take money. Vietnamese way. We understand."

"Don't give him the money unless you're sure he'll give you Xinh," he said as she stepped out of the cyclo. "I'll be waiting here."

Twenty minutes later Xinh and Thanh walked out of the building, arms around each other, chattering away and smiling. Xinh looked a little tired but the overnight stay in jail hadn't affected her charm any.

"I humbly thank you, Captain Steve, for help me. You good man. I cry last night think you maybe no can help. I very happy you come today free me."

"Thanh had a lot to do with getting you out. She seemed to know exactly what was needed. I just followed her instructions."

Xinh patted Thanh's shoulder. *"Cam on, em."* Thank you little sister, she said.

Xinh climbed into the cyclo next to Steve. Thanh excused herself and disappeared into the throng of scurrying people, waving good-bye. Xinh opened her handbag and showed it to Steve. The .45 nestled neatly in the bottom among her feminine things.

"Maybe you had better give me that thing," Steve said with a worried look.

"You take." Xinh pushed the handbag at him.

Steve thought for a moment. "Well, on the other hand, you seem to know how to handle it pretty well. You go ahead and keep it. I won't even ask you where you got it."

"I keep?"

"Yeah. You keep. After what happened at the restaurant, I'll feel a lot safer with you packing that cannon. Never know when we'll need it again. Going somewhere with you is like being accompanied by a personal bodyguard."

"I take care you. For sure no one hurt you when Xinh around," she said with finality, almost like an oath, as she looked at Steve commandingly.

She gave instructions to the driver and they pulled away, down the middle of the crowded street. Steve leaned back in his seat, Xinh holding his hand, relaxed, watching the swirling crowd of Vietnamese going about their daily business as they had for hundreds of years. This war isn't going to change any of these people, he thought to himself. What the hell are we doing here?

He looked at the young girl beside him. How had this all happened? Just last year he was home, back in the States, eating hamburgers and drinking cokes, engaged to a fair-haired American girl, attending concerts, shopping in air-conditioned malls, and watching Monday-night football. Now it was Nam. "Nam." He whispered the word, carefully measuring the sound. "Vietnam," a strange foreign sound. An alien place with cyclos, raven-haired women with pretty long eyes, napalm, *nuoc mam, di di,* gook sores, Buddhist pagodas, Katusha rockets, spring roll, and girls with peculiar names like "Xinh." Nam; a moment in time. How had it happened? Why was he here? And who was this girl beside him? His head hurt thinking about it. An aberration in his time line? Or was time pulling him along toward his destiny, only to become a confused memory? The cyclo rolled on, the driver pedaling as he had for centuries.

Xinh remained quiet, sensing Steve's mood, alert to his wistful gaze. She detected his unfulfilled longing, his yearning for more familiar surroundings—for his own people. Her heart filled with love for him and she softly stroked the back of his hand. Someday he will leave me. My time will become a memory too—like his. He will return to his fair-skinned girls. He will. But I will still dream. Yes, dream of some day becoming his good wife and bearing his children. My dream. I will live it while he is still with me, and time has not yet become a memory.

But she decided that part of him would remain with her forever. She would not be content with a memory. She would see to it that he planted his strong seed within her fertile young body, and she would nourish it until she became heavy with child. Then she would be comforted. The memory would live.

Even as a child she had cherished the intense desire to grow up quickly and become a wife and mother. To take care of a man, to bear his child. Her desire had matured, been blown into a hot flame. Her craving would not be denied. It was greater than the war, greater than the Vietcong. Her need had its roots in the ancient past, springing from the age-old Asian concepts of femininity. And physical desire was calling to her now, heavy in her veins, urging her on.

She was in love, so terribly in love, and she wanted desperately to express it.

"I love you, Steve." She moved forward a bit and sat at the edge of the seat, her shapely body twisted at the waist so she could look squarely at him. "You maybe little sad, want go home America? Back 'real world,' you call it."

"You always seem to know how I feel, what I'm thinking, don't you, little one?" He craved a cold Jonathon apple, to feel it deliciously pop and squirt between his teeth. A good apple always snapped back at you, Dad had always said.

"Xinh do. I love you. Feel what you feel. Want share with you."

Steve winced inside. He felt crazy uncomfortable when she talked like that.

"Thanks, Xinh, but right now I'm a little confused about Vietnam and what I'm doing here—what any of us are doing here."

"You hate Communists? You hate Vietcong?"

"Hate them? I don't even know who they are. How

can I hate someone I've never known. I wouldn't know a Vietcong if he came up and stared me square in the eye."

Xinh had to bite her tongue to keep from laughing.

"You like Vietnamese people? Vietcong?"

"Not so much. They're strange. I think they scare me a bit."

"Steve want be free . . . live?"

"Sure I do. What kind of question is that?"

"Vietcong same. No different. Like me maybe." She bit her tongue harder. "They people too. Want live. Marry. Have family. Need love too. You think so?"

"I think so."

The cyclo pressed on through the horde of legs, bicycles, Hondas, Vespas, and French Renaults. Women trotted along the walks with baskets full of unusual fruits and vegetables. Dried and fresh fish and meats, live ducks and chickens were hawked from straw mats spread on every available space along the street. The unique, pungent smells of Asia filled his sinuses, desensitizing him to his familiar middle-class hygiene.

Overhead, the intense blue of sky. Billowing columns of white cumulus building in the east. A faint hint of breezes moving ahead of the coming showers. F-4s banking over the low hills. Pretty, swaying *ao dais* mixing with army green.

The driver pedaled through the center of town and into the countryside, where the people and pavement, brick and mortar gave way to water buffalo and red earth, hooches and palms. Xinh motioned to the driver seated behind them to stop. Steve looked around.

"Why are we stopping?" he asked.

"You see. Xinh have surprise. You see real Vietnam now."

"The real Vietnam? What's the real Vietnam?"

"What GI never know. Come, I show."

They stepped out of the cyclo and the driver turned around and headed back to town. Steve stood in the middle of the broken road, watching him as if he were being abandoned. At that moment he felt like the foreigner he was, naked and vulnerable, with no rights.

"You come," Xinh said, motioning to him from the deep grass along the irrigation canal, her hand waving up and down. He could never get used to that wave. In America it meant good-bye. Here it meant come.

Through the grass Steve could see a footbridge in the distance, spanning the canal. It led to a narrow path that traveled along the paddy dike. He stepped off the road and down into the grass. Xinh reached out and grabbed his hand, pulling him forward. Instinctively he pulled back.

"Where are we going? I'm very uncomfortable here, Xinh," he said, uncertainty in his voice.

"You afraid?"

"Frankly, yes. I'd be a fool if I wasn't. I don't know what's out there. Do you?"

She walked back to where he was standing and stood very close, looking up at him, her hair hanging down over the front of her small breasts. She brushed a few strands from her high cheeks.

"This my country. I know what out there," she said, pointing through the grass. "You come me, be O.K. You go alone, maybe not O.K."

"Oh, yeah. What makes you so sure?"

"You think I no take care you. You think I let you get hurt. Who take care you restaurant last night? Who?" she said angrily.

"You did," he said sheepishly.

"You better believe it, GI," she said, pushing a miniature finger into his broad chest. "Anyone try hurt you, I kill them. You remember, no forget! You safe any place you go Xinh. Any place Vietnam."

He stared at her incredulously.

"Now you follow me."

He followed.

Chapter Ten

Xinh led Steve through the tall elephant grass, parting the way with her body and pushing the dense cover aside with her arms. He followed close behind, marveling at the smoothness with which she moved, unhindered, through the grass, not missing a step, as if this were a routine jaunt through the six-foot-high blades. He noticed that she had taken off her shoes, and the small footprints she left in the soft, moist earth revealed the evenness of her strides. It was obvious this was her territory. She was just as at home in the bush as she was on the dance floor.

Steve stumbled along, slapping at the grass, following in Xinh's tracks and complaining under his breath for allowing himself to be told what to do by this little elf. His discomfort was compounded by not being able to see more than a few feet ahead. He would have felt much better carrying an M-16 in the spooky grass. He was a setup for an ambush, had this been a field operation. High up in the seat of his Phantom he never thought about these things.

Much to his relief, they finally reached the canal and climbed onto the first paddy dike. Xinh with her shoes in her hand led the way over the rickety bamboo span crossing the canal. She literally bounded like a rabbit along the two narrow poles, covering the thirty feet in a flash. She waved Steve over from the other side.

Steve started across then changed his mind. He took off his shoes and tossed them to Xinh. By this time she was unable to hold her laughter. He frowned at her. With trepidation and arms held out like a tightrope walker, he started over the six-inch-wide bridge. Xinh jumped up and down, squealing with delight and encouraging him on, clapping her hands.

Slowly, inch by inch, he negotiated the wobbling bamboo. About three quarters of the way he stopped to adjust his feet, lost his momentum, and began to teeter. Xinh rushed out to steady him, but it was too late. The two of them, arms circled around each other, crashed over backward into the canal.

Laughing and dripping wet, they struggled up the bank and lay in the grass to catch their breath. Xinh took off Steve's clothes and squeezed out the excess water, spreading them out to dry on the bank.

"I love it. I haven't had so much fun since I was a kid," he said.

Xinh walked to the edge of the canal and stood there for a few minutes throwing pieces of bamboo into the green water.

"Tell Xinh about Steve girl live America." She looked down at her hands. She didn't turn to face him.

Steve put his hands on her shoulders and turned her around. He saw that she was biting her lower lip.

"I don't want to talk about her," he said.

"She pretty girl—yes?"

"Yes. She's pretty."

He could see her teeth pressing harder into her lip. Her eyes remained fixed on her tightly clenched hands.

"What color her hair?"

"Blond."

"What color that?"

"Yellow."

Her hands were turning white. He thought she would twist her fingers off.

"Oh . . . yellow." She pressed her toes into the grass. "That pretty. American girl have pretty yellow hair, blue eyes."

"I'd rather not talk about American girls."

"My hair black. My eyes too."

"Yes . . . very black."

"What you think about that?"

"Pretty."

"Yellow hair, blue eyes more pretty."

Some of the color had returned to her hands. Her eyes were closed.

"Steve, American girl have lots money too—like American GI?" She rubbed one bare foot over the other.

"Xinh, please."

"Vietnam girl poor."

She opened her eyes and looked directly into his pale blue ones. He returned her steady glare. Those long, soul-searching eyes—eyes of command—penetrating his ethos. He looked away.

"You love her?" She didn't expect an answer.

Steve pulled her down beside him. He kissed her long and deeply, and felt her little heart pounding wildly against his bare chest. He pulled away her *ao dai* and made sweet, tender love to her. Only the elephant grass saw. And Xinh nearly died with pleasure, giving her man the ultimate gift.

Afterward they lay on their backs looking up through the grass at the clouds rolling against the dense topaz sky. The air was still. He raised her up. That was when he saw it—the angry raw scar crawling the length of her spine. He recoiled. Circular-shaped blotches covered her otherwise perfect buttocks. Napalm had burned quarter-size holes through the skin into the muscle tissue.

Somewhere deep in his soul a primeval thing screamed and welled up and clawed at his throat. There are no names for such a thing. It is the core of the individual to which we pay lip service. It is the stuff of life itself—what makes us human, or inhuman. It is the totality of a person's experience reckoned with, filed, and forgotten. It makes every man truly different from all others—and makes him the same.

Not in the first minute, or the second, or the third did the thing happen to Steve. But then it was there. The high g turn. The stick in his gloved hand, the thumb settling on the release button, the flash and roll of liquid fire . . . Suddenly it was back, the look of the sun, the rising smoke, the radio calls, the tree lines; and their faces—all of them—the men, the women, the children. He could see it all, looking down the pulsing red throat of a beast . . . his throat.

He sunk to his knees, wrapping his arms around her

legs, his tears wetting her thighs. The thing was here—all the moments coming together into a single moment of truth—and it seared his mind like a seething caldron of churning, swirling, fiery jellied gasoline. It lay there, saying its say, untouched, flowing out of his eyes. The fuse, after sputtering wetly, had flared and caught.

He turned her around, parting her long tresses like a curtain that hid a secret, and forced himself to take a long, lacerating look. Her beautiful golden body perfectly sculptured, was indelibly stamped with the signature of war. Still on his knees, he raised both hands and placed them gently on her back, sensitively tracing with spread fingers the terrible glistening wound along the path of the burning napalm, feeling her writhing pain as the stuff ate through her young flesh.

She held still, embarrassed by her nakedness and the discovery of the ugly blemish on her beauty, but understanding Steve's need to saturate himself with the mutilation as a sort of atonement. She was no stranger to the casualties of war. She inflicted them and had them inflicted on her. She watched her comrades fall, and accepted her own injuries philosophically. They came with the job.

When she felt his hands stop trembling she turned around and knelt facing him. She asked him to fix her hair. She showed him how to pull the long, wet tresses together over her back, twisting so the water ran out in rivulets. He loosened the twist at the ends and she shook her head a few times, spreading the silky threads into a wide, black fan over her back and shoulders. When it was dry she showed him how to braid it into a long rope.

Dry again, she clothed Steve and smoothed out her *ao dai*. Still barefoot, she led the way down the paddy dike. Steve's emotions calmed and he began to notice the beauty surrounding him. Fields of shimmering green rice, framed in rows of tall coconut palms and thick stands of bamboo, soothed his war-torn brain. Here and there the Vietnamese worked their fields with heavy, snorting water buffalo, or walked the narrow paths with hoes and rice bundles slung over their shoulders. Above was a brilliant tropical sky of pure azure blue studded with columns of intensely white puffy clouds.

Steve reached out on impulse and caught Xinh's flowing hair. For the first time since beginning his tour of duty, Steve realized how beautiful Vietnam really was. The sun was on his flesh and the breeze came up and fluttered his shirt sleeves.

The time passed quickly as they walked from rice field to rice field along the dikes and tree lines, and through large areas choked with melons, chinese cabbage, and rows of leafy rau and white radishes. Soon they came to a slow, meandering green river lined with bamboo and beautiful flowering tamarind trees. Children were playing along its banks and swimming in the eddies, shouting to each other and gaily laughing. Farther down, a group of women were pulling eels and flat-bellied fish from the current. They argued good-naturedly over who had the best catch. Steve had stopped to watch and Xinh had to pull him away, so engrossed was he in their activity.

They continued their journey, following the twists

in the river and enjoying their conversation, Xinh answering the many questions Steve asked about Vietnamese country life and the customs of the people. His eyes were being opened to the real Vietnam and he liked what he saw. He wanted to know more. He became aware that everyone seemed to know Xinh and that they all had a word or wave to give her as she passed. He edged up closer to her just as they turned a bend in the lazy river. A picture-book hamlet was revealed.

"Xinh, this is a wonderful place. It's so beautiful here and everyone seems happy."

"Yes, very beautiful. My country beautiful place. All Vietnam like this one time when no war. Everyone live together in peace, grow rice, raise children, and love."

Steve grew quiet for a moment, thinking over her words, wondering why governments wouldn't leave people alone.

"What is this place? I like it."

"You say you want see real Vietnam. I show you real Vietnam. This my village. These people raise me. They bring me here from Binh Duong after father, mother, family killed by artillery, napalm. I live here many year. They take care me. I love them. They love me."

Walking underneath a spreading woody vine, Xinh reached up and plucked a row of brilliant red and purple floral bracts from a hanging branch.

"Bong giay," she said, holding the flower up to Steve's nose.

"Bong giay," he repeated. The flower had a sweet, strawberry redolence.

"Mean paper flower your language."

They walked on.

"Your favorite?" he asked, pointing to the thin, parchment blossoms.

"No. Tamarind Xinh like. Thanh like too." She put the *bong giay* blooms to her cheek.

"What do they look like?"

"See," she said pointing to a large tree with pinnate leaves and red-striped yellow flowers.

"Pretty," he said.

"We eat tamarind flowers."

"No kidding."

"Can eat seed too," she said. "Make candy."

They stopped and looked at the long seed pods hanging from the Indian date. The pods were too high for Steve to reach. He patted the yellowish trunk.

"That's a fine tree."

"Steve have flowers live in America?"

"Oh, sure."

"You have best one?"

"What, Xinh?"

"You know—best one—fa . . . vo . . . rrrr . . ."

"Favorite?"

"That what I mean—best one." She patted the tree trunk like he had.

"I don't have a favorite." He touched her hand. "No. No favorite."

She put the floral bract in her hair and looked demurely up at him. His blood rose.

"I want to kiss you." He tried to pull her toward him.

"No can do, GI." She pushed him away.

"Why not?" Her hand was still on his chest.

"No can do."

"Back there at the canal we—"

"That back there. We here now."

"But, Xinh."

"No, GI." Her hand stiffened against his chest. After a time a playful smile cracked the corners of her lips. She patted his hand.

They left the river and headed into the sleepy hamlet with the mud-brick huts and thatched hooches.

"I take you see my uncle. He hamlet chief. Live there," she said, pointing to one of the larger, sturdier-looking dwellings. "We get something eat, drink. Talk."

Steve obediently followed, unusually excited and increasingly interested by all of this, knowing that he was experiencing a rare look into Vietnam's bowels.

Coming up to the house, Xinh motioned for Steve to wait under the overhang while she went inside, scattering ducks and chickens in her path to the door. Inside, he could hear Xinh and several people engaged in excited conversation. A few children had taken up positions around him, smiling and studying his uniform.

Steve, feeling uneasy, tried to make friends with the children until Xinh reappeared, followed by a wizened old man and two beautiful women; one elderly and the other only a few years older than Xinh.

"This my uncle Dong, his first wife Hoa, and his second wife Hao," Xinh said introducing Steve to the family. The three politely bowed, palms pressed together in front of them, never taking their eyes off Steve. All three spoke English, the old man having been educated in America, Xinh informed Steve.

Steve was taken inside and given a chair by the younger, second wife, Hao. He noticed that by Vietnamese peasant standards Uncle was living rather well. His furniture though old, was made from polished hardwood, probably teak or mahogany. He had a floor, uneven red-brick tile, not the usual bare earth found in most village houses. His walls were thick, and pole beams covered with a thick layer of palm thatch formed the roof. The windows were shuttered. There was a heavy plank door with a metal latch. And, of course, the two beautiful wives adorned his home.

The main room, in which they were sitting, contained the kitchen with its earthen stove set in the rear. A back entrance led to the hamlet's community well. The house had a small bedroom, and a bathhouse stood a few feet outside the rear entrance.

As soon as Steve and Uncle were settled with glasses of homemade Vietnamese gin and smoking pipes, Xinh and the two wives enthusiastically turned to preparing the afternoon meal. They were soon joined by several neighbor women and some young girls who brought more food and lent a helping hand. Their husbands, coming in from the fields, brought chairs or just squatted around the floor, eager to find out about the American flyer Xinh had brought into their midst.

So it was with a great deal of curiosity and interest that Steve was invited into the hamlet chief's home. As word of Steve's visit spread rapidly throughout the hooches, the uncle's home quickly filled with people inquiring about the old man's health, returning articles they had borrowed and now found it convenient to return, or dropping off a few eggs or a basket of mangos. Some supposedly stopped to ask counsel of their sage.

Xinh and the ladies had no trouble keeping everyone's rice bowls filled with noodles, steamed vegetables, and *nuoc mam* pork. As the crowd grew so did the food supplies being provided by the curious. A festive atmosphere developed and the Vietnamese overflowed to the yard surrounding Uncle's house. Children played, old women chewed and spat betel, young women gambled at Tu Sac, and the men drank milky gin and smoked.

People crowded the windows and doorways, while others squatted on the floor around Steve and the old man. Two urchins had ensconced themselves on Steve's knees and a third nestled between his legs. Women admired his good looks, and the men discussed his decorations, respecting his courage and skill.

By now, Steve had begun to wonder how many of these cheerful, bright-eyed villagers were covert VC. He was acutely aware that many Vietnamese were in one form or another emotionally tied to the Vietcong. Having relatives on both sides of the conflict made it difficult to choose which ideology to support, so most Vietnamese, particularly the country folk, chose to ride the fence, supporting the government during the day and the VC at night. To them, the government was corrupt, brutal, and exploitive—but tolerable and fatherly when you learned to deal with it. The VC, on the contrary, though uncompromising and often ruthless in their methods, offered to revolutionize the country by ridding it of well-known and wide-spread bribery, selling of political favors, immoral behavior, fraternization with foreign devils, and other improper and debilitating conduct. They promised to place the country in the control of the people and to punish those who exploited them, a popular notion among the common folk who made up the majority of Vietnam's population.

By the time the sun began setting behind the tamarind trees, casting long shadows through the hamlet into Uncle's open door, Steve had developed a new sense of awareness and understanding of Vietnamese life. He had forgotten his earlier suspicions and entered into unguarded and free expression. And they, finding him friendly and open, reciprocated with great quantities of affection and conversation. They taught him colloquial phrases and words to add to his growing proficiency in their language, took him for a walk through the hamlet, proudly pointing out their community improvement projects—a new well, a meeting house, and the beginnings of a new irrigation system for the farms—all very impressive and well engineered. These were industrious and resourceful people, family centered, dedicated to each other, and committed to the land.

"Where do you live?" asked the little girl sitting on his knee. Her serene and untroubled, deep black eyes looked innocently into his round blue ones, exploring their strangeness. He was the first American she had seen. Steve had excited a queer wonder in her.

She realized he did not naturally belong to this place.

Steve thought for a moment, then said in Vietnamese: "I come from a place very far away. Across the ocean. A place you will never see."

"What are you doing so far from home?" she asked in childish honesty.

Steve could sense all ears tuning in on his answer. He looked around the room. All eyes were glued to him. No one stirred. It was very quiet and the evening gloaming covered the hamlet in a dim half-light. Then came the soft rains pattering on the palm roof.

"I don't know, I just don't know," he finally said.

Part II

The End of Innocence

"Forgive me . . . please . . . someone forgive me."

Chapter Eleven

He shook his head trying to clear it of sleep.

"Time wake up, Captain Steve. Two o'clock. Time wake up."

He tried to focus on the houseboy.

"Two o'clock morning, Captain Steve."

He lifted himself onto one elbow, looking around the black room. The cobwebs wouldn't clear.

"Good morning, Captain Steve. Time you get up." He switched on the small overhead light bulb and placed Steve's shoes and clothes within reach on the bed. "You wake now?"

"Yes. I'm awake," Steve said dully.

Satisfied, the boy left to wake another pilot.

Steve rolled over and sat on the edge of the steel bed. The 2 A.M. wake-up came early. He shook his head again. Special day. What was it? He rubbed his eyes. Secret mission. Cambodia. The Skull. He was leading. Right. That was it. He was leading. He was wide awake now. He jumped up and did a few deep breathing exercises. He quickly washed and shaved, pulled on his jumpsuit and hurried along the rock walk between the barracks to a breakfast of powdered

119

eggs, bacon, and coffee.

The officers mess was empty. Most of the pilots wouldn't get their wake-ups for another two hours. They were sleeping through while he and the planners and his flight leaders worked out the strike. His mind became a squirrel cage of activity. Must make sure that there were enough strike aircraft and that ordnance, radio frequencies, aircraft crews, and call signs were given final approval.

He wasn't very hungry, but he ate anyway, knowing he would need the breakfast later—when he got into action. He forced down the watery eggs and gulped his black coffee. He spread his hand. Steady as a rock. He mustn't forget to double-check with the ramp guys and analysts to be sure that each flight had four aircraft—two elements in each. The squirrel cage hummed. He couldn't afford any stragglers today. Not on this one. He needed max bomb coverage, and he wanted full coordination and support for each flight. A flight with too few eyes would weaken the squadron's security; he needed mutual support within each element. The Skull was no place for straying aircraft. He finished off his toast and downed the warm orange juice.

Walking to the OPS center he had mixed emotions about his wisdom in agreeing to lead the strike. He wasn't sure if he was ready for this much responsibility. But Wing had given him first crack at the job since he was the most familiar with the Skull and its Vietcong sanctuaries just inside Cambodia. He had flown several low-level reconn missions into the heavily defended area and pretty well knew target locations and the best ingress and egress routes.

Much to everyone's surprise he had been fired on by SAMs and radar-controlled triple A. And two Soviet-built Migs had been scrambled against him. His cameras brought home the evidence.

Washington had approved the strike. It was to be top secret. Only the strike pilots, the wing commander, and a few specialists were to know. If any of the strike force were shot down inside Cambodia, no rescue effort would be launched. Therefore, Washington wanted the Phantoms flown by single, unattached officers, captains and below. There would be no acknowledgment of the attack.

Inside the operations building, Colonel Tramaine and his staff of specialists were fine-tuning the strike. They briefed Steve on the technicalities of the mission, much of which he already knew. Tramaine pulled him aside afterward to explain the political complexities involved. He added that a promotion was in order upon completion of the mission, if successful.

"I know you're not the kind of officer that's impressed by these kinds of things, Steve, but I want you to know that we have been thinking of giving you your oak leaves for some time now. The only thing in the way has been your age—too young—but I think I can swing it after this mission. You've got an outstanding career ahead of you, boy. You're a fine pilot and an outstanding officer."

"Thank you, sir. I do the best I can."

"I know you do, Steve. And I'm proud of you. You've helped us a great deal over here. I don't know how much that's worth to you. It's a crummy war, and I'm probably the only one that appreciates your effort. Certainly damn few people back home do, and I often wonder if Washington is even behind us, with all their bungling and interference."

"Yes, sir. Too many restrictions. The pilots complain a lot about the selection of targets and the 'protected' areas like Xuong Song and the others. Isn't there anything we can do about it?"

"Maybe your strike today into Cambodia and hitting the sanctuaries is the start of lifting these restrictions. I don't know. Good luck, Steve. Hang tough."

"Thank you, Colonel."

They saluted each other and he watched Tramaine leave the building and disappear into the early morning darkness. Good man. Wish he were leading the mission instead of me, he thought to himself. I hope I can pull it off. I have to pull it off. I have no choice.

He called together his eager flight leaders and they began going over the fine details in the squadron room with the planners. Reconnaissance photos and maps were again studied in depth, probing for the best approach, altitude, cruise speed, attack angle, and egress route. The truck parks and storage areas were easily identified from the infrared photos, and his sensitive cameras had also recorded the locations of surface-to-air missile sites and antiaircraft gun emplacements. Finally the strike plan began to fall in place. The maps and charts were made; weather was verified; bomb loads, routes, and technical data were finalized; and Colonel Tramaine gave his approval.

The first light of dawn was beginning to creep across the still rice paddies when Steve called in all his pilots for the final briefing.

"If you're not scared you'd better ask yourself some serious questions. Most of you haven't flown against modern weaponry and heavily defended targets, your missions having been primarily ground support against poorly equipped VC. But this morning you're going to come up against a more sophisticated enemy—the North Vietnamese Army, heavily fortified and entrenched in their jungle redoubt at the confluence of the Ho Chi Minh and Sihanouk Trails in Cambodia."

He paused and looked at their faces. No emotion. Well, what did he expect? Panic?

"Watch your ECM indicators and call out all SAM launches."

"SAM launches! SAMs, this far south?" someone said in disbelief.

"Frankly, it surprised us. But the photos have clearly identified several sites—and I had one fired at me on my last reconn run. Also, watch for Migs."

"You're kidding!"

"Migs?"

"Affirmative. Apparently, they've moved a few down from the Hanoi area along with the SAMs and triple A. No one knows who's flying them. Maybe Russians or Cambodians. More than likely NVA," he said.

"Good grief."

He moved to the wall map of South Vietnam and Cambodia. He stabbed the Skull with the pointer. "Here's your target. Along this valley, just inside the Cambodian border. It's a vast staging area for resupply and troop movements into South Vietnam.

The NVA and VC operate with impunity from these sanctuaries."

"What happened. How come we get to hit 'em now?" a young lieutenant wanted to know.

"Who knows? Washington gave the approval, the order coming from the White House. It's top secret. You're not to talk to anyone about this mission. It never took place. Understood?"

Heads nodded.

"If you're hit, get back over the mountains into Vietnam. If you buy it in Cambodia there's nothing we can do. *No Rescue*. You're on your own. In any event, if a pilot has to bail out, the closest plane will follow him down, give him cover, and pinpoint where the chute hits. If he comes down on the Nam side, everyone else get altitude and call Rescap. Go light on the fuel." He paused. "We can all take turns on the tanker until we get the choppers and Spads in and out. No loners Capping. Support each other. No sense in losing more ships than necessary."

"There's nothing we can do for each other, then, if shot down inside Cambodia?" another pilot asked, wanting to be absolutely sure of the order.

"Roger that. The order is clear: *no rescue*. All you can do is confirm any chutes and cover for the guys until they can get to good cover and hide out."

No one spoke. This was a situation they would rather forget.

"We're going to hit them hard; we'll try and get the job done the first time around. If not, we're going to have to go back again. We'll be loaded up with five hundred and thousand pounders. I'll lead us up through Phum Long and then make a right turn at Siem Xop, coming up the valley from the south," he said, tracing the route with the pointer. "Egress through Buong Thuy, here, and then up along the river." He looked around the room for questions. All eyes were fastened on him. "My call sign will be Eagle. Hensley on my wing. Stoner, number three. Pete, four. Billy-Joe will lead Comanche flight. Tranari, Chicago flight. Camacho, Kingfish flight. Any questions? . . .O.K., get your gear and mount up in fifteen minutes."

The F-4 drivers stood. Steve stuck his charts and maps and photos of the target into his big knee-pockets and then got together with his flight leaders and discussed last-minute tactics. That done, he stopped off for a cup of coffee and went to the toilet.

Steve entered the fast-filling equipment room. He removed his jewelry, wallet, and pocket junk, leaving only his dog tags to identify him. He put on his lightweight flight suit, then zippered himself into the g suit with its many pockets. It carried flares, knives, compass, rations and other survival articles. He stepped into his flying boots and buckled a Colt .38 pistol and ammo belt around his waist. The survival vest went on next. It had more gear in it, including two bottles of drinking water and the survival radio with its beeper, which gave off a most unnerving distress signal—a disagreeable and painful noise that alerted all pilots in the area that a comrade was down. The parachute had a beeper too.

He picked up his hard helmet, kneepad, parachute, and a bag crammed with operating procedures and checklists; then he climbed into the truck that took him to the flight line and his waiting aircraft.

"Everything ready to go chief?"

"Roger, sir. Our baby looks good," Kelly said, snapping a salute.

"No leaks?"

"None."

He strolled around the death machine, shaking the bombs and external fuel tanks, looking for anything his crew chief might have missed. The Phantom seemed to literally pulse with lethal energy. It was like a race horse heaving against its bridle waiting for the rider to mount.

"How's it going Kelly? How's the new grandson?" He had a few minutes to kill before engine start and felt like talking.

"Oh, just great, Captain," he said, pulling the well-worn picture from his wallet and handing it to Steve.

"He hasn't changed since last week," Steve said.

Kelly laughed. "I show this picture so often I forget who's seen it. He's a great kid. He's going to be a jet jockey too."

"Is that right? What makes you think so?"

"Because I want him to be."

"You already lost two sons flying, Sarge. You sure you want your grandson to take the risk?"

"Only lost one, Captain. The other's in Hanoi. The kid's father. He'll get out. And he'll fly again. We're an Air Force family and my grandson's going to continue the line. You can make book on it. You ever fly against Hanoi, Captain?"

"Yeah, Kelly. I've been north. Flew MigCap out of Korat and Da Nang."

"Rough, huh?"

"That's where I got those two red stars," he said, pointing to the Mig kills painted on the splitter plate. "Your sons—flying Thuds?"

"Yeah, 105s. Rod took a direct over the Red River. A SAM. He never got out. Went straight in. Four months later Bobby went against the rail yards at Than Hoa. He ate flak all the way on his bomb run. They say he was burning when he dropped his load. Hit the target too. He bailed out, but the commies picked him up as soon as he hit the ground."

There was an awkward moment of silence. "Hear you're leading this morning, Captain. Good luck." Kelly climbed up the ladder to give the cockpit a final check.

Steve was thankful that Kelly had decided to break off the conversation. He didn't want to hear any more. It was time to be alone. He was about to put in several long, grinding hours of hard work and he was tired of talking to people. He walked away from the Phantom and reached for a smoke. The starry sky was beginning to blue and the pallid glow of dawn cast an eerie backlight along the rows of waiting aircraft, silhouetting the deadly F-4s against the low hills and shadow-covered fields of golden rice. Racks of bombs stood in a line.

He took a deep drag on the weed and slowly exhaled. The guns would be zeroing in on him. They knew he was coming. They would watch him on their radar while he crossed into Cambodia, then pick him up visually, training their triple A on him as he led the squadron along the ridge, making the turn down the long valley. Waiting for him . . . tempting him . . . bringing him into range . . . into the wall of steel. Even now he could hear the shrieking flak wildly bursting around the canopy, causing him to involuntarily shrink in his cockpit, to make himself smaller, to try to avoid the hits that would surely penetrate his armored refuge.

There would be no surprise. They knew he would eventually fly the gauntlet, come against their guns. He could feel fear trying to overcome him. It gnawed at his gut. It was like a tightening band around his head. He had seen others give in to cowardice only to be devoured by their own guilt and self-condemnation. They did penance in search of forgiveness but were forever blemished by their violation of eternal law. He was scared. The responsibility was overwhelming. Could he hack it? Sixteen ships and their crews were depending on his leadership to get them in, and get them out.

It was time to go. Time to launch into the gloomy thickness of the tropical dawn and head for the guns. His private hell for the next few hours. He field-stripped the cig, and checked his g suit and survival vest. Now came the transformation—to convert his fear to determination, to stubborn persistence and unwillingness to acknowledge defeat. His conversion to a professional combat pilot with the skill, courage, and tenacity to get the job done. There wuld be no compromises. Someone had told him to go and he would go. It was his job.

Diluca was already in the back seat going through his preflight check. Steve climbed up the ladder and let himself down into the armored seat. Kelly leaned over the canopy rails and helped him strap in. He handed him his helmet and mask. Steve began plugging into the weapon: Oxygen, life-support system, radio transmitter; and the secret Target Acquisition and Designation System (TADS) that was fitted only to his aircraft.

It was hot in the cockpit and he sweated profusely. He smoothed his wavy hair back and adjusted the sweatband. The helmet went on with a few twists. Then came the deep breath and buttoning down. After adjusting his .38 and vest he hit the starter button, kicking the twin J-47 General Electric engines into life. Up and down the line each aircraft commander fired up his Phantom, creating a deafening turbulence of sound. The air was filled with the sweet, harsh smell of jet fuel. He was nearly blind with perspiration.

Chapter Twelve

Kelly plugged in his face mike to the Phantom's belly, producing the familiar high-pitched secondary signal in Steve's earphones.

"Ready for pretaxi check, Captain."

"Roger, Kelly."

The crew chief rushed back and forth along the pulsing F-4, checking the aircraft's responses to Steve's operations inside the cockpit. Fifteen minutes later Kelly gave him the go signal. Steve began the countdown with each flight:

"Chicago one."

"Rog, Eagle. Tranari, go."

"Kingfish one."

"Camacho, go."

"Billy-Joe."

"Uhhh, Roger, lead. Comanche all set."

"Binh Hoa tower, Eagle ready to roll with sixteen," he said.

"Roger, Eagle. You are cleared for taxi. Proceed to arming area."

He brusquely threw his head back to break the tension in his neck and signaled the ground crew to pull the wheel chocks. The engines reverberated with power. Kelly stood in front of the aircraft, tattooed arms held high and barrel chest expanding through his sweat-soaked shirt. When the crew was clear, Kelly cocked his right arm and set it into rapid motion, signaling Steve to pull out behind another Phantom. He moved Randall swiftly onto the crowded ramp.

Kelly's jaw set and the old veteran's back stiffened to rigid attention as the bomb-laden F-4 turned the corner. He shouted through the roar of engines: "We're all riding with you, Captain. Give 'em hell."

Steve snapped a parade salute in return, and headed for the arming pit, open canopy pointing into the Indochina sky. Diluca was busy in the back seat checking out his radar and weapon systems.

The air and ground vibrated with the intensity of sixteen twin jet engines rolling into the busy arming area. A young crewman wearing ear protectors pointed to Steve and signaled him along the painted double lines to a spot at the edge of the tarmac. Hensley taxied in next to him, being led by another airman. Each Phantom rolled into position, nose pointed into the rice paddies, engines screaming. It was terribly hot on the pad and the crews were bathed in sweat.

Steve checked his gun and bomb switches, being certain they were all on SAFE. He raised both arms over his head and the two-stripers leaped under the aircraft checking to see that none of the ordnance had jostled loose, that there were no hydraulic or fuel leaks, that the F-4's skin was tight, and generally that she was A-O.K. to make the mission. Satisfied, the pad sergeant nodded his head and the crew pulled the safety pins from the bombs, armed the fuses, and set the switches. Steve was now hot. The sergeant signaled him off the arming pad and the next Phantom pulled into position as Steve throttled up and swung onto the runway into run-up position, Hensley close behind.

"You ready, Hensley," he said into the RT, looking across the open canopies at his wingman pulling in alongside of him.

"Rog, boss." Hensley gave a wave with his gloved hand.

Steve took a final pull from the drinking tube, checked the dancing gauges, and wiped away the heavy streams of sweat from his eyes. He jerked the black oxygen mask around, snapping it to his face. "Tower . . . Eagle leader . . ."

He pulled the sun visor down over his eyes and made a final adjustment to his flight helmet.

". . . cleared for takeoff. Good luck."

He hit the hydraulic and the open canopy slowly let down, locking shut. He was sealed off. Just him and the ship now. Just the familiar hum in the earphones. The butterflies played with the inside of his stomach. Was he up to it? He had to be. It would be all right when he got in the air. The challenge flooded over him. Sixteen crews, thirty-two men, including himself. Could he pull it off? Hensley was waiting. His squadron was waiting—lined up behind him. Thumbs up. Full throttle. Power up. Takeoff roll—and the burner light is on for everyone to see. It's a go, guys! The dance has begun. We're going!

The butterflies fade away with the blast-off. The transformation takes effect. Up, up, and away! Super Pilot. *Shazam!* Billy Boy Batsun has become Captain Marvel! He's invincible now. The fears mysteriously disappear at the moment he feels lift-off. Up come the wheels. The settling "bump" into the fuselage. Confidence surges through him. The Phoenix rising from its own ashes. Power incarnate, rising on wings of death. Higher, higher, higher. Slipping the surly bonds of earth. Poetry in motion. Flight. The intense irrational reality of a dream. Incongruous imagery. Unnatural combinations mixing with natural emotions.

Everything that's important is in front of him now. All else is left behind. *The mission.* Get to the target . . . and get out. Oh, the closeness of it all. The sweet edge of immortality—toying with the fringe of death, carrying it under his wings. Hunters in search of prey. He never felt more alive then he did at this moment.

Start the play, big guys. Bring it around. Move it up. And keep thundering. No stragglers this trip. Not with Captain Marvel at the throttle. Got to keep thundering. Stupid war! Who said that? Keep it moving. Somebody said to go—so we go. Tankers twelve o'clock and high!

He circled. Big mamma, big bird, nursed her fledglings. He waited his turn on big mamma, watching each eaglet drop away with a full bag of war juice. Now it was his turn. Steady boomer. Don't pierce me in the wrong place with your beak. Gag. Fumes filling the cockpit. Won't just one of these air refueling operations go right. The first light of day stabbed the horizon. Good morning Southeast Asia! Arghhh! The fumes are getting worse. Back off. Let someone else take his turn. Cycle off the boom and try again. If only these thunderheads would go away. Top cell, your turn. Get the strike force gassed up, boomer, and get us on the road. More bouncing around. Won't this ever end? Vertigo. Revert to instruments.

"O.K., it's breaking up. Anyone still thirsty? Kingfish?"

"Negative."

"Comanche?"

"Negative."

"Chicago?"

"All full."

"Compass Call, niner-one-four. Fox-fire TBD . . . all flights. Thanks, Big Bird."

"Roger, Eagle lead. See you on the way home. Good luck." The blunt nose of the tanker disappeared into a thunderhead below. The strike force formed on Steve, made a climbing turn west, wheeled around, and streaked for Cambodia.

The columns of thunderheads rose from the deck and climbed above thirty thousand feet. It was a bumpy ride and he was continually checking his instruments and pumping new data into his navigation gear to bring the force together in the best possible shape for their run on the target. Were the gunners awake?

About the time they passed over Vinh Hoa the weather began clearing and it looked like it would hold all the way to the Skull. There was still some broken cloud cover but patches of green rain forest were visible in between. Thai-Chau slipped underneath his ship as he corrected a few degrees and swung onto the Tra Oc river. He switched to secret frequency.

"Big Safari, this is Eagle leader. Do you read?" No answer. He made the call again. "Big Safari, Eagle lead. Approaching with strike force Alpha-niner-one." Another moment of silence. Then abruptly came the static reply from ground station Cambodia.

"Eagle leader, Big Safari. Charlie-zero-niner. You are cleared for strike. Repeat. You are cleared for strike. Have you TDX on strike frequency *Two-Zero*. Buella-one. Coordinates niner-five, three-seven.

"Roger, Big Safari. Charlie-zero-niner, TDX two-zero, Buella-one, niner-five, three-seven. Proceeding to target."

He flipped back to squadron frequency and reached for bombing altitude. Sixteen gloved hands deftly squeezed back on their sticks and Eagle squadron rose.

"Let's go to strike channel. Check in." Pause.

"Eagle."

"Two."

"Three."

"Four."

"Chicago."

"Two."

"Three."

"Four."

"Comanche."

"Two."

"Three."

"Four."

"Kingfish."

"Two."

"Three."

"Four."

Thirty seconds of silence.

"Cambodia dead ahead," Diluca said.

"O.K., let's get rid of the tanks, guys."

Thirty-two wing tanks were jettisoned, tumbling earthward, streaming fuel.

"Eagle one . . . Comanche. One of my indicators is sputtering like crazy!" came the excited voice.

"O.K., we've got a prelaunch warning. Five miles. Strong indication."

"Eagle . . . Chicago lead. I've got strong guns ahead."

"O.K., SAM is up! Strong signal. One o'clock."

"Which Comanche has SAMs?"

"Comanche four."

"Eagle lead . . . Chicago one."

"Go ahead, Chicago."

"Guns still strong. New signal at eleven o'clock."

"Kingfish one . . . Kingfish two."

"Go."

"Got another one at twelve. Weak signal. Fading."

"No, that's Chicago."

"Roger."

"O.K. Another SAM is up. He's at eleven o'clock. Four miles. Strong indication . . . fading . . . O.K., he's no threat."

"Keep it moving. Bring it around. Bring it around. Looking good, baby."

"Captain, I've got bogie contact bearing two-seven-zero, range eighteen miles," Diluca, his Weapon Systems Operator, said in the back seat.

"How many?"

"Looks like . . . four . . . no . . . two more just came on the scope. We've got six now!"

"Roger." He looked over his right wing at Hensley. "Eagle two . . . Eagle one. Any other friendlies supposed to be in the area?"

"Negative. We're the only aircraft fragged on this one."

"Roger. Eagle leader to all Eaglets. We have bogies bearing two-seven-zero, range fifteen miles and closing. Heads up! Camacho, take your kids high."

Behind him, Rudy eased back on the control stick and four Phantoms climbed to altitude to fly high cover. Eagle squadron thundered on.

A minute went by. "Bogies two-seven-zero, range now ten miles."

"Eagle one, bogies still two-seven-zero, nine miles."

"Eagle one, bogies two-seven-zero, eight miles."

"Eagle one, bogies now turning to one-eight-zero and attacking!"

"Eagle one, I've got bogies visually."

138

"Who's got the bogies?"

"Camacho."

"Who? Camacho?"

"Kingfish has bogies."

"Where?"

"Twelve o'clock high on reciprocal heading."

"Kingfish has bogies too?"

The situation was becoming confusing. Wish that guy would stop asking questions, Steve thought to himself.

"Kingfish . . . Eagle. Altitude of bogies?"

"Above me—two thousand."

"Rog, Kingfish, you're CAP."

"I've got them now—Chicago two—moving to one o'clock."

"Anybody identify them yet?"

"Negative."

"Chicago three . . . Chicago one. Negative."

"Eagle one, crossing into Cambodia. Beginning ninety-degree turn. Comanche, move it up."

"Migs! I've got Migs!"

"Whose got Migs?"

The question boy again. Steve was getting irritated.

"Kingfish four has Migs."

"Coming around on the ridge. *They're rolling in*!"

"Do you have them, Eagle?"

"*Tallyho*! Six Migs, three o'clock and attacking."

"Can you split them, Tranari?"

"Negative, too much angle off."

"It's up to you Camacho."

139

"Roger, Eagle. Damn, they're pretty."

"Go get 'em Rudy."

"Keep thundering!"

First Lieutenant Rudy Camacho, leading Kingfish flight, was flying high cover. He watched the six Mig 17s commit themselves, cutting down into the inside of Eagle squadron's turn—fast—maneuvering for firing position. His F-4s, slow and heavy with bombs and fuel, broke into the communists.

"Kingfish one . . . Kingfish three. Shall we jettison our load, Rudy?"

"Negative. Keep your bombs. Let's see how many we can get on the first pass. You're free to unload if they come around again."

"Keep moving! Keep it going! Bring it up Billy-Joe," Randall said.

"I've got a SAM launch, Comanche one."

"Good grief!"

"Coming up at you Billy-Joe."

"I've got him."

"Another light. Off to the left, nine o'clock, strong signal." The action intensified.

"Watch the SAMs. Breaking left— *Now*!"

"Where're the Migs?"

"Camacho's got them. Still at three o'clock. No. Two o'clock."

"Got 'em."

"Christ. Kingfish still have their bombs!"

"Clean-up, Kingfish. You're still—"

"Bring it around, Eagles. . . . We've got two SAMs. Positive launches. Headed up. Move it around."

"ECM picking up strobes on the ridge."

"Triple A locking on. Strong signal."

The goof balls began arching up. Globs of red tracers floated in a long curve, feeling for the range of the strikers.

"Good grief!"

"I'll take the leader." It was Camacho. "Go bore-sight."

"Roger," his WSO acknowledged."

"Do you have lock-on?"

"Not yet . . . coming around . . . coming around . . . analog . . . O.K! He's locked up. Cleared to fire!"

Camacho pulled the trigger and one of his big AIM-7 radar-guided missiles dropped out of the fuselage well. A second later, its rocket motor ignited and the missile leaped ahead, accelerating out to Mach 3, trailing a long plume of white smoke as it guided on the lead Soviet interceptor. At the same time, Kingfish three fired his own missile.

"Chicago two . . . Kingfish engaging Migs." The tension was almost unbearable.

"They're breaking off!"

"He's split them."

"Missiles away! Good track."

"No. They're going to miss—too much lead."

"Keep it moving, guys. Keep it moving."

"No, good track . . . pulling good lead!"

"Keep thundering. Bring it up Tranari."

"We're taking fire from the ridge, Eagle."

"*Flak! SAMS! MIGS!* The radio was filled with calls.

"Good grief!"

"Keep it down."

"Splash! Splash! We got 'em."

The two Sparrows simultaneously crashed into the two attacking lead Migs, instantly setting them afire. They both nosed over, falling off into a long spiral, trailing dense black smoke and burning furiously.

"Nice going, Kingfish."

"Who got the Migs?"

"Camacho and Kingfish three."

"Rudy. Do you have the other four?"

"Negative, boss. They split for the river."

"Eagle lead . . . Comanche four. Migs nine o'clock going away. . . . Now they're turning around."

"Got 'em. Watch the flak. Get back down here, Tranari. We can out-thunder the Migs now. Trim up for the bomb run."

Another minute passed. "Eagle lead . . . O.K., guys, there's the valley. Coming off the ridge . . . starting left turn. Keep it moving." The stress mounted.

Steve began going over dive angles, airspeeds, and target photos. He leveled off at bombing altitude. He had been right. Everything the NVA had in the area was waiting for him. It was worse then he had expected. His hawklike eyes pierced the jungle canopy below, searching for the emplacements and gun pits as he screamed into the target area at six hundred plus, lining up for his flak suppression run. It was his job to flatten the guns so his guys could get a clean strike on the target. He looked at the photos again. There. Where the two roads converged, that was the big battery. The imprint was fresh in his

142

mind from his past reconns.

He climbed over the top, rolled inverted, and looked down through the top of his canopy. He was the point. Draw their fire. Identify the gun positions. Then paste them. He hung there, suspended in the seat harness, waiting for the muzzle flashes. He floated on his back, a sitting duck, tempting the gunners, bombs jiggling on their racks. Then came the winks of light—a few here, a few there—one after another, building to a climax. Small stuff. He wanted the big ones.

He waited. Come on, baby. Slowly the flak began to blossom. Like black flowers. The wall of metal popped and screamed and crackled around him. The blood coursed and pulsed in his head and neck. He couldn't hold the position much longer. Come on, baby. Where were they?

"Comanche one . . . I've got an indicator light on you, Eagle," Billy-Joe said.

"Another . . . and another, Steve." It was Tranari.

"Three revving up, Eagle lead," came the unidentified voice.

"Positive launches! Positive launches! Three dust clouds directly below you, Eagle."

"Break, Eagle. You've got three SAMs rising! Coming up at you."

Suddenly all the big 85s and 100s opened up. Couldn't wait, huh? Itchy fingers. O.K. Now! He kicked hard rudder, sticked it, and lit his afterburner. He carved out a big swath of sky, arching down like a hunter's arrow, guiding on the blazing lights. He set his jaw determinedly, his teeth were clenched. His eyes raced once more over the indicators and switches. Sweat poured down his face. Good setup. You're going to get it, baby!

"Migs are back, Eagle." He ignored the call.

"Whose got the Migs?" Shut up! When I get back the first thing I'm going to do is find out who that guy is and—

"Chicago three." Keep thundering, damn it!

Down he came, riding his chariot of fire. Prometheus unbound. Down, down. Good angle. Watch the airspeed. The flak screeched. One SAM dizzily faltered, then spun out, unable to adjust to his wild dive. Another began to crazily gyrate, curved earthward, and tumbled into the jungle canopy. The third went ballistic, streaking for the sun. Behind him Eagle squadron thundered, coveying up, bringing their birds around for a good run, waiting for him to blow a path through to the target.

"Hensley. You still with me?"

"Rog, Steve," came the metallic reply. Damn good wingman.

"You take the two on the left. I'm going for the ones on the right."

"Rog."

The gun pits floated into his sights. A little correction. Another moment. *Now*! Off came the thousand pounders, whistling through the dense air. Crump! . . . Crump! . . . Crump! Crump! Crump! Flames. Smoke. Dirt and debris. Flying skyward. Secondary explosions around the pits. He pulled hard and cranked around. Crump! . . . Crump! . . . Crump! . . . Crump! . . . Crump! Hensley's bombs

144

exploded into the target. He dipped his wing and rolled off.

"Two . . . one."

"Go."

"I see all guns down."

"Roger. All guns down."

Chapter Thirteen

Coming off the target, Steve yawed the ship, pulled hard, and jinked to throw any remaining gunners off. Hensley maneuvered in an opposite direction, also jinking from side to side, calculated to further confuse the gunners. But they needn't have worried. Their bombs had done a thorough job. The batteries were silent.

"Let's bring it around. I think I saw something back in there." They pulled up, converted into a split S and headed back into the valley. "Light your burner."

Down he came, head swiveling, looking. Browns and greens flashed by the canopy. The ship bounced hard in the heavy air, low on the deck. Difficult to handle. One false move this low and it was all over. He whistled along, past the now-silent gun pits. Then . . . there! Off to the left. Trucks! Trucks! And more trucks! All loaded. Deep under the jungle canopy.

"You see that Hensley?"

"Roger. Must be getting ready for something big."

"Chicago lead, this is Eagle. Have new target

for you."

"Eagle, Chicago one. Go."

"Do you see my smoke?"

"Negative."

"I'm at your one o'clock, low, angels five," he said, looking up through the Plexiglass at Chicago flight passing over him. "Beginning strafing run on truck park. You'll probably see some fireworks. Bring your gang in behind me. Kingfish and Comanche continue to primaries."

"Roger, Eagle."

"Rog."

"Roger."

Steve gave a quick glance back. His three flights of Phantoms had positioned themselves well for the bomb run. They looked real good. He pushed his nose over and shot down the long valley again. His finger settled on the trigger. The trucks came into view. The Vulcan gun exploded and the big Phantom shuddered against the hammering shock waves. The trucks grew in the gun sight. Several more bursts. The tracers arched out in long red streaks. *WHOOM! WHOOM! WHOOM!* One truck after another blew apart, sending fiery pieces into other trucks, igniting them. A chain reaction of eruptions. *WHOOM! WHOOM!*

Hensley rolled in, cannon shells ripping into the vehicles. More explosions. Black smoke and raging fire billowed into the air. An inferno.

"Can you see that, Chicago? . . . Don't miss!"

"Got it Eagle. Good show. Did you leave anything for us?"

"There's still plenty in there. Big ammo and

148

supply dump west of the trucks. See if you can get it."

"More Migs. Ten o'clock high, Comanche . . ."

"Which Comanche has the Migs?"

"Comanche four."

"Got 'em. Keep it moving, Comanche."

"Comanche one, Comanche four. I've got a hung tank. It won't blow."

"You with him, three?"

"Roger."

"Check him over. Keep moving."

"Migs closing."

"I've got a Mig 21 at two o'clock. Correction . . . one o'clock."

"Do you have those Migs, four."

"Roger. Can't keep up. Tank won't go."

"Get rid of it! Shake it off!"

"No good, lead. It's stuck," came the steely answer.

"Migs closing."

"Eagle, Comanche lead. We're in trouble. Migs moving around to our six o'clock. Four's got a hung tank, and my speed's dropped off."

"Comanche, Eagle. I've got you." He lit his AB and reached for attack altitude. "Break when I tell you. Drag the Migs out about half a mile. Can you hold speed?"

"Will try. But four's straggling. He's a sitting duck. Migs are pushing within the six thousand foot limit."

"Roger, Comanche. Hang tough. Keep it moving."

"Kingfish has a launch light."

Steve had Comanche flight visually now. If they could only hold their speed for a little longer maybe

149

the Migs wouldn't get the edge they needed. Just one more minute and he'd be in position . . . But with Comanche four slowing the other three with a hung tank . . . well, it was going to be close.

"Chicago, two Migs at eight."

"You have eight o'clock for Chicago?"

"That's right."

"Kingfish three, you're clear."

"O.K., Comanches, they're moving past our nine o'clock to seven. Beginning attack. Eagle, you got that? Migs are all over us!"

Steve didn't want to lose the mission now. It was a clean, open run on the target, except for the Migs. Keep your bombs guys. I'm almost there. Don't jettison them. Not yet. You've still got speed. Just hold it awhile longer.

"Chicago, Migs level. Moving to six."

"Launch light fading. No threat."

"Kingfish, you're clear."

"Roger."

"Keep thundering. Move it around."

"Chicago beginning run. Start your music guys. Make it sweet."

"Good grief, the 21 is flying formation with us!"

"Forget it. We'll take care of him later. Here we go. . . ."

Joe Tranari and Chicago flight dropped out of the sky on their bomb run with a frustrated Mig 21, unable to gain the advantage he wanted, making up an unwelcome fifth member in the group.

Billy-Joe and Comanche flight were fast running out of room. Up to now he somehow had not allowed the Migs the turning advantage they needed to blow him away. He had kept his bombs but his number four was in big trouble and was in desperate need of speed. He would have to jettison his load if Steve didn't arrive soon.

"*Junetime! Junetime!*"

"Kingfish has a launch light. . . ."

"Four o'clock, two miles."

"*Junetime! Kingfish. Junetime!*"

"*Kingfish,* break left—*Now! Junetime!*"

"Oh, shit! I'm hit. Good God, no!"

"Which Kingfish is hit?"

"Kingfish two."

"*I'm burning! Eagle, I'm burning!*"

"Kingfish two's on fire."

"Stay with him, Camacho."

"Jettison your bombs, Kingfish two. Clean-up. You've still got your bombs," Steve yelled, watching the spectacle below him.

"Eagle, Comanche. We've got Migs at our six o'clock. Where are you?" Billy-Joe cried.

"Kingfish lead, two. I'm going into the bomb run with you before I bail out. I think I've got enough altitude. I'm keeping the bombs."

"Two, you're burning and smoking badly from the aft fuselage," Camacho said. Big hole on the right side where the tail fin joins." Camacho pulled in closer to look his wingman over. "SAM did a job on you. How's your hydraulics—controls steady?"

"Tightening up, but she's still responding. Pressure fluctuating."

"Can you get altitude?"

"I think so."

"O.K., give it a try—if she holds together. And go

through your procedures to get that fire out. You might get lucky."

"How do I look now? Fire light seems to be dimming."

"Still burning—not so bad now. Pieces still falling off."

"Maybe I can starve it out when I dive-bomb. I'm sticking, boss. I can't get back over the border no how. Might as well go this way as any."

That guy's got brass balls, Steve thought to himself. From his perch high above he could see the strange and awesome scenario unfolding below. Dense smoke and fire covered the target area. Tranari and Chicago flight were rolling into their dive-bomb run with a determined Mig driver flying wing on number four. Eagle three and four, Steve's second element, were crossing directly below Chicago, lining up on their own target. Camacho and his Kingfish were cranking around, echelon left, behind Chicago, number two a sheet of flame. And bringing up the rear, in big trouble, was Billy-Joe's Comanche flight. Two hungry Migs were bore-sighting his number four who was limping behind off to the right with a hung fuel tank on his left wing.

Steve really needed another few seconds to be in optimum position to take on the Migs, but Comanche four had run out of time and it was now or never. He rechecked his gun switches and his eyes flashed across the instruments. He was approaching supersonic just as Comanche flight and the Migs went into a thin haze below him.

"Comanche four, Eagle one—*Break right, now! Dive for the deck! I'm rolling in.*"

The break was instantaneous.

"O.K., Hensley, let's take these guys."

He dug in the Phantom's stabilator and unloaded. "Light your AB!" Now he was in combat velocity. Mach .9 . . . 1.0 . . . 1.1 . . . 1.2 . . . 1.3. The gs tugged at his head. The g suit inflated. He pushed it to the limit. The cockpit began turning gray. He kept muscling over the stick. The F-4 gained more energy. Six gs . . . 7 gs.

"P-p-pull h-harder, four." His speech broke up in the high g turn. Comanche four tightened his turn. "Drag . . . them . . . out . . . another . . . few . . . s-s-seconds."

"Which way you breaking, Eagle?"

"Just keep them turning. Am I clear, Hensley?"

"Roger."

He wanted these two bad. Get in close. Maneuver with them. Then hose them with a single, long burst. Surely they had seen him by now. He was rapidly closing the range. The reticle was nearly centered as he continued to roll with the Migs. They loomed larger in the optical gun sight.

"Reverse it!" he shouted.

Comanche four instantly obeyed and the lead Mig floated nicely into Steve's sights. He squashed the trigger and the big Vulcan cannon again exploded, vibrating the Phantom's innards up and down its airframe. The 20-mm cannon shells raked down across the Mig's nose and back along the canopy, killing the pilot. Chunks of sheet metal and parts of the canopy blew off into the slip stream, revealing the Mig pilot slumped over his controls, oxygen mask still in place, white scarf wrapped around his neck, flapping in the open air behind him. Fuel began streaming from ruptured tanks, vaporizing in a fizzing cloud of fumes. A thin line of white smoke trailed out from around the Mig's wing root. Now it changed to gray. Then black.

Steve yawed his ship to the right, quickly coming around on the communist wingman. Before he had a chance to center the reticle, the Mig's canopy popped off and the pilot ejected.

"Well, I'll be a . . . Hensley, did you see that?"

"I did. But I don't believe it."

"He came out right in front of us! That smart S.O.B."

He fired a long burst into the pilotless Mig and watched it blow apart in a fireball. He rolled over and came back around, thundering past the pilot floating down in his parachute, lighting his afterburner as he went by.

"Maybe I scorched him a bit," he said. "Smart S.O.B."

He jerked around. Billy-Joe had throttled back and number four was climbing into position.

"O.K., Billy. It looks like you're clear now. Bring it up and get your ducks in a row."

"Roger, Eagle."

"Eagle, four. Thanks."

Back along the valley, the target sector was covered with mushrooming gray and black explosions. A string of five hundred pounders slid off the last of Chicago flight as they turned and wheeled for home.

Steve pulled the map out from inside the knee-pocket where he normally kept it, and glanced over the targets again. It looked like he was pasting them good. Now, if Camacho and Billy-Joe could hit their sectors with the same success that he and Tranari had . . .

"How's your fuel, Hensley?"

"Joker."

"Let's take it around one more time and cover for Kingfish and Comanche."

"I think all the Migs broke off."

"Roger. Let's keep patrolling until we hit bingo."

"Kingfish one. Eagle lead. How's your number two."

"He's still smoking. Fires out though. He's going into the run with us."

"Tango! Tango! This is Eagle leader. I've got one Phantom hit bad. Going into bomb run. Pilot and WSO may have to eject."

Pause . . . static . . . "Eagle leader, this is Tango. On station with two. No RESCAP inside Big George. Can he make it to little George?"

"Tango, Eagle leader. He's hit pretty bad. Could go down any time."

"Eagle, Tango. Repeat. No RESCAP inside Big George. Sorry."

Long pause.

"Roger." He knew what the answer was going to be, but he had to check anyway. Do everything you can for your guys.

"Kingfish, Eagle. You copy Tango?"

"Roger, Eagle."

"Chicago, Kingfish. You take any ground fire on your run?"

"Negative, Kingfish. Target clear."

"Roger. Green 'em up, Kingfish, and let's do it."

Camacho rolled in on his target and salvoed his bombs, followed by his number three and four. Kingfish two, smoking badly, hung back for an instant then rolled in behind four. He looked good all the way but just as he dropped his bombs and was pulling through the dive, the Phantom began coming apart.

"Lead, two. This is it, Rudy. I'm going to have to leave her. She's breaking up."

"Try for more altitude."

"I can't make it, Rudy. She's froze up."

"Kingfish two is going out! Cover him."

Then he heard it. The lonely wail of a lost soul. What every fighter pilot believes will never happen to him. The incessant screech of the beeper cut through the air waves announcing to Eagle squadron that one of their guys was out of his ship and falling. Steve could do nothing but listen. The most depressing, helpless sound in the universe. His gut ached for Kingfish two. The terrible agony of being separated from your comrades. Falling . . . falling . . . falling. No longer invincible. An Eagle shot from the sky. Falling, falling—into the hands of your waiting enemy. Your talons pulled. What was going through Kingfish two's mind at this moment? His wife. His five-year-old son? His brother and two sisters? How his mother used to tuck him in at night? Read him stories? Dad bringing home his first football? Kingfish two. Oh, God how he hated it all. Stupid war! Damn war! All the king's horses and all the king's men couldn't put Kingfish together again. Deep inside, down in the hidden corridors of his heart, the small, pitiful and lonely soul of Steve

Randall cried out like a child to his God, "Please, Lord, help Kingfish two."

"Big Safari! Big Safari! Strike leader alpha-niner-one."

"Strike leader, this is Big Safari. Go ahead."

"Aircraft hit. Crew bailed out. . . . Zulu-five-niner-three. Have covering force in area. Will cycle off tanker. Can you help?"

"Negative, strike leader. Your guys are on their own."

Bastards!

"Tango. Tango. Eagle lead. Did you copy Big Safari?"

"Eagle lead, Tango. Roger. It's a hell of a war."

Bastards!

The two parachutes, their large colorful panels contrasting against the dark foreboding green of the hostile Cambodian jungle, floated lazily over the smoking battle zone. Five hundred feet overhead Billy-Joe waggled his wings in salute then rolled into the target. What remained of Kingfish two's Phantom fell off on its left wing and plummeted down, trailing a long blanket of dense smoke.

"Big Bird, Big Bird, this is Eagle leader. Is your gas station open?"

"Roger, Eagle. On station and open for business."

"Kingfish two is down. We're going to stay with him as long as we can."

"Roger, Eagle."

"Anyone bingo?" he asked.

"Chicago two."

"Eagle three."

"Comanche one."

"Comanche four."

"O.K., hit the tanker," he said. "Kingfish, you MIGCAP. The rest of us will cover Kingfish two."

"Roger."

Steve watched the two chutes drop onto the ridge about two hundred meters apart. The beepers immediately cut out and Kingfish two's voice came over the emergency channel.

"Kingfish two is down and we're both O.K."

"Kingfish two, Eagle lead. Get out of sight. We'll stay in the area as long as our fuel and ammo hold. We're cycling off the tanker."

"Roger, Eagle."

Steve made a pass over the downed men, pinpointing their position.

"There's some movement below. People coming up the ridge. Can you see them?"

A few moments of silence.

"Roger, Eagle. We see them. We're moving out. Can you cover us?"

"Will do . . . and good luck," he said quietly, almost reverently.

As Kingfish two broke cover and sprinted for the top of the ridge, Steve could see the soldiers at the bottom leap forward in pursuit. He came in low and hot, lining up at the edge of the forest, where it gave way to the rocky slope, at the point where the communists had to pop out.

Run, Kingfish two! Don't let them get you. Remember your young wife and your little son. They need you. Run Kingfish two! Run! Run! Keep running. Keep moving. Don't stop, even when you feel you can't take another step. Go until you collapse. Then go some more. The Vulcan gun pounded . . . dum-dum-dum-dum . . . dum-dum . . . dum-dum-dum-dum-dum-dum-dum-dum. I'll buy some time for you. Run, Kingfish two, run. Remember your little boy . . . dum-dum-dum . . . dum-dum-dum-dum-dum-dum. The tracers burned through the fetid air, tore through the forest cover and exploded into the communist infantry. Run, Kingfish two, run. Don't let them catch you. Run until your lungs burst. Run until you drop. Then run some more . . . dum-dum-dum-dum . . . dum-dum. Get down here you guys. Don't let them get him. A comrade has fallen. An Eagle is down. Help him get home to his family. Run, Kingfish two, run. The tears were streaming down his face. *Bastards!* Leave him alone. His finger turned white on the firing button. Help him, guys . . . dum-dum-dum-dum-dum-dum-dum. He wept unashamedly. He wept for Kingfish two. For all the Kingfish twos. He wept for himself.

Bang! The ship lurched heavily. *Bang!* The Phantom buckled again. The red fire-warning light blazed in his face. The sharp, violent smell of burning jet fuel. Rpms on the right engine bouncing off zero. Now the left gone. Hold the circuit breakers in, Diluca. Restart. Restart. *Damn it, restart!* Got to get altitude. Can't punch out this low. Hydraulics . . . gone. Flame-out! Flame-out! This is it. Time to go. The smoke. Can't see. Where are the handles? He pulled. Xinh . . . Oh, God, Xinh . . . we never had enough time.

Chapter Fourteen

Xinh stared numbly into the sky. A big void began expanding in the pit of her stomach. No. It wasn't so. She would wait. He just needed a little more time. His airplane would appear any moment now, banking over the low hills, rolling into the final approach as it had every time she had waited for him. Her eyes pierced the blue horizon. Steve. Please, Steve. Come home. She would will him back.

No one paid any attention to her. The pilots and crewmen just walked by not even giving her a glance. She watched them closely, waiting for someone to tell her, hoping that no one would tell her, knowing without being told. Her eyes involuntarily pulled away from the empty sky, focused on each tail number down the line of now-quiet Phantoms, and finally fell on the vacant parking space again.

Suddenly she was running, rushing after the pilots, going from one to the other, pulling at their g suits, shouting, crying, "Where he? Where my Captain Randall? Please. Please. Where my Captain Randall?"

No one said a word. Each just looked dully back

into her pitiful face and said nothing, allowing her to tear at their clothing and gear, not lifting a hand to stop her from pounding on their big chests with her tiny hands. The mission hadn't taken place.

"Where my captain?" she screamed, tears pouring down her face. "Please. Please. Tell me. Where my Steve?"

Each man's gut ached for her. Each wanted to take her aside and explain to her as best he could his final moments. For that was how he would want it when his number came up. Comfort my lady. Tell her how it happened. Answer all her questions. Then seal it up forever. Life goes on.

But they couldn't do this for Steve because the mission never took place. And each of them silently looked through blurred eyes at poor Xinh clinging to the truck as they pulled away from the flight line. She fell to the ground still begging them to tell her what had happened to her captain.

The lightning flashed and the thunder roared, and uncle's house shook along its ancient foundation.

When Xinh was a child, elders of the village had told her stories about past generations of her family that had occupied this very site upon which uncle's house now rested. For centuries her relatives had been born here, took husbands and wives here, raised their families, died and were buried here.

And now with the heavy monsoon rains beating on the house she recalled those stories and it seemed to her that she could feel the pulsing rhythm of her ancestors passing from one generation to the next, their voices quietly calling out to her from the driving storm . . . comforting her . . . sensing her loss . . . sharing her agony.

She sat motionless beside the oil lamp, her eyes transfixed on the swaying, rain-drenched palm trees being wildly buffeted by the raging winds. The night had metamorphosed. A spiritual transmutation hung in the rains, spanning generations of time, altering the moment. Yellow light from the lamp cast dancing, sagging figures on the whitewashed walls around her, and the night moaned its lamentations.

The little girl inside of her wailed in grief-stricken agony, afraid and lonely, mourning her loss. Steve *oi*. Where are you? Are you alive? Dead? No one will tell me.

Uncle Dong sat in his straight-backed teak chair smoking his pipe and sipping at a cup of the bitter green tea. His two wives were in the next room occupied in low conversation, sewing by the light of an oil lamp. The wind howled and the storm unleashed its fury against the small house. If only the rains had come yesterday she thought to herself, he wouldn't have gone. The mission would have been grounded and he would be here today with me.

"You were in love with him?" her uncle asked, getting up from the hand-carved chair and shuffling over to her. He sat down, and she reached over to pour him some more tea. He took off his embroidered Chinese slippers and curled his thin legs up underneath him on the wooden divan next to her. She relit his pipe. He drew in a long breath. "You seemed to be in love with him."

163

"Yes, Uncle. I loved him."

"Very much?"

"Oh, yes. Very much. I loved him very much."

"And how did he feel about you?"

"I think he loved me too."

"You don't know what happened to him?"

"No. Nothing. No one will tell me anything."

"With your contacts at the base, no one is able to help you?"

"No one. I think it was some sort of secret mission." Nobody knows anything about it, except the pilots, and they ignore me."

"I see," he said, drawing pensively on his pipe. The rain continued to lash and beat about the old house. "Would you feel better if you knew his fate?"

"Oh, yes, I most certainly would," she said looking at him hopefully.

"You know, these things are often best left alone. Worse things could come of them if you pry."

She said nothing.

"Maybe it's best you forget about this Randall."

"No," she wailed. "It's impossible for me to forget him, ever. It's unthinkable." She was on the verge of tears again.

"I've never questioned you about your VC activities, Xinh, but I would think that it can not go well with you if your superiors know how you feel about this American. I have no quarrel with the Vietcong. They have given me a good life here as hamlet chief and I know, though you have said nothing to anyone, that it is through your efforts that we are allowed to live peacefully in the 'dragon's mouth.' But still, the Communists are vengeful people, and above all else, they always maintain strict control over their subjects. There are never any exceptions, and extinction is the usual course of events for those who violate their trust. Do you agree?"

Xinh thought for a few moments before answering. She looked up at her old uncle and her long eyes were very sad. "Uncle, what you say is true, and I'm afraid that I am already in disfavor with my superiors. My commander has tried to have me eliminated, at least once over the past few days." She related her narrow escape with the Dao Dua at the restaurant.

"Ah, I see," he said, touching her tenderly on the shoulder. "So they know."

"Yes, they have known almost from the very beginning. Captain Randall and I tried to meet secretly, but they found out. My commander informed me, however, that it was permissible to continue seeing Steve on the condition that I dupe him into supplying me with military secrets and vital information which I would, in turn, pass on to the VC high command.

"And have you been obeying his orders, my child?"

"I have been putting him off. Each time I've been asked for the required information I've made excuses, unable to betray my lover. I tell him that I need more time, or that Captain Randall has refused to discuss certain sensitive matters."

"And what has he said to this?" uncle asked, taking another sip of the bitter tea and cautioning Xinh with his eyes to speak low, motioning to the open bedroom door.

"He has said nothing. But I can sense that he has

grown impatient. Being a crafty man, he has played me along while at the same time planning my demise."

"He has seen through your excuses?"

"Yes, for sure. And therefore, I have outlived my usefulness to him."

"This is much more serious than I suspected," her uncle said. "What is it you plan to do?"

"All my hope was in Captain Randall. Now that he is gone I don't care what happens to me." A bolt of lightning flashed through the house electrifying the air with a powdery blue fluorescence.

"But you can't give up, my child. Don't give up," he said firmly.

"But what can I do? There is no hope, Uncle." She looked away.

"There is always hope, child."

"Where do I begin? Where do I start? I'm blocked in every direction I turn." She sat on the floor cross-legged, rocking back and forth, tightly grasping her knees with her arms.

"You start by finding out what happened to your Captain Randall. That's where you start. That will be your purpose. That is what will sustain you. Keep you going. And when you find out, your next step will be clear. You will know what to do when you find the answer."

Xinh stopped rocking. She slowly lifted her head from between her legs and looked out at the thrashing storm. A glowing luminescence bathed her skin. "Yes . . . yes," she said slowly. "Yes, Uncle, I will find out what happened to him." She got to her feet. "Thank you, Uncle." She quietly circled her arms around the old man and kissed him. "Oh, thank you."

"Follow your heart, Xinh. It will never fail you. Listen to the still, small voice of God. When you look to the left hand and then to the right, you will hear a voice behind you saying, 'This is the way, walk in it.' Follow your heart. This is not a matter for the intellect."

"Uncle Dong, listen to the wind."

"Yes, it blows with a thousand voices." He looked toward the door heaving on its homemade hinges.

"Where does the wind come from, Uncle?"

"From the north—beyond Vietnam—from the high mountains of China. I remember stories from my youth."

"Will you tell me a story—like you used to by the river Phu Cuong in Tay Ninh?" She edged up to him.

"Tay Ninh. Yes, I remember Tay Ninh." His eyes grew distant in memory. "It was a wonderful time. All my nephews and nieces gathered around my feet like ducklings."

"And Duc and Thanh." She pulled her thick hair over her shoulder.

"Yes, Duc and little Thanh. How is Thanh?"

"She's fine, Uncle."

"And Duc?" He fingered his pipe.

"Gone."

"Ah, yes . . . gone."

"Is the tree still there, Xinh?"

"The tree, Uncle?" She smoothed the ends of her hair.

"Yes, the tree."

"I'm sorry, Uncle. Which tree?"

"The tree we would sit under when I told the stories." He reached out and touched Xinh's hair. "Your hair was always long and shiny, even as a child."

"I haven't been back. But it must still be there, it was so big," Xinh said.

"The biggest tamarind tree I have ever seen. My mother made the best candy in Vietnam from its fruit."

"Maybe we can all move back to Tay Ninh and live like we used to," she said.

She sat cross-legged on the floor again and began massaging the old man's feet. Uncle was deep in thought.

"We were very happy then," Uncle Dong said.

"There was much rice." She put the slippers back on his feet.

"And *chom chom* and lichees."

"But we were poor," Xinh said.

"Always poor—but happy."

"Yes, very happy, Uncle."

"Very happy, Xinh."

The violent storm had passed and only soft rains were heard on the hamlet roofs. The wind died down; and then a full moon broke out from between the clouds and bright stars could be seen sparkling like newly polished diamonds in the velvet sky. She fell peacefully asleep on the divan.

The following day broke bright and clear. Xinh went to work and solemnly told Thanh that it was

168

important that they talk right away. They went off base to an innocuous, bored-looking restaurant in Binh Hoa City where they could talk privately. Thanh's nose began twitching with anticipation. They ordered two bowls of pho from the weathered Korean waitress whose face was as flat as a dishpan. Xinh shifted uneasily in a crude, worn-out chair, resting her elbows on the table top. The hand-axed slab wobbled on unevenly cut legs. The Korean shuffled back, limping on one broken sandal and dropped a stained teapot on the slab.

"I talked to him," Xinh said. She put her hand on the teapot and with a fingertip began tracing the outline of the dragon painted on the cracked porcelain. "I told him that he can't change God's mind. God never forgets." She picked up the pot. "Want some tea?" Thanh noticed that Xinh's hand trembled while pouring the tea.

"God never forgets," Xinh repeated. "He never forgets, right Thanh?" The green liquid splashed onto the table top, missing the cup.

Thanh took the pot from Xinh and finished pouring the tea.

"I suppose," she muttered without looking up.

"I said God would remember everything we've done. God's no fool . . . he's been watching us . . . and he doesn't forget." She picked up her teacup but couldn't get it to her lips.

Thanh watched curiously. "Take it easy," she whispered. "We'll get out of this."

"He didn't understand. I told him that we would have to pay. But he didn't understand. He doesn't even care that we know. He'll try again." She grasped

169

the cup with both hands and quickly gulped the tea down. After a minute her hand stopped shaking and she sat erect. "He wants me to continue with the planning and digging, but he's going to try again."

"Sure he will. You know that." Thanh poured more tea. The hot steam rose between them veiling their child faces.

"You're awfully calm," Xinh said.

"They're after you, not me," Thanh said with a wry smile.

Xinh leaned across the table motioning for Thanh to draw closer.

"Thanh, I've come to a decision about something and I need your help. But I want you to know that you are definitely under no obligation to say yes. I will never think any less of you if you refuse."

She glanced around the room. A Chinese with a short queue, green tea soaking his thin, chin beard, stared dully past her. Beside him was a bamboo cage holding two white doves.

"We have been through a great deal together, sister Xinh, and I owe you my life." Thanh stuck her finger in the tea and licked it. "You took me in and cared for me when my family was gone and I had nowhere to turn. You gave me rice and shelter. You clothed me. You have become my home. I have fought beside you in the jungle and along the paddy dikes. You have saved me from danger many times. I cannot refuse you. I will do as you ask."

"So be it." Xinh bowed her head toward Thanh. There was a pause. "You have touched my heart with your kind words."

"What is it you wish of me?" Thanh asked.

170

Xinh poured some *nuoc mam* sauce into a saucer and broke a small red pepper into it. She stirred the contents with the end of a chopstick. "I must know what has happened to Captain Randall. We are certain he was on a secret mission."

Thanh quickly became animated and sat on the edge of her chair. She slapped the palms of her hands on the slab table top. "Yes, we know that much," she said brightly. She reached behind and gathered her hair into three overlapping folds. She piled the black heap onto the back of her head and jammed a long, four-toothed comb into the folds to hold them in place.

"And we know he never came back from that mission. Judging from what information we have been able to gather, it appears that he was shot down."

A small boy jumped from his mother's lap and ran over to stand in front of Xinh.

"Correct. But we don't know where," Thanh said.

"Nor do we know his condition—alive or . . ." Xinh couldn't bring herself to say the word. She held out her hand to the boy.

"And if alive he may be injured or a prisoner. Possibly both," Thanh said. She pulled the comb and the velvet waterfall tumbled down her back.

"If we discover this to be the case, it is clear what I must do next." The boy ran back to his mother.

"But you can't do that." Thanh stuck her fingers in her mouth and looked at Xinh in horror. "You will be—"

"I must go to him. I must find him and bring him back."

"Oh, Xinh. How can you possibly? . . ." She replaced her fingers with a mouthful of hair.

"I must. I will—if he's alive."

There was a long silence.

"I'm getting out," Xinh said. "It's only a matter of time before they get me. I'm getting away while I can. Maybe you want to think over your decision now that you know this."

Thanh picked up her chopsticks and tasted the sauce. "No, Xinh. My future is molded to yours. I have no place to go either."

"All I'm asking you to do is help me find out what happened to him. I'm not asking you to do any more than that. You may still have a future with the VC."

"No, Xinh. If they're after you, they're after me too. They know where my loyalty lies. I will go with you into Cambodia if necessary. Even Laos. Or wherever we have to go to get the truth. And I'll help you bring him out if he's alive."

"I can't make it without you, Thanh." Xinh patted her cheek.

"But the attack on Bien Hoa," Thanh suddenly remembered. "The Tet offensive, and everything we've worked for. The supplies and NVA reinforcements will be coming in soon from our Cambodian sanctuaries. They're expected any day now. The Ho Chi Minh and Sihanouk trails are bulging with munitions and the order to jump off can come at any hour."

"That's it! That's it!" Xinh suddenly sat up stiffly and clasped her head with both hands.

"What? What is?"

"The sanctuaries. Cambodia!" She said in an

172

excited whisper, leaning toward Thanh. "That's where Steve is. He's in Cambodia, shot down. That's why it was a secret mission. The Skull has always been a thorn in the Americans' foot." She stopped for breath. "They've been afraid of escalating the war—angering the Cambodians, stirring up trouble for themselves and sentiment for the Communists in the rest of the world. They've been afraid of bombing our sanctuaries. But Steve did it. I know that's where he is. I just know it!"

The Chinese with the bored eyes tilted his head back and snorted. A cavernous mouth studded with gold teeth gaped open and he yawned.

"Shhhhhh, not so loud," Thanh said, looking around. "I think you may be right. I will begin making inquiries of our contacts in border provinces and villages arund Thai-Chau and Tra Oc. They will be sure to know of any raid into the Skull and of any Americans shot down." Thanh rubbed her nose with the flat of her hand.

The Chinese struggled to rise from his stool and bumped the flat-faced Korean, knocking a plate of noodles out of her hand. She clubbed him over the head with a gnarled fist, knocking him back onto the stool and upsetting the cage. The doves escaped in a flurry of feathers and flew wildly around the restaurant.

"How long do you think it will take you? Oh, Thanh, I'm so excited."

The doves landed on Xinh's table, cavorted back and forth a few times, then flew out an open window.

"I can be back in three days with all the details."

A tender hush drifted between them. Not an

173

embarrassing silence, but one of understanding and commitment. They said nothing more—only felt—and their feeling touched, and it was good. The dedication between these two girls went beyond friendship and childhood memories. Its roots were buried deep in their mutual suffering, their loneliness, and the absence of a childhood. It reached into the trenches and the everyday dangers they shared in their savage guerrilla war; and it found strength in their desperate need for love, for someone who cared, and someone to care for.

The bowls of steaming *pho* arrived. Xinh spooned in the *nuoc mam* for both of them, and Thanh separated the delicate *rau* leaves from their stems and mixed the leaves into the noodles and meaty broth. Xinh added the bean sprouts. Thanh added the black bean paste. Finally, they exchanged chopsticks. It was a common ritual they frequently practiced. Even in the simple preparations of a meal they expressed their affection and dependency on each other. They began to eat, each knowing that they had begun an adventure whose outcome could very well end in misfortune for both of them.

Chapter Fifteen

Xinh agonized through the next three long days. When on the eve of the fourth day Thanh had still not arrived, Xinh was nearly blind with desperation. The fifth day came and went. Then in the early morning hours of the sixth day Thanh gently shook Xinh from a fitful sleep. Xinh was beside herself with joy, having been convinced that her loyal friend had met with disaster.

"Thanh! Where have you been? I've been worried sick. You said you would be back in three days. What happened?"

"He's alive, Xinh. He's alive."

Xinh broke into a flood of tears and grabbed Thanh and hugged her.

"Oh, Thanh. Are you sure?" she said, clutching her friend close to her.

"I'm sure. The communists are holding him in Pak Mek, near Buong Thuy, about thirty miles inside Cambodia."

"Did you go there? Did you see him?"

"No. But the strike was confirmed by many VC that I talked to and they said that a Captain Stephen

A. Randall, USAF was shot down and captured. Two others shot down in another plane were run down and killed."

"Pak Mek village. That's where he is?"

"That's right, Pak Mek. That's why I'm late getting back. I had to confirm that he was there and it took me the extra days to locate someone who had actually seen him."

"You found someone who has seen Steve?"

"Three people!"

"Three?"

"Yes. They were transporting supplies from the sanctuary that Steve had bombed and they saw the entire battle. They said the Phantoms destroyed everything. There's hardly anything left—armament, ammunition, supplies—all destroyed. The offensive is going to suffer badly."

"No matter. What about Steve?"

"Well, during the height of the bombing a Phantom got hit by ground fire and the two fliers bailed out. When they landed on the ground another plane flew in low to protect them, strafing the soldiers who were attempting to capture the downed airmen. The second Phantom was immediately hit and the pilot and radar operator bailed out. That was Steve and the man named Diluca."

"Is Steve all right?"

"Well, apparently he was pretty low when he ejected. The three VC I was telling you about joined up with an NVA patrol and found Steve sitting up against a tree, entangled in his parachute shrouds. He had a broken leg—the bone was sticking through his boot. He had vomited over himself and all his

176

strength seemed to be gone. But when the soldiers approached him, he raised himself the best he could with his back against the tree trunk and feebly tried to unholster his gun, weakly shouting something nasty at his captors. One of the men easily kicked the pistol from his hand and he collapsed. His radar operator, Lieutenant Diluca, was found dead in a nearby tree, swinging from his parachute."

"I'm going to him, Thanh. I'm going to get him out of there and bring him back."

"I'm going with you."

"No. You've done enough already."

"I'm coming with you, Xinh. You can't get him out alone."

"I think I can."

"He's got a broken leg. And you don't know the route in. You will need me."

"You're determined to come?"

"I am."

"All right, so be it. I'm familiar with most of the territory east of the Skull but the country across the Tra Oc river is foreign to me. Do you have any suggestions on how we get to Pak Mek and Steve?"

"Well, I know this much. Cau-Mong is a good jumping off place from Vietnam into Cambodia. It's on the Tra Oc which is navigable up to Buong Thuy. From there we will have to walk through dense rain forest to Pak Mek," Thanh said.

"We will need the jungle knives."

"Yes, and at least three days rice inside Cambodia."

"How will we get up river?" Xinh asked.

"I saw many small river boats powered by

outboard engines similar to those we have used in the Mekong Delta. We can easily steal one for our use. The engines are quiet enough at low speeds.''

The two girls left it at that. They were used to living and fighting in the jungle for weeks on end and whether it be Vietnam or Cambodia it was all the same to them. Jungle was jungle.

Xinh had been as far as the Tra Oc River with her unit on operations and had trained in the Tay Ninh hill country where she had first met Tang. Yes, the territory was all very familiar to her. And the early memories were still vivid.

Xinh felt that they should immediately set out for the frontier. But certain events were to postpone her departure.

There was a gentle rap on the door.

"Who could that be so early in the morning?" Thanh whispered.

"Shhhhhh."

They waited in silence. A second knock was not heard. Instead, a slip of paper was passed under the door. Quiet footsteps . . . someone quickly walking away.

Chapter Sixteen

Xinh threw the light linen cover back and sat up in the middle of her bed. She always slept in the nude when at home, and her sleek bronzed body glistened in the metallic dawn light seeping through the open French doors. She parted the mosquito netting and cautiously placed her bare feet on the cool tile floor which sent an involuntary shiver up her shapely legs. She slowly walked to the door, her natural sway obvious, and picked up the note.

"It's from Tang," she said unemotionally.

"What does it say?" Thanh asked.

Xinh returned to the bed and slipped back under the sheets. She handed the slip of dirty brown paper to Thanh.

"We've been summoned to the quarry," Thanh said with surprise.

Xinh lay back on her pillow and began counting the revolutions of the black ceiling fan, trying to separate the four blades while they slowly turned in the dim light. The stillness of the drab little room tightened around the two worried girls.

"The quarry," Xinh said.

They quietly watched the growing light of day expanding on the bare walls, not talking, telepathically communicating with each other like they always did during the so many unexpected crises of their young lives. There had been so many turning points and periods of strain, so many emotionally significant events they had shared together throughout the years, so many decisive moments in which their response determined whether they lived or died.

"Let it be," Thanh whispered.

Their hearts touched. They knew what they must do.

It was well past the curfew hour when the girls slipped through the perimeter guards and crept to the forest edge. If discovered they would be shot on sight. But they had traveled this route so often that the exercise was little more than a nuisance now. It posed no threat to them and the way through had been completely committed to memory. They knew the location of every mine and strand of barbed wire. If necessary, they could silently crawl undetected into each listening post and fighting hole, kill the occupants without a cry escaping their victim's lips, and move on without the slightest hesitation. They knew they could do it because they had done it before. Many times. Young men the same age as themselves. The surprise in their eyes. The wild look as they struggled helplessly against cold steel imbedded in their spines. It only took a flash in time. Quick. Thorough. Not a noise came from the holes.

They trained me well and I've performed to their

great satisfaction—a perfect model of loyal Communist youth. And I loved it. My seduction had been complete, Xinh reflected. I could never think of being anything but what I am. The NLF has been my whole life. She breathed deeply, trying to clear her head with the heavy humid air. I've been impetuous. Filled with hate and revenge. Forever marked by impulsive vehemence. She scanned the heavy foliage, letting her pain-ridden eyes adjust to the black jungle interior. Can time ever wash the past out of my memory? Can I ever begin anew, fresh and undefiled? A heart-sinking melancholia swelled in the pit of her stomach. Her head spun dizzily and nausea gripped her. She bent over and retched out her insides. Thanh reached out to steady her but Xinh waved her off. She collapsed on the ground, sitting on her bottom, breathing heavily. She retched again. She wiped her perspiring face with her scarf. Everything they have taught me will be turned against them. I will atone.

After a few minutes she stood, steadying herself against Thanh. Still breathing rapidly and holding tightly to her friend, she pulled the two double-edged, triangular-bladed knives from her waistband and handed one to Thanh. They pulled up their pajamas and tied the knives to their pretty legs, loosely at the calf so a quick pull released the weapon into the hand. They raised up and looked back at the perimeter. Holding hands they stepped into the jungle and the inky blackness immediately swallowed them up.

Once they passed the listening posts and were well into the jungle they pulled out their tiny bottle lamps. They each selected an appropriately shaped leaf as a light reflector and attached it upright next to the opening of the perfume bottle with a rubber band. The stopper was removed and the wick pulled through the opening and ignited. The slow-burning kerosene cast a soft glow that effectively illuminated six feet of trail ahead, enough to provide satisfactory visibility for rapid travel, yet remain difficult to detect by unfriendlies.

After an hour of brisk walking in this manner they came to a juncture in the forest path which led through the familiar VC village of Vinh Son. There the girls refilled their kerosene lamps, ate a bowl of rice, and continued on for another two hours. They passed through more hamlets and small villages, encountering numerous trail junctions and crossing several canals. The last trail led to a large rock outcropping of about one hundred acres. It rose above the jungle and spread in several directions. This was the quarry; its name taken from the time-honored village practice of digging rock from the massif to build foundations for their small homes in the surrounding countryside.

Xinh and Thanh left the path at this point and skirted the edge of the quarry, coming out at the extreme north end of the rocky terrain. They bedded down in a large grove of bamboo. About three hundred meters to their front was the well-concealed main entrance to the underground arsenal with its many rooms and maze of interconnecting tunnels. Smaller entrances and escape hatches were strategically located throughout the system as were the hidden, bamboo air ventilation tubes that jutted up a few inches above the soil. "Pop-up" hatches covered by thick turf were positioned to provide deadly cross fire from interlacing, mutually supporting automatic weapons. Slit openings were also provided for individual riflemen.

Surrounding the entire perimeter of the quarry were varying levels of booby traps, punji sticks, and claymore mines, all ingeniously placed and masterfully concealed for maximum effectiveness. If necessary, the fortress could be successfully defended against a large, numerically superior force by a handful of VC. The entire redoubt had been designed and engineered by Tang. It was his masterpiece—a monument to his invincibility, dedicated to his "immortality."

Dawn was still several hours away. Xinh rolled over and lay on her stomach, parting the bamboo so she could see in a direct line to the entrance. Her ears rang from the bone-penetrating silence. She thought of Uncle Dong. The minutes dragged on—and they waited.

Unknown to Xinh, the ubiquitous Rat-face and another Vietcong agent had been in Vinh Son since sundown waiting for her to pass through. Tang's two thugs watched from the hamlet shadows while she and Thanh refilled their jungle lamps and sat down to a quick meal in one of the hooches. Later, the men followed them at a safe distance all the way to the quarry. They now sat silently in a clump of trees, stationed about one hundred meters from the bamboo grove where the girls, unsuspecting, had concealed themselves.

For weeks Rat-face had lusted after Xinh. He felt that he must possess her youth and beauty at least once before snuffing out her light forever. If Tang had let him have his own way he would have kept Xinh in a hole for at least a week, violating her at will, satisfying himself until he was burned out. But Tang had given him explicit orders to quickly murder her without ceremony, making it clear that if he failed on this second attempt he himself would be executed.

Now this madman crawled through the grass toward the unknowing Xinh, his loins ablaze with passion. He would crawl two meters and lay motionless for a complete minute before crawling another two meters. It took him a full hour to cover the distance. Ten meters from the grove he pulled himself up into a squat and got his bearings. Then at a prearranged signal he and his equally depraved and wanton partner rushed into the bamboo and viciously leaped on the two girls before they had a chance to react.

While Rat-face held his pistol to Xinh's head, Thanh was expertly hogtied and dragged off to another section of the bamboo. Her lithe little body strained and twisted at the tight bonds; her wide eyes flamed with hate. Wild, animal-like screams escaped from her throat in great spasms of convulsive loathing. A cold sweat poured from her and she shuddered with fear.

"Xinh! . . . Xinh! . . . Xinh! Nooooooooooooooo! Help me. Don't let him do this to me. Oh, God . . . Xinh! Noooooooooo.

Xinh lay on her back, not moving a muscle, trying to collect her wits. Rat-face's gun was pressed to her temple and he had her arms pinned with his knees.

The swiftness of his attack had momentarily paralyzed her thinking. Irrational, confused thoughts raced through her head. Her first efforts were those of a trapped, wild animal lashing out in terror, fighting for freedom like Thanh.

As Rat-face felt her resistance subside, he gradually released his hold and raised up. For a long time he stared at her motionless on the bed of grass. His long, narrow eyes penetrated the blackness of the night, pinning her to the ground, lapping up her beauty like a wild dog drinking at its trough.

"Ah, you have been a foolish girl, my pretty one," he said, studying her closely. He knelt back down and pushed the automatic in her face, his lips only a few inches away from her own. She nearly vomited from the foulness of his rancid breath. He smiled, revealing two rows of broken, rotted teeth. She willed herself to stare back into his eyes, untrembling. By sheer strength of will she forced her body not to quiver. She smiled back at him. This seemed to please him.

"You are going to make me happy now, aren't you, my dear?" Again the gust of fetid breath, making her feel light-headed. She nodded, smiling as sweetly as she could. His eyes seemed to glaze over and the terrible odor from his mouth intensified. His jaw went slack and his black tongue flopped out to the side. His breathing began coming in short gasps. She continued to smile, but the involuntary trembling in her body was impossible to control now. It seemed to heighten his excitement. Deep in the grove, Thanh screamed in terror.

Xinh spread her legs slightly, encouraging Rat-face to lie between them. He quickly slipped into the opening she had made for him, still pressing the gun's muzzle into her face. Then he shifted it to the side of her head and placed his sour mouth on her lips. She arched her body and began pulling down her pajama bottoms. Nothing else was necessary for she wore no underwear. Frantic with expectancy, he reached underneath and began helping her remove them, mouth still attached to hers.

The loose pajamas came off easily. When they reached her ankles she removed them the rest of the way with her bare feet. She spread her now naked legs as wide as she could and swung them up over the small of his back. With gentle pressure she forced him down on her, ankles locked together, her body quivering under his heavy weight. She felt the gun relax against her head, then drop to the grass; but it was still gripped in his right hand. Heaving like a buffalo, he fumbled for himself with his left hand.

Ever so slowly, she inched her hand down along her right thigh until it came to rest on the knife handle attached to the outside of her calf, just below the knee. A slight, imperceptible jerk—the steel was free in her hand!

Legs still locked tightly around his undulating body, she brought the knife point up along his back until it rested only a half inch above his spine, just below the spot where the backbone enters the skull. Then—*down*! With all the force she could generate in her arm and with the added power of her muscular frame arching upward, and at the same time squeezing his body into hers with her legs, she swiftly thrust the sharp blade deeply between the vertebrae, cleanly severing his spinal cord.

Rat-face's eyes rolled back in his skull and his head fell heavily onto her shoulder, a stinking froth bubbling from his gaping mouth. She turned her head from the hideous sight and heaved with all her strength to push the limp form from her. Though Rat-face wasn't a big man, his dead weight was difficult for such a small girl to manage. By bringing her leg underneath him, placing it squarely in his crotch, and lifting with her thigh, then pulling his head by the hair and twisting her body, she was able to squeeze out from beneath him.

Thanh had not stopped screaming for Xinh. Raging oaths and muffled cries for help broke through the stillness of the night. Xinh hurriedly pulled her pajamas back on. She twisted the knife free from the back of Rat-face's neck and stealthily made her way through the bamboo in the direction of Thanh's hysterical screeching.

About seventy-five meters into the grove, in a small clearing, Thanh lay on her back, hands and ankles awkwardly tied together behind her back, legs forced wide apart, pajama bottoms pulled down below her knees. Her perverted tormentor, completely nude except for his sandals, was on all fours, dog fashion, in front of her, holding a flaming cigarette lighter. Thanh let out another wild scream and shouted an angry oath. The man moved the flame closer between her legs. Thanh was thoroughly terrorized, writhing and trembling on the ground like a helpless animal. Each thrust of the flame into her private area brought a new burst of agonized outcries and searing pain.

Xinh stepped catlike from the edge of the clearing into the open behind the man. She crouched, knife hand extended low. The flame flickered across Thanh's face in time for Xinh to catch the recognition in her eyes. Thanh erupted into long, animal-like howls and terrible shrieks to occupy the Vietcong's attention.

As silent as death itself, Xinh swiftly reached forward, slipped her cupped left hand under the man's chin and pulled back with all her strength, exposing his throat to the quick, deep slice of the long knife blade. Still holding the flaming lighter, his leering, masochistic smile faded into a look of surprised terror, while all his tomorrows spilled out on the ground. She left him flopping around on the dirt, ejecting gurgling sounds from the deep incision, clutching at his neck.

Tears were in Xinh's eyes as she cut Thanh free and closely examined the cruel torture burns.

"Not so bad, sister. I think . . . I . . . can walk," Thanh said.

"No. I don't want you to move. I'll go into the quarry and get a medical bag. I won't be long."

"Be careful, Xinh. Tang is down in there."

"Don't worry." She carefully wiped the blood from the dagger and tied it back to her leg.

"Hurry."

"Yes, I'll be quick. I'm sorry about this, Thanh. I should have been more careful."

Thanh wiped a tear from Xinh's cheek. "It's O.K. I'll be all right."

Xinh pulled Thanh's pajamas back up and made

her comfortable. She patted her face and put the dying agent's pistol in her friend's hand.

"Rat-face is dead and this one is about gone," she said, pointing to the unconscious man on the ground. She tucked Rat-face's automatic in her waistband and headed for the river.

Chapter Seventeen

Feeling her way with her hands along the river bank and being careful not to trip any booby traps, Xinh came to the shallow depression she was seeking. It marked the location of the narrow underwater entrance. The river eddied here and the edge was heavily grown over with broad-leafed vegetation and thick grasses. She retied the knife to her leg, testing the knot for the exact tension and quick release she desired. Then, taking the automatic from her waistband, she pushed the spring catch in the handle and pulled the clip. Eight rounds. Full. She checked the action, muffling the sound with her hand and her cotton pajama blouse. She returned the clip to the housing. Satisfied with the condition of her weapons, she crawled to the edge of the bank and peered into the oily blackness below. She waited for a full five minutes for any sounds that would signal danger; then she silently slipped into the water.

The slow current carried her a few feet along before she recognized the touch of the vine rope that would lead her into the tunnel opening. Feeling it brush by her face, she caught it in her free hand and swung up against the bank. She submerged, pulling herself down along the rope, until she was ten feet under the surface and had located the round opening in the channel wall. Then, she released the rope, swam through the hole, and floated to the surface inside the quarry.

At first she lay motionless in the water, listening and letting her eyes adjust to the darkness. After a few minutes her pupils had satisfactorily widened and she could see the reflection from an oil-burning lamp flickering off the walls of the tunnel in one of the rooms directly ahead. She crawled out of the water onto the floor of tunnel number two and began to grope her way along the dank, moldy passageway toward the dim, yellow glow. The earthy smell of stale underground air was heavy in her nostrils and her small feet searched uncertainly along the cold, slippery surface.

After ten minutes of painfully inching her way through the dark tunnel she had come a sufficient distance to recognize that the light was coming from one of the two main galleries storing heavy munitions. She could see the two ladders, one leading to the upper gallery level and the other dropping down to the lower floor.

Reaching the ladder, she quietly ascended to the jutting gallery platform and lay flat, looking over the edge. She still couldn't see the source of the light so she stood in a crouch and moved carefully along the platform, holding onto the crude bamboo railing as she passed in front of a rock colonnade.

Below her in the middle of his throne room,

surrounded by piles of mortars, heavy rockets, and boxes of explosives, sat the invincible Tang. He was sitting at a rough table writing in what looked to Xinh to be a journal. An AK-47 was stretched across the table in front of him. He stood up from his writing and smiled to himself, putting the pencil down on the open ledger. Still smiling, he slowly studied the stockpiled munitions, his eyes roving over the stacks of cases and loose artillery rounds heaped around him. He walked into the piles and strolled among them, stopping here and there to caress a mortar tube or rocket round. Then his gaze turned to the huge gallery itself, made notably strange and mysterious by the brooding flame from the kerosene lamp. He looked up at the shovel- and pick-marked ceiling. Xinh darted behind a rock pilaster. He reached out and rubbed the damp wall with his open hands, admiring his monument, a lasting evidence and reminder of his achievement— his memorial stone, erected in remembrance of his power and authority.

The VC underground supply depot was indeed an engineering marvel. The three levels with their twelve rooms, three large galleries, and twenty interconnecting tunnels had been excavated completely by hand more than fifty feet below ground level. Each room had its special designation. Mortars and rockets. Rifles and machine guns. Recoilless rifles and RPGs. Dynamite, mines, and plastic explosives. Small arms ammo. Artillery rounds and grenades. Medical supplies. Rice stores. Clothing and equipment.

Tang returned to the table and again buried

himself in the paperwork. Xinh peeked out from behind the rock column and then began creeping along the gallery platform. Tang looked up from the ledger. Xinh flattened. He went back to writing. Xinh inched her way across to the opposite side of the gallery and waited breathlessly on the landing. After a few minutes her nerves quieted down, and catlike, in the open, Tang with his back to her, she began to descend the earthen stairs out of the wall. Rat-face's gun was tightly held in her hand.

Slowly . . . slowly . . . quietly . . . not a noise. She eyed the AK-47. Could he reach it in time? She wanted him alive. But he was quick and . . .

Tang leaped for the rifle! Somehow he had detected her presence. She fired a warning shot into the table top. "Stop, Tang, or the next one goes into you." He froze, back still toward her. Cautiously, she moved around in front of him and kicked the rifle off the table, out of his reach.

"So it is you," he said with a sneer. "Amazing. You're simply amazing. I underestimated you."

Xinh said nothing. She just stared at him, letting the reality of what had happened sink deep into his sinister brain. For ten minutes they just faced each other without saying another word. Xinh's eyes never wavered. Slowly, the sweat began beading on Tang's face. Fear began to show in his eyes. His usual arrogance and invincibility faded away. He was quivering. She remained still. Finally he couldn't take it any longer. He broke the silence. Inwardly she gloated.

"Why don't you just shoot me and be done with it?" he said, glaring at her, eyes livid with hate. His ashen face showed the humiliation of being captured by his prey.

"Shoot you! That would be undeserved by such a great and noble figure as yourself, the man destined to lead us to final victory. You deserve a much better end then that. Shoot you! Oh, no. You are worthy of a much better death than mere shooting. That is so common, Comrade Tang. So . . . unimaginative. You need to enter the next life with something more inspiring. Something grand to announce your arrival into *hell*!"

With that she ordered him to lie face down on the floor. At first it looked as though he might rush her, forcing her to put a speedy end to him, but his animal instincts clung to life, holding out for a few more precious minutes.

"Spread your arms and legs!" she ordered, pushing the gun into the back of his head and running her free hand over his body, checking for concealed weapons.

"I was mistaken about you, Xinh," Tang said, sputtering with rage. Xinh pushed his head down into the dirt with the gun. "I took you for a mere country girl, willing to follow me for a few crumbs. I was wrong. Your ambition goes far beyond anyone's imagination. But I question your intelligence," he raved, spitting out a glob of gravelly dirt dripping with saliva. "My death will not open the door for your ascendancy to my throne of power. Surely you expect my superiors to investigate. And you would be the first they would question. In short order they would discover your plot. Then it would only be a matter of time before they caught up with you and scattered your young bones in the hills to poison the wild dogs. May your soul wander aimlessly forever in a foreign land for this, Xinh!" he shouted.

"Think what you will, Tang, you son of a pig, but my ambition ends with you." Pulling his hair she jerked him up to his knees. She moved the gun down to the small of his back. "Now get up!"

"What are you doing? What are you going to do to me?" he cried.

"Something fitting." She pointed to the cases of dynamite. "Start carrying cases to the top of those rockets," she said, waving her gun at the 122-mm rounds neatly stacked in the middle of the arsenal.

Tang's raging now turned to pleading. "Don't do this to me, Xinh. We can work something out. Can't we?"

"Move!"

After he had piled four cases of the explosives side by side on top of the rocket mound she told him to stop.

"Now climb up on the cases and lie down on your back."

"No, Xinh, you can't do this," he begged.

"How much mercy did you show Thanh and I? How much! And to all the others who outlived their usefulness to you? How much, Tang!"

Xinh wired the crazed Tang tightly to his throne. Then she climbed up where he lay spread-eagled over the top of the dynamite and rockets.

"Any last words, comrade? A final speech to your loyal subjects, your majesty," she said, kowtowing to him and waving her hand over the assemblage of weapons and ammunition. Tang spit in her face.

Xinh patiently wiped the drool away with her pajama blouse. "That's so unbecoming of you, Tang. Such a venerable leader as yourself should be able to say good-bye in a more graceful manner. But on the other hand, what can one expect from a mental degenerate whose father was a crawling serpent and whose mother was a whoring dog."

Tang screamed vile oaths and twisted angrily under his bonds while Xinh carefully went about her deadly business, connecting the end of the fuse coil to one of the boxes of dynamite. "Your flesh will rot until the maggots die of starvation, you she-devil," he raved, almost out of his mind with terror.

Xinh picked up several more coils of fuse, and began carrying bundles of dynamite from open cases to the other rooms. After many trips back and forth she finished setting charges throughout the caverns and passageways, being meticulous about placing double and triple charges in the piles of ammunition. She unrolled the coils from each charge and spliced them into the main fuse; an akward but effective method, given the materials she had to work with. They had run out of electronic detonators and wire long ago. She purposely spliced in the fuse leading to Tang last so he would hear each explosion, like the ticking of a clock slowly counting off the fleeting moments he had left to live. The length of fuse began and ended in his room.

Having completed the demolition work, Xinh followed a small passageway to the medical stores and got the burn medicine and dressings she needed to doctor Thanh. As she was about to leave, Steve came to her mind so she went back and grabbed a

197

complete U.S. combat medic's bag.

In the equipment room she picked up her Chinese 56 and Thanh's AK-47, along with some extra clips of ammo. She stuffed the medical supplies, some rice rations, net hammocks, and a few other items into a rucksack stamped "U.S." and then made her way back through the labyrinth to Tang.

"Xinh!" he yelled, surprised to see her again, halfway hoping that she had decided to spare him and had left the quarry. Seeing her, despair flooded over him again and he began shouting, one moment cursing her, the next wailing a lament. She ignored him, concerned now only with completing the preparations for revenge against the Vietcong whom she had once faithfully worshiped as the only source of truth and hope for her people.

She dropped several grenades into the rucksack then picked up the kerosene lantern. Tang raised his head and watched her with bugging eyes, his vocal cords paralyzed with fright. She lit the fuse with the lamp flame. He saw it sputter, then catch. His voice returned and he shouted another foul oath.

Xinh hitched up the pack, slung the weapons over her shoulder, and unceremoniously walked out, carrying the lantern by its wire handle. The last thing she heard from her VC commander as she left him shrieking in the dark was, "Xinh come back. You can't do this to me. Please come back . . . *you rotten bitch!*"

She ascended the ladder for the last time, climbing up to the secret exit in the top gallery. The slow-burning fuse sparked behind her. Tang's screaming oaths echoed through the tunnels like ricocheting bullets.

Then she was outside in the fresh air. She quickly clambered from the opening into the dawn, took a big suck of air, and raced across the open ground into the bamboo grove. She paused for a few moments, listening. All was quiet. She whistled the call of the *gio-gi* bird. It was returned.

She covered the remaining distance very quickly. Thanh was lying as she had left her, gun still in her hand, the dead VC sprawled in his own blood.

"We've got to get out of here!" Xinh cried. "Can you walk?"

"I can. Let me lean on you. What happened? You were so long."

"Tang," she said, out of breath.

"I was worried."

"No time to talk. Got to move. Quickly." She helped Thanh to her feet. The girl winced from pain.

"Can you make it?"

"How far?"

"Just a few . . ."

She didn't finish the sentence. The earth swelled and heaved under them, knocking them both flat. The explosions ripped the earth wide open. Fire and smoke leaped from its ruptured bowels as the quarry convulsed in great spasms that shook the whole region. Dirt and rock showered down on them. The two girls lay prone, hugging each other.

"Are we going to die, Xinh?"

"Not yet."

Another eruption tore through the redoubt, exposing a gapping hole in the rock. Then another . . . and another. The air was thick with smoke and debris. Fires were breaking out on the surface. The explosions continued unabated as the arsenal fed upon itself, devouring its insides. They couldn't breath in the choking air.

"We've got to get away," Xinh gasped. "Come on."

Partly carrying and partly dragging Thanh, she somehow managed to get into the safety of the trees. There, they fell down, exhausted and breathing heavily.

"Are we safe here?" Thanh asked. She was shaking.

"Yes, I think we're safe now."

"Where's Tang?"

"Down in that," Xinh said, waving feebly in the direction of the quarry. I'll tell you all about it later." She sighed tiredly.

Back inside the quarry, the booming explosions continued, the fortress destroying itself. But the girls didn't hear it any longer. Like two children, arms wrapped around each other, they had fallen asleep. . . . Do you forgive me now?

Chapter Eighteen

The spent girls hid in the jungles of Binh Duong licking their wounds. Xinh patiently applied salves and root extracts to Thanh's burns which luckily turned out to be less serious than she had initially suspected. Applications of *nuoc mam* hastened the healing. Her own wounds, from the struggle with Rat-face and from flying rock from the exploding quarry, were superficial and had quickly healed. They rested.

Visions of a future spun round and round in Xinh's tortured mind. Each time she thought about it the tense band around her head tightened, causing her to nearly faint from pain and loneliness.

"Steeeeeeeeeeeeeeve." She threw herself on the ground, pounding it with clenched fists.

Thanh knelt beside Xinh, loosening her hair. "We'll find him, sister. We'll find him," she said, touching her shoulder.

Xinh turned her tear-streaked face to Thanh. "You understand, don't you? We can never go back."

"Yes, I do." She pulled Xinh's hair back from her face and tied it with her checkered guerrilla scarf.

"It's going to be all right. You'll see."

Thanh got up and began rummaging through the rucksack. After digging through the grenades, ammo clips, and assorted supplies, she found Xinh's small bag of personal items. She loosened the nylon drawstring and took a jade-studded Chinese comb from the bag. She untied the scarf and sat down cross-legged behind Xinh. She began combing her hair with long, even pulls of the wooden heirloom. She watched the silky black strands cascade over Xinh's shoulders with each stroke of the comb, the ends settling on the leaf-covered ground around her bare feet. A few drops of coconut oil made her lovely hair shine like a raven's wing.

The pretty little Saigonese remained in her place and without interruption went on smoothing Xinh's hair, calming her nerves, talking to her in quiet tones, trying to take her mind off Steve. She reached into the bag again, brought out a worn picture of a venerable Cochinese ancient dressed in ceremonial raiment, and handed it to Xinh. With loving eyes Xinh looked at the picture of the old woman for a long time. It had been a while since she had last visited grandmother. She missed her familiar husk-like smell. It brought back the secure feeling she remembered when she was a child. Sometimes, when she had been lonely and whimpering in bed, the old woman would part the mosquito netting and motion for her to come to the comfort of her arms.

"Xinh oi. Di ngo khong?" Xinh darling, can't you sleep? she would say. *"Lai day con,"* come here to me, child. And Xinh would jump from the poor wooden bed and rush to her Ba Ngoai.

202

Grandmother would then turn down the oil lamp and secure the mosquito net while Xinh snuggled under her arm, falling quickly asleep with Ba Ngoai's pleasant scent lingering in her dreams.

But her most vivid memories of growing up in Vietnam were not connected with the carefree joys that most children experience during their early years. She mostly remembered hard work, fear, insecurity, and grinding poverty. Sad and lonely because of isolation from playmates and youthful activities, deserted by her mother, and never knowing her father, she lived a miserable, wretched life of near hopelessness. She remembered always being alone, bereft, and forsaken.

Yet through it all, grandmother had been there to wipe away the tears and comfort her. Ba Ngoai was the only family she had ever known and it was through her persistent dedication to Xinh's future that she had been able to rise above her poverty.

Grandmother was sometimes drunk on homemade rice wine and milky colored gin, and occasionally she would beat Xinh with the stinging bamboo stick. But she never lost sight of her responsibility to the little waif. Xinh had been a sickly child. Born with a deformed foot, for many years she crawled or scooted on her little bottom unable to walk. Every night after putting her own children to bed, Ba Ngoai would place Xinh on her lap, heat her hand over the charcoal fire, and massage her granddaughter's crippled foot. Eventually this primitive method forced the rigid foot to yield enough so that Xinh was able to use it. Walking on it made the foot more and more normal until, in adulthood, there was only a tiny trace of a limp.

Then there had been the open, running sores—so shameful and they hurt so much. "Gook sores" the GIs called them. Ba Ngoai tenderly treated the inflamed tissues with salt packs or sometimes she rubbed kerosene oil from the lamps into them.

Xinh would cry out; "Please grandmother, no more . . . hurt! hurt!"

Then Ba Ngoai would caress her but she would leave the packs on. "I'm sorry child, but they must stay on. They will heal the sores and the hurt will go away."

Xinh was thankful that only a few scars still remained and that they were in unnoticeable places.

Through all this, Xinh was required to work. It was still painful for her to recall the depressing memories of having to rise from her bed of palm leaves before the light of day and trudge with her little aunts and uncles to the train station to sell bread and tea to the passengers. Standing barefoot in the depot, wearing her dirty, tattered dress with her malnutritious belly protruding, she would beg the people to buy her *ban mi* and *nuoc tra*. The humiliation was often unbearable and large tears frequently streaked her dusty cheeks. If she saw someone she knew she would hide until they passed.

When the last train of the morning pulled out she would return home and give her grandmother the few piasters she had earned. If any of the bread was left over, a piece was given her along with a bowl of rice for breakfast. Then she would leave for school, walking along the paddy dikes, stopping now and then to watch other peasants planting the young rice in knee-deep water and plowing the paddies with their ponderous water buffalo.

In school she was often so tired that she would fall asleep in her seat. An application of the teacher's stinging bamboo switch usually forced her to stay awake, though her frail body cried out for rest. Nor did her suffering end after school. For she had to retrace her predawn steps. At the station she peddled bread again, this time to the returning passengers on the afternoon and evening trains.

It wasn't until late at night when the last train pulled in that little Xinh turned from the depot to face the long walk home. If she was lucky, grandmother would be home waiting for her with a bowl of rice and a slice of fish with a few pieces of *rau*, the vegetables she liked so much. If Ba Ngoai wasn't yet home from scavenging the countryside she would wait in the dark watching the rat poke its head in and out of the hole in the middle of the dirt floor.

And the cycle continued the next day, seven days a week, three hundred sixty-five days a year, until one day she realized that somehow she had survived the terrible circumstances of her childhood, and had emerged, in her adolescence, a striking beauty, fully recovered from the debilitating environment in which she had grown up.

Her tenacity for life and her persistent hope to break the vicious cycle in which she was caught, brought her through the ordeal healthy and strong and filled with determination to improve her life.

Xinh affectionately ran her delicate fingers over grandmother's picture, being careful not to let her long fingernails scratch the glossy finish. She remembered with tenderness that Ba Ngoai now looked at her with great love in her old eyes, never failing to say when she visited her, "You have grown up to be a beautiful woman. I never thought you would live."

She gently placed the photograph back in the bag. I will go see my grandmother when I get back from Cambodia, she thought to herself. I will bring her a basket of *xoai* and some *cam*, her favorite fruit. She will need money too. And tobacco.

The day's first rays of sunlight streamed in through the forest trees warming her smile. She sat quietly watching the crimson ball chin above the horizon while cooling morning breezes wafted loose threads of soft hair across her high Asian cheekbones.

How wonderful it would be to have a husband to share these gentle moments with. Steve's letter stared at her from the open bag. It was dated four months earlier from Da Nang where he had been temporarily transferred TDY to fly MigCap missions over North Vietnam. She picked it up and read, picturing him sitting next to her:

Dear Xinh,

I have been away for a week now and I miss you so very much. I'm told that I'll only be up here another few weeks, at least until the replacement pilots arrive from the States. I'll be taking a few of them over Hanoi with me on their first missions. Then back to Binh Hoa and Xinh.

Got another Mig today. Disintegrated (get out your dictionary, honey—it means blew up into little pieces) right in front of me. Poor guy didn't have a chance. While I watched the missile track him I found myself wondering what his last thoughts would be. Did he have a beautiful girl like you back home who wore pretty *ao dais* for him. Was he married? Children? I hoped that he would get out O.K. But he didn't. No chute.

Someday this dumb war is going to end, Xinh. Then maybe your people can get back to the business of living, regardless of who wins. Personally, just between you and me, I don't think there are too many who really care who wins. They just want to stay alive.

I feel sorry for your people, Xinh. They're caught in between. No voice. No say in their destiny. Never knowing their future. Controlled by the Chinese. The French. The Japanese. The French again. The Communists. The Viet Minh. The Americans. Will it ever end?

I'd like to take you out of all this, back home with me, if we both live through it. But maybe you won't want to come. I've never asked you. I love you.

> Hoa Binh,
> Steve

She held the letter to her breast and closed her eyes. No, he had never asked her. And she had never brought up the subject when he had returned from Da Nang. America was so far away. Would she like it? She carefully folded the letter and returned it to the bag with her grandmother's picture.

Thanh finished combing Xinh's hair. She gave it an expert, short twist and retied the checkered scarf.

Xinh stood up.

"It is best we get started. I think we are well enough to travel now."

"Yes, sister," Thanh said, taking down the hammocks and placing them in the rucksack.

"We will travel as much as we can during the day, keeping to the forest trails. Be alert for American patrols. And remember, every Cong in Binh Duong is looking for us. They may already have picked up our trail."

"Yes, sister. We will move faster when the sun goes down."

Xinh shouldered the pack and handed Thanh her weapon. She picked up her own rifle and the two girls started off at a trot, Xinh out in front and Thanh following twenty meters behind.

They headed west over the dense trails toward Cambodia, being impelled by an inner force, spontaneously reacting to familiar environmental stimuli that guided them through rain forest and tree lines, and occasionally across the open paddies. They skirted the villages and hid in the undergrowth. They never slowed their pace, except when sensing danger, and it wasn't until the sun had moved into its zenith that they stopped for a rest.

The girls, toughened by the strict self-discipline and self-denial of guerrilla warfare in the Southeast Asian jungles, suffered little physical discomfort from the torrid heat and hostile terrain. Their lives were marked by simplicity and the avoidance of comfort and luxury. And they were undaunted by pain and danger.

An American GI normally consumes the contents

of his two canteens within a few hours of beginning a field operation in the bush. He never runs except when his life depends on it, his heavy, burdensome equipment, the searing sun, and the near hundred percent humidity sapping most of his energy. Xinh and Thanh carried no water and had tasted none since morning. They had been running four hours.

Instinct suddenly sent the girls crashing off the trail.

"Quick—over here—this way."

"I'm right behind you—hurry."

"Down, down—get down."

"Give me another clip."

"Here—take it. Shhh, here they come."

"Keeeee . . . keeeee," cries the kite hovering in the torpid sky, flexing its black talons.

They lie in the long grass on the embankment. A dull, metallic "thunk" and the bolts come back on the Chinese 56 and AK-47 pointed down the forest path. Xinh watches a smile creep across Thanh's steely face. She licks parched lips and her eyelids flicker twice then drowsily slide closed.

"Americans," she purrs in her soft, husky voice.

Then comes the sound of heavy boots on packed earth, the swish and clank and clink of metal and the rush of canvas. They trudge past, flak jackets open at the chest, some shirtless, some with sleeves cut off, biceps exposed. Young like themselves, eyes lizard fast, dressed in jungle greens. Death and pain so close . . . innocent, unknowing.

Thanh pulls the pin on a grenade and lets it tumble down the embankment.

"Keeeee . . . keeeee." The kite suddenly locks its

wings and falls earthward in a plunging dive.

The heavy grenade rushes through the grass and rolls into the open. Dirt and rocks are dislodged. The young infantryman turns. His skin is peach soft on his beardless face. He lifts his two arms, extending them toward the bouncing, khaki object, rifle dropping to the ground. His mouth forms a wide O.

"Keeeee . . . keeeee." Hooked claws sink deep.

The explosion tears the air—shrieking metal fragments and fire splinters. The arms remain reaching for the explosion, up, as if in prayer. The boy's body falls away, bloody stumps hanging from its shoulders, leaving the hands and arms suspended in the air.

M-16s pop and spit. An M-60 begins its rhythmic thumping. Rounds crisscross through the grass, chopping down the blades in wide swaths. Lips turn blue with fear. Young faces drain into colorlessness. Trembling fingers hold down triggers and barrels burn hot in adrenaline-swollen hands.

Xinh forced her head down into the hard dirt. The sharp rocks and woody twigs bit into her cheek. Rifle rounds thudded into the ground, splattering her with debris. Her nose was filled with the thick smell of dry grass and dirt.

"We will have to pull back."

The deep-throated pounding of the M-60 cut through the popping of M-16s. Exploding bullets ran up the slope to her.

"We are pinned down, sister. We can't pull back."

The machine gun tore a furrow a few feet in front of them. Xinh inched back from the edge of the depression she had fallen into. A burst from the M-60 froze her.

From the corner of her eye she could see a fire team maneuvering around to the right to outflank her. A bullet ricocheted off the hard ground and spun a few inches over her head, whining loudly.

"Can you see them, Thanh?"

"Yes. There are four of them."

"If they get to the top of the embankment we're finished."

"I can't do anything."

Xinh rolled over on her back. The shooting dropped off momentarily to let the four men move out of the line of fire. It was the few seconds of time that Xinh needed.

"Now Thanh!"

Quickly the girls were on their knees, pouring withering fire into the soldiers creeping up the steep slope. The fusillade caught the four men by surprise, and they scattered in confusion, falling and rolling back down the incline.

"Pah! That was close." Xinh was flushed.

The blood coursed through her veins. No experience could compare with the adrenaline high of combat. Her nerves were right on the surface and every cell in her body screamed with excitement; every sound was amplified beyond its normal range. The smells were heady.

"*Ehhhhhh!*" One of the soldiers lay in the open, unable to move, gut-shot. The sun beat down on him. He held his stomach, screaming, entrails curled around his fingers. Xinh could see him over the lip of the depression where she and Thanh were hunkered down.

211

"Why don't they come to get him?" Thanh said. "I can't stand his screaming." She put her hands over her ears.

From her high position on the embankment, Xinh had the advantage of position and the Americans were reluctant to move from what cover they had. But they had the advantage of fire power and kept her pinned to the slope.

Thanh had edged into the depression so that she now had a better field of fire and the protection of a large rock. Whenever a soldier would rise up, she would lay down a few rounds, forcing him down again. "How many do you count?"

"Looks like about twelve." Xinh rubbed dirt from her eye.

"Have you decided how you are going to get us out of here?"

"I'm thinking."

The M-60 began thumping again, but the rounds were going high and wide.

The soldier on the slope hadn't stopped screaming.

"Can you see him from where you are, Xinh?"

"Yes. Why?"

"Kill him. I can't stand to hear him anymore."

Xinh said nothing.

"Why don't they come to get him?"

"He's in the open. No one wants to take the chance."

"*Ehhhhhhhhh!*"

"Shoot him, Xinh."

She looked at Thanh then back to the wounded soldier. "His screaming demoralizes the others. They

212

will be afraid and won't fight hard."

"How long can they stand it? It's creepy."

"Kill me, somebody kill me," the man shouted. "Please . . . kill me . . . *ehhhhhhhhh*!"

The M-60 opened up again. The bursts were nowhere close.

"That gunner must not be able to see us."

A soldier got to his feet, a belt of ammo slung around his neck, and ran for a tree. Thanh's bullets chased him all the way to the tree, nipping at his heels. A moment later he crawled out with a medical bag. A red cross was emblazoned on the case.

"What do you think?" Thanh looked over at Xinh.

"See what he does."

The man skillfully maneuvered up the slope, sprinting across open spaces and falling into depressions eroded in the earth or behind rocks.

The girls ducked down as suppressing fire raked them.

"Shall we let him?"

"Let him."

The soldier reached the shot man and lay flat. He glanced up the slope.

"What's he going to do?"

"Shhhh," Xinh said. "Listen."

The wounded man finally saw his buddy. "Shoot me, Jack! Please, shoot me!" The sun was cooking hot.

Jack reached into the bag, then jabbed the screaming man with morphine. He placed extra Syrettes into the private's hand and crawled back down the slope along the same route he had come.

"Thanh!"

"What?"

"The Americans will not wait much longer . . . they are getting restless. We have been lucky so far. We must go now."

Thanh was frowning. "How can we get out of here?"

Xinh looked over her shoulder. "It's only a few feet to the top of the embankment. Throw two grenades; then run. I'll cover you."

"What about you?"

"I'll do the same. You cover me from the top. When I reach you we'll get away down the back side and double back toward the quarry."

"The quarry!"

"We have no choice. The Americans will be right behind us."

"And the Cong will be in front of us," Thanh said.

"It's our only chance. We can't stay here."

The M-60 gunner was hauling the weapon into the open.

"Now, Thanh, do it now before it's too late!"

Thanh slipped the sling over her back and pulled the pins to her last grenades. She looked over at Xinh.

"Now!"

She flipped them down the hill and Xinh spit lead up and down the line of Americans.

"Go, Thanh, go!"

Bullets whizzed around Thanh and plowed into the dirt, tearing the grass to shreds. She threw herself over the top of the embankment, chest heaving, mouth gasping for breath. She crawled back to the crest and began pumping shells down the slope.

Xinh picked her targets, took a deep breath and

heaved the grenades with all her might. *Whoom! Whoom!* She was up and running, bulllets whining and ricocheting around her. It seemed an eternity passed before she fell over the top. Panting, next to Thanh, she opened fire.

"We'll take a few minutes to catch our breath."

Thanh was busy reloading. Two soldiers tested the open ground, moving toward the hill.

"They're getting tired of being held down."

Another American moved out.

"Let's go!"

A final burst from the AK and the 56, and the girls were gone; two shadowless forms withdrawing from the grass, crawling down the low ridge and phantomlike, gliding away, along the back side of the hogback.

Hitting the tree line on a dead run, they found the path again and settled into a jog. The patrol would recover fast, the Americans always did, and they would call in their gunships, the widow-makers, and the little 03 observation planes to hunt them down. Xinh was always amazed at how persistently the Americans pursued even one VC. Body count was what they called it. The big noses were always talking about the body count. Sometimes a dead buffalo was counted when they couldn't find any dead VC.

The girls took turns carrying the rucksack. Thanh got more nervous each yard they retreated.

"I don't like going back this way," Thanh puffed.

"I don't like it either, but we have to." Xinh's feet padded lightly on the path. "The only way through these hills is back there. The big noses have that blocked, so we'll just have to swing around to the quarry and look for another way into Cambodia."

Thanh tilted her head back. "Listen . . . hear that?"

"I hear it." Xinh looked up through the break in the trees while she ran.

"They don't waste any time do they?"

The familiar whumping of helicopter rotor blades pounded the air, sending shock waves through the forest. The two guerrillas ran faster, sticking close to the shadows.

"Tired?"

"Not yet."

"Thirsty?"

"No."

They ran, putting distance between themselves and the patrol. The gunships crisscrossed the paddies and tree lines searching for Xinh and Thanh. The girls held to the jungle path, closely watching the breaks in the tree canopy.

"Look, Xinh!"

Two Hueys had landed, disgorging their loads. The fresh troops were running through the paddies at an angle that would cut off the girls' retreat.

"This way." Abruptly Xinh turned off the path and headed through the trees, up a hill, and then down into a narrow valley. She stopped to catch her breath.

"I don't know this place." Thanh was looking around, worried.

"I do." Xinh drew a long breath. She was sweating heavily. "Tang had some tunnels about five hundred meters from here. There's food and ammo. We can rest and hide." She adjusted the rucksack.

Suddenly her body went rigid and her eyes grew wide. She grabbed Thanh by the neck and pulled her to the ground. Xinh flattened beside her.

"We're trapped!" Thanh pointed the AK out of the foliage at the force of advancing Vietcong.

"Hao's out front, Tang's second in command." Her eyes were cold and dead.

"Minh and Dong are with him." Thanh looked at Xinh, waiting for her order. "They'll see us soon. Make up your mind."

"I'm going to try something, Thanh. I don't have time to explain, just trust me."

"I trust you."

"We may not make it out of this one. You can tell that Hao's been searching for us for days."

"Maybe we can surrender to the Americans."

"They will just turn us over to the ARVN and we will spend the rest of our lives in the tiger cages at Con Song Island."

"That's worse than being killed." Thanh screwed up her face.

"I have another plan."

Caught between the Americans and the revenge-seeking Vietcong, Xinh realized that her options had run out. Thanh lay beside her, trigger finger impatiently flexing, her bottom wiggling back and forth.

"Pick a target. I'll take Hao."

Thanh nodded. *Pow*! Minh dropped. *Pow*! Hao toppled to the ground. The VC scrambled for cover, giving Xinh the few seconds she needed.

Xinh was quickly on her feet, Thanh right behind

her, flying through the forest, dodging trees and jumping bushes. Back over the same ground she raced, knowing that the U.S. troops were waiting in ambush for her.

The Vietcong were on their feet.

"It's Xinh."

"Get her!"

"Cut her belly open and feed her entrails to the dogs!"

"Make her die slowly!"

The crazed VC tore after her, screaming their rage, delirious with hate like a pack of rabid wolves.

Down the narrow valley and up the hill she ran. She stopped at the top of the hill and looked back, standing in the open, fully revealing herself to the VC. The guerrilla queen fired a few times, turned and ran along the ridge, then disappeared down the other side. The Cong roared their hate.

"There's the trail," Thanh said as they came to the bottom of the hill.

"The American soldiers are just ahead."

Xinh fired a few shots to alert the Americans. She stopped for a few seconds, waiting for the VC who were unaware of the presence of the U.S. troops, and leaving them no doubt about the direction of the chase.

Thanh, catching on to Xinh's clever plan, smiled. "Your ancestors will be dancing in their tombs before this day is over."

"The sun has not yet set, little sister."

The trail entered a heavily treed stretch and the forest closed in. Xinh sensed that this was the location of the Americans' ambuscade and quickly threw herself into the dense foliage. She crawled into a shallow ravine, waiting for the trap to spring. Her chest beat hard against the ground.

"We've become soldiers without a country," Thanh murmured. "Everyone is our enemy now."

"We are warriors of the twilight, neither in the light or the darkness," Xinh said softly.

The Vietcong were stupidly bunched on the trail. Leaderless, they had become an undisciplined, noisy mob, each man wanting to personally get credit for murdering Xinh.

They ran by her, their sandaled feet slapping hard against the packed dirt trail, twenty of them their minds working as one; *Kill Xinh!*

"When?" Thanh whispered.

"Soon."

The last Cong ran past.

Whoom! Whoom! Whoom! The front door of the trap swung shut. *Pow . . . pow . . . pow . . .* Screams, yelling, shouting, confusion. Firing from the helicopter assault troops was heavy and accurate.

The intense smell of exploded gunpowder floated through the trees, reaching Xinh's nose. Her face hardened. This was one battle she would stay out of.

Like a thick fog, the predictable blue smoke rolled down the trail and sifted upward into the canopy. Beams of sunlight spread through the smoke, creating a surrealistic glow that transformed the rain forest into a fantasy of bright, dancing particles.

The VC fell back along the trail, stumbling, falling, bleeding. Xinh's eyes were cold and blank, like a shark's.

Then the back door closed tightly. The patrol

came up fast from behind, blocking any hope of retreat and fired point-blank into the guerrillas. The Cong were falling everywhere, M-16s mercilessly cutting them down in their tracks.

One guerrilla, shot through both shoulders, arms useless, fell on an American and buried his teeth in the soldier's neck, shaking it like a dog with a bone in his mouth.

Xinh watched without a trace of emotion. Her wooden eyes were focused on a puppet show in Tay Ninh, under the large tamarind tree. She was sitting in grandmother's lap. She held the rag doll tightly to her and stroked its yarn hair.

Xinh could see from her hiding place in the ravine that all the Vietcong had been killed. The American teenagers sat down in the gore and smoked. Some laughed, some stared, some lay down, and others vomited. Others shared their canteens and slapped each other on the back.

The helicopters returned. The child warriors climbed in and flew away.

Sluggishly jogging along the forest path as the sun receded above her, Xinh's worried eyes searched the land for a defendable campsite. She saw a large banyan tree two hundred meters off the trail, rising above the jungle canopy. Without breaking stride she plunged into the foliage leading away from the track.

Reaching the foot of the massive tree, Thanh helped Xinh off with the rucksack. The girls didn't stop to catch their breath, but clambered over the huge trunk buttresses and crawled up into the lower heavy branches of the banyan. Like two little monkeys they playfully chased each other over the thick limbs, swinging from the aerial vines.

Sitting on a high branch, she said to Thanh: "Steve used to call me his 'young rice.' He wrote a poem about me. Want to hear it?" Xinh began reciting from memory, not waiting for Thanh's answer.

> Bit of a sprig
> So innocent and pure,
> Ripening to harvest
> 'Til age sublime;
> Sight of your loveliness
> God's perfect cure,
> Blessings from the Khan
> Sweet youth divine.
>
> Sweet girl of the fields
> My life you ease.

Thanh clapped. "Very nice."

The girls could have played like this until nightfall, but as usual, they had to cut their recreation short and turn their attention to more practical matters. The most imminent need was water. In a few minutes they found what they were looking for: a cavity in the bole of the banyan. Thanh placed her hand into the fist-size opening and brought it back dripping wet with rainwater. She picked a leaf from the tree and shaping it into a scoop, dipped it into the bole and drank the pure, crystal water. Taking turns, the girls drank their fill

221

then returned to the ground.

No further words passed between them. The heat of the day was upon them and they would sleep until the trees began casting long shadows across the clearings. They finished stringing their hammocks and Thanh built a small fire while Xinh cut two twelve-inch sections from a length of growing bamboo. She then carefully made a three-inch lengthwise incision through the bamboo wall of each section with her knife and stuffed the hollows with rice, adding a few drops of water from the banyan bole. The fire had burned down to a bed of coals, to which she added the bamboo rice cookers. Within thirty minutes the puffy white rice began to bulge through the slits. The girls broke open the bamboo and using their fingers, heartily consumed the contents. A few slices of dried cuttlefish and more water from the bole rounded out the noon fare. Xinh smiled at Thanh, patted her tummy, and rolled into her hammock with the Chinese 56 lying across her chest. Within seconds she was asleep.

Xinh and Thanh lay quietly hidden in the underbrush on the banks of the Tra Oc river separating Vietnam from Cambodia. On the other side was the Skull, the oddly shaped land mass that thrust eastward into Vietnam like the bony head of a skeleton for which it was named. There was still enough light available from the last rays of the disappearing sun for the girls to see the beautiful deep jade green color of the wide river. Waiting for darkness they rested in the foliage, admiring the Tra

Oc's shimmering beauty.

The territory covered in the past few days to get to the Cambodian frontier had been familiar to Xinh. But the miles that lay ahead were completely unknown to her except for the map in the rucksack and the crude descriptions Thanh had received during her reconnaisance. Somewhere in that wild interior was Steve.

From their concealed position, the girls anxiously watched as the wings of night chased the hot, torpid breath of day from the land, drawing forth cooling breezes that rippled the surface of the Tra Oc and brought a welcome relief from the suffocating humidity. The water slapped against the bank in front of them and the outline of the river runner could be seen bobbing in its shallow berth a short distance away, tied to the prop root of a verbena. The first evidence of a quarter moon poked its crescent above the jungle canopy on the Vietnamese side as Xinh and Thanh crept out from the thick growth and silently made their way along the river's grassy edge to the river runner. As quietly as two river eels the girls slipped neck deep into the water, expertly pushing the narrow craft ahead of them. When the current had caught the river runner, they edged around the gunnels so that the boat was between them and the Vietnamese shore. There they hung while being carried farther midriver, away from the winking hamlet lamplights and cooking fires.

Xinh nodded to Thanh and they pulled themselves over the gunnels into the boat, on top of their weapons and equipment. After a few minutes of lying prone, Xinh reached over and fired up the small motor. She quickly grabbed the tiller, turned the river runner into the current, and accelerated upstream. The little French-made outboard purred, a reassuring hum, while the long, extended drive shaft rapidly turned the propeller behind the boat.

"Fortune is with us," Thanh said, poking her finger into the gas tank. "It's full!"

When they had gotten out of rifle range from the village, Xinh cut the engine back to economize on fuel and to reduce noise so they wouldn't draw undue attention to their presence.

Rrrrrrrrrrrrrrrrr, the little engine stuttered along, cutting a narrow wake through the green water and propelling the girls upstream into Cambodia where new dangers lurked. They crossed over midriver and guided the boat by the shadowy outline of the opposite shore. Thanh squatted in the bow and kept a sharp lookout for dead snags, sandbars, and protruding rocks.

"What should we do if we run into Cambodians?" Thanh wanted to know, bringing her rifle up.

"Nothing, if they're Khmer Rouge or country peasants. They have nothing to do with us."

"Kampuchean government troops?"

"Avoid them," was Xinh's answer. "We take no chances with them, nor with any Vietcong or North Vietnamese regulars."

"Isn't the Cambodian government shaking hands with North Vietnam and the VC?"

"Not anymore," Xinh said.

"Why not?"

"The Americans have come down hard on Prince Sihanouk and the Kampucheans for letting the NVA operate from the sanctuaries."

"So why are we still able to work the sanctuaries?" Thanh asked.

"Sihanouk doesn't want to antagonize the North Vietnamese leaders. He has enough trouble with the Khmer Rouge Communists."

"Looks like he's going to let the Americans do his dirty work by giving them permission to bomb the sanctuaries."

"I suppose so. Steve's raid was the first. And that was supposed to be secret," Xinh answered.

"They can't keep that secret for very long."

"No. It was stupid to even try. For all their technology, the Americans are surprisingly dumb."

"Politically?" Thanh asked.

"Yes. Politically and militarily."

Several hours later the river suddenly began to narrow and the jungle closed in around them blocking out what little navigating light they had from the moon and stars. Xinh instinctively cut the engine down to a putter, just enugh to make headway. The river was almost motionless here. Thanh tightened her hold on the AK-47.

Chapter Nineteen

The smell of the tiger was heavy in the air as Xinh wedged the river runner into an opening in the bank. The boat was scraping bottom and they had just about run out of river. Thanh arched her neck and sniffed the stagnant air. It was oppressive, smelling of rot. Her acute sense of smell brought her to the alert.

"I smell him," she said, sniffing vigorously and turing her head to left and right.

"I can smell him too," Xinh said, also inhaling the noxious wet odor of the tiger. "Not so strong."

"Very strong. Very strong," Thanh said.

"Close?"

"Yes. Close."

"Where?"

"Out there. Somewhere out there," Thanh said, pointing ahead into the black night. She shivered.

"We can't go any farther on the river. Too shallow. Help me pull the boat on shore," Xinh said. She jumped to the bank.

Thanh threw her the bow line. Her frightened eyes continuing to search the heavy undergrowth. "He's out there."

"Come on. Help me."

The girls tugged at the rope, pulling the water skimmer onto the bank. They pushed and struggled, hauling it back into the foliage where it would lay concealed until their return.

"Get me the lighter and the map."

Thanh reached into the rucksack and brought them to Xinh. She flicked the PX-purchased cigarette lighter with her thumb. The flame sprang up, casting a frightening glow on their faces. They huddled over the spread map.

"Where are we?" Xinh asked.

"Here."

"No, we're not. That's too far north. See where the river ends? Farther south."

"That's a different river," Thanh said.

"So it is."

"Where are we then?"

"I don't know."

"Wait. Look here." Xinh brought the lighter closer to the map. They pushed their heads together. "See. Here's Ban San Talat," Thanh said, stabbing the map with her index finger.

"And here's the upper Tra Oc. And here—" Xinh followed the course of the river with her finger nail— "is the Siem Pang tributary we took about five miles back."

"How far have we come?"

"Looks like about twenty miles. It will be dawn in a few hours."

"We've been traveling that long?"

"We should get some sleep."

"Where?" Thanh asked, looking disturbed.

"Right here."

"Are you kidding. With that damn thing crawling around out there?" Thanh said, jerking her head toward the jungle.

"Don't worry about it," Xinh said.

"*Don't worry about it*!" Thanh cried.

"Shhhhhhhh. Not so loud."

"You know tigers as well as I do, Xinh. Remember that one in Tay Ninh? Ate Linh half away and the next night dragged Binh into the river and drowned her before we could reach her. Craziest thing I ever saw. I never thought tigers could swim."

"They're thick in the Michelin Plantation, you know."

"Are they, Xinh?" Thanh's elfish nose started twitching. She had a hypnotic attraction to tigers. "Tell me about them."

"My grandmother was a cutter, on the rubber trees, and one evening after everyone had left, this big male Siberian crept out of the bush and began stalking her. She could see him, behind her about three hundred meters, inching up on her on his belly, moving from tree to tree."

Thanh's eyes got as big as rice bowls. "My god! What did she do?"

"First thing she did was wet her pants."

"No kidding!" Thanh moved up as close as she could to Xinh, touching her cheek with her own, eyes searching the night. "Then what?"

"Well, Grandmother figured since she was the last one to collect her rubber pots and her section was farthest from the rest, no one would hear her screams.

229

And if she started running, the tiger would quickly run her down."

"So what did she do?" Thanh asked, petrified with horror.

"She screamed and ran."

"She did? *Troi oi*! What did the Siberian do?"

"He was after her like a shot. Just like she imagined. But as she was running she spotted a tree—the right kind, small trunk, high branches. Tigers can't climb trees, you know."

"I know, I know," Thanh said. "Go on."

"Grandmother leaped onto the tree and pulled herself up to the top. The tiger slammed into the tree, clawing and roaring and spitting all at the same time."

Thanh's mouth was wide open, her long eyes as round as Chinese teacups.

"Grandmother stayed in that tree, screaming all night, with the tiger clawing and biting the trunk and trying to get at her."

"Great God, Xinh. How terrible for the old lady. How did she get away?"

"The workers returned the next morning. The cat decided there were too many to handle, so he reluctantly slunk off into the forest. Grandmother was a nervous wreck when they climbed up into the tree and brought her down. She couldn't move, paralyzed with fear. They had to carry her home. She never went back to work in the Michelin grove."

Thanh was exhausted from the story. She lay up against a tree and took a deep breath. "Xinh, we can't stay here. That son of a bitch is going to eat us both if we do." Suddenly she cocked the bolt on her Russian

Kalashnikov, leaped to her feet, and fired a wild burst into the blackness.

"Thanh! You idiot!" Xinh tore the rifle from her hands. "Now everyone in Cambodia knows we're here."

"Tigers scare me, Xinh. I'd rather fight a hundred ARVN or Americans than have to face a tiger."

Xinh could see that she was really afraid. She knew many Vietnamese believed that a tiger was a ghost endowed with demon powers. Apparently Thanh was one of them.

"All right. Help me gather some wood. We'll keep a fire going all night."

"Can't we just leave? Keep moving?"

"Where to? How? We have to wait till daylight to get our bearings. And that animal is going to stalk us as soon as we leave the river. Be reasonable, Thanh!"

"Yes. I suppose you're right. It's best we stay right here." She began picking up dead wood and piling it while Xinh unsheathed the long jungle knife from the rucksack and hacked out a clearing for their camp.

Throughout the night while the girls lay in their hammocks and periodically fed the fire, they could hear the tiger coughing and circling around them. Thanh, totally spent, finally fell asleep with Xinh holding her hand and telling her stories of old Vietnam she had learned as a child. Xinh stayed awake keeping watch and feeding the fire. Once she walked to the outer edge of the ring of light cast by the fire and looked into the two yellow eyes that watched her from twenty meters away. The big cat growled low and the eyes disappeared just as she got the rifle to her shoulder.

Finally gray dawn began to creep in among the dusky trees, bringing an eerie ground fog that hung about three feet above the river. Long arms of vapor crawled over the banks into the undergrowth to lie motionless until the day's heat burned it away.

Xinh lay in her hammock watching the depressing stuff move in from the river like the long tentacles of an enormous octopus. She looked over at Thanh. Fast asleep. She thought about waking her but changed her mind. Let her sleep. She would need it.

Looking around, she saw no trace of the tiger. She walked a few meters around the camp, rifle ready, but the animal had apparently left the area. She came back and threw some more wood on the fire to help take the chill out of the veiled morning.

Everywhere she looked the heavy dampness created an air of mystery. Moss and vines covered the trees, and the jungle floor was thick with ferns and broad-leafed Araceae. The air literally breathed danger in every direction. She let Thanh sleep another thirty minutes then reached over and gently poked her in the ribs with the barrel of her rifle.

Thanh moaned and turned away.

"Thanh. Wake up," she said, poking her again.

Thanh rolled over and rubbed her eyes. "Where's the tiger?" she immediately asked, reaching for her rifle.

"I don't know. Gone I think."

Thanh sniffed the drugged air. "I can't smell him anymore." She got up and stretched while scanning the Araceae and ferns. She looked up into the trees, just in case. Satisfied, she laid the rifle against a tawny palm and squatted beside the warming fire.

"Well, little sister, where do we go from here?" Xinh asked, spreading the map on the ground between them. "What did your informants say to do when we ran out of river?"

Thanh studied the map. "Do you agree we followed the right tributary?"

"Yes. There's no doubt it's the right one. All the landmarks check out and the distances match."

"Then we are right here," she said, handing a piece of rice cake to Xinh and placing the knife point on the map exactly where an indistinct blue line abruptly stopped and seemed to disappear into the paper. "About ten miles from Pak Mek." She moved the knife point to the village's position.

"The jungle's too thick. We'll never make the ten miles."

"There's supposed to be a track crossing the river channel somewhere close to where it dries up. Probably just a short distance from where we are right now," Thanh said.

"Where does this track lead?"

"Right into Pak Mek."

"Let's pray we find it. Traveling ten miles overland without a guide in this country would find us lost in ten minutes."

"And if we don't find it?"

"We'll have two choices. Turn back or strike out cross-country."

Xinh reached up and cut down a clump of green bananas from the tree to which one end of her hammock was tied. She pulled off two large ones and covered them in the coals. She selected a half dozen more and placed them in the rucksack. "Let's wash."

A few feet away a clear stream emptied into the shallow river. The girls took off their clothes and began splashing each other down with the cool water. They soaked their scarfs and rubbed the dirt and dust from their bodies. Xinh walked downstream a few feet and stepped into the main river and felt around the thick bottom mud with her toes until she located the hard shells of freshwater clams. She reached down and dug out a few, tossing them to Thanh who placed them on the hot coals with the cooking bananas.

After finishing their refreshing bath in the brook, the girls combed out their long hair and used their scarfs to tie it up out of the way. They redressed and sat down to a hearty guerrilla breakfast of roasted green bananas, river clams, and some rice cake left over from the previous day's lunch.

"Good?" Xinh asked, opening a large clam with the knife's edge and passing the half shell to Thanh.

"Very good. Even better than those served at the My Canh restaurant boat in Binh Hoa." They laughed.

"I can find some more if you want."

"No more. I'm full," Thanh said, rolling her eyes and lying back against the tree behind her.

"Me too," Xinh said, finishing off a rice cake and licking her fingers. She got up, smothered the fire with loose dirt, and returned the camp to its natural appearance.

Thanh looked over the river runner to make sure it was well hidden. She placed a few more branches around it and slung on her rucksack. She took the point, rifle resting loosely in the cradle of her left arm, and headed west following the course of the rapidly drying river.

They had been traveling only about ten minutes when the river, now beginning to pool, made a sharp bend north and the easygoing terrain gave way to dense growth. They had stopped in a clearing, their path being blocked by a huge shoulder-high mahogany log overgrown with ferns and runners. Xinh took Thanh's rifle and gave her a leg up onto the fallen log.

Thanh at this point decided she had to urinate. She laid the rucksack on the log beside her and had just pulled her pajamas down to squat on the log, letting the three-foot-long jungle knife dangle between her legs, when the tiger struck.

The deep throaty roar of the wild animal completely obliterated Thanh's pathetic bleat of surprise. The Siberian bounded twice across the clearing, lunging for the paralyzed girl. Xinh's snap shot went wild, crashing into the thick vegetation behind the tiger. From where she stood, behind Thanh and a little to the left, she could easily see the beast's flaming red eyes and angry, curled pink lips. Its long white fangs were stained a dirty yellow and its nostrils were flared wide.

Strong, heavy muscles rippled and danced under the beautiful orange and black striped coat. The magnificent beast leaped high in the air, forearms reaching for Thanh. Razor sharp, retractable hooked claws were fully extended, and its gorgeous, massive head shook violently as a roar issued from its gaping red mouth.

Thanh, unable to jump away because of the pajamas wrapped around her ankles, fell over backward wildly swinging the jungle knife. The surprised Siberian clawed at empty air, bellowing his rage. Thanh crawled out from the ferns and braced her back against the log. From a sitting position, her feet still trapped inside the pajama pants, she tightly gripped the jungle knife with both hands and held it high, poised over her head. Her eyes flashing, she prepared to meet her death valiantly.

But the tiger, having missed his kill and having lost the element of surprise, never even bothered to look back. Without breaking stride he hit the ground and was quickly swallowed up by the impenetrable cover beyond.

It had all happened so quickly. Only a few seconds. It was hard to believe that it had taken place at all. Thanh still held the knife over her head in a death grip, breast heaving violently, lips moving incoherently. Xinh slowly lowered her rifle and looked at Thanh. But Thanh's eyes were frozen to the spot where the cat had disappeared. She continued mumbling to herself, and the jungle knife never moved from its position over her head.

Xinh stepped over to Thanh and waved her open hand in front of the girl's wild eyes. They never blinked. Xinh slapped her flush on the cheek. Thanh dropped the knife and looked up at Xinh. She began shaking uncontrollably. Xinh sat beside her and took her in her arms and held her head. After a few minutes Thanh stopped shaking, got up, and pulled on her wet pajama bottoms. She pulled her rucksack down from the log and plunged into the forest, hacking at the lianas with the jungle knife as she went. Xinh stayed close, rifle ready.

An hour's tough march brought them, without further mishap, to the last remaining traces of the river channel and to the jungle track leading into the Cambodian interior. Hopefully, they would reach Pak Mek village by nightfall.

Chapter Twenty

Steve sat bent over in a small bamboo cage, head between his knees. There was no room to straighten up in the confined jail. His broken leg had been primitively set; a crude bamboo splint held it in place. It was hideously swollen, twice its normal size. An empty rice bowl lay on a board next to him. When he had to relieve himself he did so directly between the bamboo poles into the river below. The cage had a foul stench and his toothy guard smiled evilly in at him, holding his nose contemptuously. The mind searing heat was unbearable, and insidious black flies ate his flesh. Slimy river rats crawled over the cage.

By sheer tenacity and stubbornness he fought back great waves of loneliness, despair, and the wings of death. To keep his sanity he would think of home and the cool, grassy hillside where he played with his brothers when a child. He pictured himself on a lazy spring afternoon going into his mother's vegetable garden and picking juicy tomatoes, and pulling tender young carrots, and bringing them in for her to prepare for supper. He saw his mother's loving face smiling at him and heard his father's heavy hammer sing against the nails as he added another bedroom to their little house. Mom would be bringing a baby sister home about the time dad finished it.

A sweaty yellow face poked through the round bamboo bars opposite him.

"You talk soon American bastard. I cut you good," the North Vietnamese noncom said, reaching through the bars and sticking the point of his dirty blood-stained knife into Steve's swollen leg.

Steve grimaced but managed not to scream from the piercing pain. He just dully stared into space, thinking of the grassy hillside. Mom. Dad. Brothers. Again the knife jab.

"I stick you good GI . . . Nghaaaaaaaaaa!"

Steve yelled this time and kicked at the repulsive face with his good leg. He almost fainted from the pain.

The face pulled back and spit on him. "American dog. Tonight I make you talk. You tell all tonight." He left.

Steve leaned against the bars, panting heavily. Tell all, huh. What's there to tell? You saw what I did. You know where I came from. You know who I am. Tell what? Want me to confess my war crimes? Sure, Charlie. Who cares? Where do I sign? Dumb war. Xinh, will I ever see you again? No. Who cares? Shut up. I care. Name—Stephen A. Randall . . . Rank—Captain . . . Serial number—1802327 . . .

He carried on these conversations with himself to take his tortured mind off the insufferable pain and to relieve his boredom. But underneath, deep within his subconscious, the best part of Steve was clicking

240

away, working, planning, building, hoping. He wasn't about to give up. And just on principle, he wouldn't tell the communists what they wanted to know, whatever it was. If they killed him, he still wouldn't give them the time of day. Bastards.

And what about the communists? What was it they wanted to know? Probably nothing. They just wanted to terrorize him. Play with him. Use him to relieve their own boredom. Like sadistic children who drown puppies just to watch them struggle and die. He tried to stretch out, but his legs could not extend full length in the cramped jail. The bamboo poles dug into his flesh however he tried to lie or sit. He half-closed his eyes, trying to shut out the blinding sun, trying to rest, watching the rats jump across the open bars, waiting for night when the sweaty yellow face would return and stick him some more.

The sun was low in the west when Xinh and Thanh left the foot track and circled around behind Pak Mek. They squatted in the foliage and patiently studied the village for almost an hour. They changed their position several times. No sign of Steve. It was getting late. They would have to come out in the open and mingle with the people. Risky. Where was he? Maybe gone. Maybe never here.

Xinh sang under her breath while trying to count the number of people carrying weapons. The sun, an orange ball sitting on top of a coconut palm, was glaring directly into her eyes from across the village, making it difficult to see clearly. Everything was backlighted. Only outlines were visible. They would have to come out. Take the risk.

"What are you singing?" Thanh whispered.

"Nothing important. Just something Grandmother taught me."

"What is it?" Thanh asked, looking at Xinh queerly.

"A cradle song."

"Oh."

"How many NVA soldiers do you count?" Xinh asked, shading her eyes.

"Maybe twenty."

"I count about the same."

"Vietcong?"

"Could be half as many."

"Thirty all together."

"Yes. Where are the Kampuchean soldiers?" Xinh asked.

"Don't see any."

"Probably won't either. Crazy war," Xinh said, parting the bushes for a better look. "I haven't seen a Khmer either. Look Thanh."

"What is it?"

"The tamarind trees are blooming," she said, pointing to the red-striped yellow flowers. "Aren't they beautiful?"

"So pretty," Thanh said. She crawled to the tree next to her, reached up and pulled two of the blossoms. She put one in her hair and gave the other to Xinh. "Can we make tamarind candy when we get back, Xinh? With Grandmother, like we did last year?"

Xinh caressed the soft petals. "It's a bit early for the

fruit to ripen. But maybe we can find a few near Bac Co where cousin Phoung lives. Her trees always seem to bloom faster."

"Oh, good," Thanh said happily. "We must remember to use more sugar cane this time. The candy last year was sour."

"It's good sour. That's how it's supposed to be," Xinh said.

"I don't like it very sour. More sweet than sour is better."

"O.K. We'll put more sugar cane in it this time—just for you." She playfully slapped at Thanh's ear.

"Xinh, will there always be war?" Thanh asked, changing the subject. She went back to her surveillance of the village.

"I don't know."

"You should."

"Why?"

"You're smart."

"Oh, Thanh, I'm not so smart."

"Yes, you are. Tell me."

"All I know is that we always seem to be in some kind of waiting zone between disasters," Xinh said, frowning at the village.

"Who do you think is better for Vietnam? Uncle Ho or Thieu?" Thanh asked seriously, sticking an extra banana clip for the Kalashnikov into her waistband.

"They're both gangsters."

"Why do you say that?"

"They both want to be absolute masters."

"Maybe that's good. Some of us need masters."

"Don't be silly. Who?"

"Me. I need a master. I need someone to tell me what to do. Like you, Xinh. I need you to tell me what to do."

Xinh put her arm around Thanh and brushed the strands of hair from her eyes. "We are too young, Thanh. Too young to know much. I wish I had the answers."

"Is it like this all over the world, Xinh? Not just in Vietnam, Cambodia, and Laos?"

"Like what?"

"War. Like we've had ever since I can remember," Thanh said.

"I think so."

"What will become of us all, sister?"

"I don't know."

"Tang lied a lot didn't he, Xinh? He stole rice too. I saw him selling it to government troops. Did you know that, Xinh?"

"Yes, I knew that. Tang did as he pleased. I've also seen government troops selling rice to the Vietcong. Same rice maybe."

"Crazy war," Thanh said, sighting in on a group of NVA strolling through the village.

"Don't fool around," Xinh said sternly, pushing the rifle barrel down.

"Look at us, Xinh. Just a few weeks ago we were killing ARVN and American troops. Now we're shooting NVA and VC, and running for our lives from both sides. What's happened to us? What's going on, Xinh? And you know something, Xinh? I don't even mind popping off those guys out there. NVA, ARVN, VC, Americans. It doesn't seem to make any difference to me anymore. I'm just trying to stay alive. What's happened to me?" She threw down the rifle and covered her face with her hands.

"The Americans don't have the stomach for this war," Xinh said offhandedly without looking at Thanh.

"I know," Thanh said, wiping the tears from her eyes with her fingertips. I watch how they react in a fire fight. Many of the younger soldiers refuse to fire their weapons."

"Why should they?" Xinh said. "What do they have to fight for? There's nothing here for them."

"I remember being surprised by a young American at Lang Cau. I came out from the elephant grass and there he was right in front of me. He had me. There was no question about it. I can still see his big nose with the red pimples on it. He didn't shoot. Just stood there looking at me with his round eyes. I emptied half a clip into him, then crawled back into the grass. I got two more when they stupidly ran into the open to see what had happened. And have you seen how they bivouac?"

"Their bivouacs? You mean how they lie around under those funny propped-up shelter halves and temporary hooches made from their C-ration boxes, spread around in the open, drinking beer, listening to loud rock music on their Japanese radios and cassettes, and smoking dope and taking drugs?" Xinh said. "I suppose they have their reasons." Her face was expressionless, her eyes distant.

"I couldn't believe it when I first saw one. It looked like a zoo. Really, Xinh. That's what it reminded me of. A bunch of lazy animals lying around distracting themselves, trying to forget their captivity," she said with disgust. She spat.

"Maybe we're just as bad but for different reasons," Xinh said.

"What? What do you mean?" Thanh said, looking up, mouth hanging open.

"We don't think about what we do."

"What?" Thanh said, getting angry.

"The Americans believe in dissent. Like the boy with the pimply nose you cut down. What are our values? We found them in a revolution."

Thanh looked at Xinh in amazement. "How you talk."

"You don't approve?"

"I'm not smart like you. How do I know what to approve or disapprove? Where did you learn all that?" Thanh said, her lips pouting.

"All that?" Xinh smiled. "It's not much. I think a lot. I put together what I see and what I hear people say."

"You have never told me these things before."

"No. Because I am . . ." She caught herself. "Because I was a Vietcong field commander and a disciplined communist. I didn't talk about what I thought. I only talked about what I was told to talk about."

"Those NVA soldiers out there wouldn't agree with you." Thanh motioned to the village.

"No. They wouldn't. They wouldn't for the same reason you wouldn't have agreed with me either a few weeks ago."

"Is all this true, Xinh? I mean, that's incredible if what you say is true. Did you dream all this up?"

"No." Xinh stroked her rifle barrel. "It's true."

246

"I don't know about all this. I'm just a simple country girl. I don't think about those things," Thanh said.

"I never used to until . . ."

"Yes, and now look at us."

Xinh didn't reply. She shifted her weight uneasily on her haunches. Thanh was right.

"I'm sorry, Thanh," she said sadly.

Thanh looked at her from the corners of her pretty eyes. That's all right. We're going to make it." The two smiled at each other.

"Shall we do it?"

"Might as well."

They both stood up and boldly walked out of the jungle into the village.

Rifles slung over their shoulders, they waded through the paddies and arrogantly stepped onto the dike and walked past the first hooches. Old Kampuchean women squatted outside their homes chewing and spitting betel, eying Xinh and Thanh suspiciously. Naked children ran freely. Ducks and jungle fowl scrambled to get out of the girls' way. The heat was oppressive and the air thick with a sticky, penetrating heaviness. They walked on, nerves taut, trying to remain unnoticed.

The first VC they encountered was young. Maybe sixteen.

"Where's the American pilot?" Xinh asked him.

"Down by the river. What unit you with?"

Xinh's heart skipped a beat. He was here. Alive!

"Binh Duong," Thanh answered, measuring up the boy, ready to smash him with the rifle butt if he made the wrong move.

"Why do you want to see him?"

"None of your business, brat." Thanh's steely gaze cut off any further questions.

"Who's in charge here?" Xinh demanded, and without waiting for an answer, she quickly added, "Take us to him." She was startled by her own boldness, but the young guerrilla obeyed.

"Follow me," he said, and led the girls down an embankment toward the river.

Along the way Xinh marked defensible positions and possible escape routes in her memory. She noted the clusters of hooches and their arrangement, the bunkers and weapons emplacements. She counted the weapon-carrying males and females—NVA, VC—and looked for Kampuchean guerrillas. Her eyes studied the tree lines, paddies, and dikes. She got the points of the compass straight in her mind, for she knew from much experience that during the heat of a fire fight it was easy to lose your bearings and become confused. And she wasn't fooling herself. It was going to be a savage fight to get Steve out.

When the hooch clusters ended, the guerrilla led them through a group of coconut palms and along the edge of a rice paddy. They turned right following the dike. The swollen river came into view snaking through the wide flood plain. A lone hooch stood on stilts back from the river. Standing on the porch under the overhang, a very short and gaunt-looking NVA major spoke to a young Kampuchean girl, about Xinh's age. A rifleman squatted on his bony haunches at the foot of the short ladder leading up to the porch.

The communist officer's eyes narrowed at the

approach of Xinh. He waved the Cambodian teenager off. She ignored him and studied Xinh. The major looked Xinh over carefully and a smile stole across his grim face. The guard straightened. His eyes, too, mentally caressed Xinh. The girl's lip curled and she drifted closer to the skinny officer. He pushed her back and uttered some angry words at her. She remained behind him, glaring at Xinh.

"This Vietcong girl is from Binh Duong 404, Major. Says she comes to interrogate the prisoner," the VC said, looking at the officer indifferently.

"Is that so?" The major made no effort to hide his admiration of Xinh's beauty, his eyes roaming over her face and body. "Please young lady, won't you come into my humble quarters, out of the heat," he said, overly polite, taking his hand away from the pistol holstered on his hip. "You may go," he said to the guerrilla boy.

As Xinh started up the ladder she brushed by Thanh and whispered, "Make friends with the guard. Learn everything you can."

Inside the hooch, the major offered Xinh a seat beside him at the small table. "Would you like something to eat? You have had a long journey from Binh Duong."

"Yes, I would like to eat. And so would the girl with me, if you please."

"Yes, of course. Fish and rice for the two Vietcong," he said in Cambodian to the girl. She shot a fiery glance at Xinh and reluctantly left for the food. "Bring some fruit and tea also," he shouted after her. "These Cambodian women are so primitive and crude. Not at all like our exquisite Vietnamese girls," he said, oily, his eyes roving over Xinh again.

"How long has it been since you have had a Vietnamese girl, Major," Xinh said, gently placing her soft hand on his.

The North Vietnamese immediately became noticeably excited. He made a feeble attempt to control his lust, but his eyes glazed over and his breathing began to come in short gasps between words. His smile became exceedingly obnoxious. What an animal, thought Xinh.

"Too long, my dear," he croaked. "Too long." His eyes sucked her in. Xinh turned her head away, hiding her revulsion.

"Major," she went on, her right hand still over his, her left on the trigger of the Chinese assault rifle pointed, under the table, at his belly, "my superiors have reason to suspect that the Americans and ARVN have been warned about the Tet offensive; that they have specific information and details with regard to selected targets and our supply stations."

"What?" he exclaimed, withdrawing his hand from her touch. "This is disturbing news. What makes you think so?"

"The strike on the sanctuaries. It was too well planned, too close to Tet, and too accurate. They knew exactly where the targets were."

"Yes, it was devastating," he added gloomily.

"We believe that government agents posing as VC within our ranks are responsible. We further believe that these spies used special electronic equipment planted within the targets for the American bombers to home in on."

"Yes. Makes sense. The bombing was very accurate

250

and thorough." He scratched at a running sore on his arm.

"We want to question the prisoner in this regard. My assistant and I have special ways to make him talk. We have been trained for this kind of interrogation. We need details. Specific identification."

There was a noise on the porch. Xinh looked up. The Cambodian girl stood in the doorway with a wooden tray filled with food. Xinh didn't like the look on her round face. Did the girl suspect? Or was it just jealousy? Being noticed, she quickly walked in and placed the rice pot, a plate of steamed fish and peppers, bowls, and chopsticks on the table. A bowl of yellow-red mangos and ripe papaya was added. She poured tea and withdrew to a corner, never taking her eyes off Xinh. Thanh came in and joined them at the table.

"Eat," said the major. "When you have finished I will take you to the American flyer."

Xinh gave him her sweetest smile. "And after?"

"Well, we will see about that," he said. The oily grin returned.

Chapter Twenty-one

"He's out there," the NVA major said, pointing with a crooked finger to a pierlike structure supported by bamboo poles. It extended out over the river.

From her position in the open rice field, Xinh could see that the cage was lashed to the makeshift pier. A catwalk traveled along the edge of the pier and angled around the cage. She knew that the cage was portable, of the type she had built in Binh Duong to easily transport important prisoners from one area to another to prevent discovery.

"Will there be anything you will need?" he asked.

"No. We won't be long. We just want to feel him out first. The actual interrogation, when we really get down to work, will come later."

"I see. Do you do this often?"

"Often enough—as required by my superiors."

"Do you speak English well?"

"I'm understood. The Americans get my message very fast, even without the use of words," she said, smiling.

"Ummmmmmm," he said thoughtfully, developing a keener interest in Xinh. His eyes showed growing respect for the young woman.

"Chinese?" he asked, pointing to her rifle.

"Yes."

"You like it better than the Russian Kalashnikov?"

"Much better. Lighter, swings faster, and I find it more reliable."

"I would like to talk to you more about your combat operations in Binh Duong and around Saigon when you finish with the prisoner. You seem to be very experienced in military matters for one so young."

"I was trained near Hanoi."

"Oh? Where?"

"Phuc Yen."

"My father's home."

"That so?"

"Yes, small coincidence," he said, smiling eagerly at Xinh. "I will have some French cognac waiting when you return." He turned and began walking back to the hooch.

Xinh's heart beat wildly. He was down there, alive. In a few minutes she would see him. It took all her self-discipline to keep from breaking out into a run. She had come this far. Just a few more feet. Keep calm. Wait. Be patient. She fought the tears. Give me strength, God. Oh, give me strength when I see him. Then she was there. His back was toward her.

She turned to the guard. "What is your name?" she asked in English.

"Cai gi?" What? he said.

"Where do you come from?" Again in English.

"Cai gi?"

"Ong khong noi tieng Anh?" You don't speak English?

"Kong." No, he answered.

Good. She looked at Thanh. She got the message and pulled the guard aside and engaged him in conversation. Xinh stepped onto the catwalk. Her legs were shaking. She steadied herself.

She couldn't hold back the tears when she saw him. He was emaciated—dried blood on his face, on his swollen lips, and matted in his fair hair. His back was bent, unable to straighten because of the confined dimensions of his small prison. She had known his intense masculine vigor and spirit. His virility. But now he was broken and torn, weak and feeble. She was surprised at what a few days in the hands of these people had done to him.

"Steve," she whispered, her face pressed between the bars, her small hands gripping the strong bamboo tightly. She had positioned herself so the guard could not get a clear view of her face yet she could watch his every move.

"Steve," she whispered again.

He opened his eyes, trying to focus. He smelled terrible. The first thing she would do after getting him out was bathe him, she promised herself.

"It me, Steve. Xinh. No show guard you know me. Guard close."

"Xinh?" he muttered, the words forming slowly between his swollen lips. "Xinh?" He blinked hard, trying to see her.

"Cung oi." Darling. "You can hear me?"

"Xinh? Is it really you?" He started to lift his hand to touch her face, but she quickly reached in and

255

pushed it down.

"Don't. Guard see. No. Guard close. No show you know me. You understand what Xinh say?"

He nodded.

"How you feel?"

"I hurt, Xinh. I'm hurt bad. They keep cutting me and beating me. I think my nerves are broken in my back from sitting like this. I haven't been able to straighten. My leg . . ." he pointed.

Xinh reached into the cage and pulled away the torn fabric on his flight suit, keeping an alert eye on the guard. A cry escaped her lips when she saw his terribly mutilated leg. Xinh was hardened to the ravages and suffering of war, but she was forced to grip the bamboo tighter. She tried to hide her tears.

"Don't cry, Xinh. Don't cry. I'll take care of these guys when I get better."

She smiled softly at him.

"Honey, what are you doing here? How did you find me?" He began coughing and spit up some blood.

She took a deep breath, closed her eyes and said it: "I Vietcong, Steve. I be Vietcong since I young girl." There. It was out.

His mouth fell open and his eyebrows shot up. He tried to speak, but he could only stutter. "You . . . you . . . you . . ."

"Yes, me." She dropped her eyes.

The news was a thunderclap in his drowsy brain. His eyes popped wide open in surprise. He was stunned and his breathing became heavily labored.

"I sorry." Her eyes stayed glued to the bottom of the tiger cage.

"You . . . you?" His soggy mind, deprived of sleep and saturated with days of torture, was struggling to understand the full impact of what she had said. "I can't believe it. I won't believe it." The suddenness of the blow took the wind from him.

"It true."

Steve Randall, having undergone such intense pain from his captors, could not be hurt anymore. There just was nothing else that could shock him— he'd thought. But hearing these words from Xinh, the girl he loved and admired, pushed him over the brink. He was falling, headfirst, into a deep, black chasm, ricocheting off and being deeply cut by the sharp rocks of truth.

"Oh, God, no! Not you, Xinh . . . not you."

He lifted his eyes to her. She had never seen such shock in a pair of eyes. She was horrified by the effect of her words.

"Anybody but you." His whole system had gone into shock and he was shaking uncontrollably. "Why? Why? Why?" His teeth were clenched and his hands twisted and pulled at the bamboo bars.

"I try many times to tell you. I want tell you. I want run away from Vietcong."

"You whore; you VC whore!" His hands gripped the bars until his knuckles turned white. "How could I have been so stupid?" The blood rose into his neck, turning it purple.

She suddenly realized that he would kill her if he could get his hands on her.

"I no want hurt you."

"Ha!"

"Please, no laugh at me."

"Ha!" He had a coughing spasm.

"My heart always true to you."

"Damn you." He pounded the bars.

"No say bad words to me." She lifted her eyes and brushed the hair from her face. "I want take care you."

"You only care about getting information from me. You're working with the rest of those shits."

"That not true." She hung her head. "I so sorry, Steve."

Steve sighed deeply and wiped away some of the blood with the back of his hand. He coughed again. His head dropped.

The river bamboo hung limply in the stifling heat. Not a breath of fresh air stirred. The jungle was tomb quiet. A sampan drifted lethargically with the sluggish current, its occupant slumped over the oar-rudder.

"Sorry? Are you? Look at me. Aren't you the reason I'm here—half dead?"

"No. Not true. But I kill many your countrymen. You kill mine too, and—"

"Shut up, Xinh. I just want to get out of here."

"That why I here. I love you, Steve. I always love my *cung oi*. You forgive, Xinh? Please, you forgive?"

"Can you get me out of here, Xinh? Can you really?"

"I get you out—somehow." She stood and turned to leave.

"Xinh." His eyes softened and the hardness went out of his face.

"Yes?" She squatted back down beside him. Her face only inches from his behind the bars.

"I . . . I'm . . ." The words caught.

"No talk. I take care you. Tonight." She reached into the cage one more time and let her hand rest on his, watching the guard closely.

He looked down at her delicate long fingers. He felt her tender caress. His tears fell onto her soft, golden skin. She left her hand as long as she could, letting it comfort the tortured man. Then she got up and briskly walked back along the catwalk to the bank where Thanh was keeping the guard occupied.

"Let's go," she said, grabbing Thanh by the arm. She looked at the guard's sweaty yellow face with hate in her eyes. She visualized him cutting and beating the helpless Steve. "Don't abuse him anymore. He's too weak. If he becomes any weaker it will be impossible to get any information out of him. You should have known that, you imbecile." She jerked around and headed for the major's hooch, pulling Thanh with her. She made a mental note that she would deal with yellow-face in a very special way tonight. The noncom stared after her, scratching his head.

Inside the hooch the major lay on his dirty cot, the Cambodian girl beating his bare back in rapid motion with the open palms of her hands. He turned his head and watched Xinh enter through the open door.

"Not gentle like a Vietnamese woman's hands," he said, sitting up. The girl sat on the edge of the cot, legs crossed under her skinny bottom, saying nothing. Again the hate stare.

"I would like the American given food and water. He is almost dead and cannot be interrogated in his

259

condition. It would be senseless to even try."

The major said a few impatient words to the girl. She reluctantly got up, casting an evil glance sideways at Xinh as she brushed in front of her.

Xinh turned and watched her fill a cracked porcelain bowl with rice. "Put some fish and vegetables in it," she said firmly in Kampuchean country dialect to the girl. The Cambodian sneered at her. Xinh walked straight up to her and slapped her full in the face knocking her back a few feet. The major roared with laughter. The girl, obviously more hurt by her man's mocking rejection than by Xinh's blow, reached into her bosom and brought out an eight-inch knife, which she clutched in her dark-skinned hand.

Thanh quickly moved between the girls and shoved the muzzle of her AK-47 into the Cambodian's flat nose. The major, still laughing, got up from his cot and pushed the girl outside. There were a few heated words on the porch, the girl arguing her case. But she was finally banished from the premises, the major's arm pointing toward the center of the village.

"These Cambodians. So stupid and primitive," he said, coming back in. "I apologize for her behavior." He grabbed Xinh's hand and pulled her to his cot.

Thanh finished preparing the food and placed it on the tray with chopsticks. On the way out she filled a half coconut shell with water from the large clay water pot by the door and added it to the tray. Without looking back she walked out to feed Steve.

*   *   *

260

The sun crawled down from its resting spot on top of the coconut palms and vanished behind the tree lines. Dusk settled on Pak Mek village. Cooking fires twinkled between the trees and the chickens found their roosts under houses. The ducks waddled into the undergrowth and tucked their necks into soft feathers. Children hungrily sat, chopsticks and rice bowls in their laps, watching the white, steaming, delicious stuff puffing in family cauldrons, waiting to fill their bellies. Soldiers settled in with their warm hooch maids.

Xinh poured the major another cognac. He was becoming melancholy, and very drunk.

"My mother was a toad of a woman."

"Oh?" said Xinh, lifting the cognac to his lips.

"Dull, boring, completely without imagination. The only thing she had going for her was her fidelity."

"That's not too bad," Xinh said.

"She had a face that looked like a monkey's."

"How charming."

"No, no. You don't understand. You're making fun," he laughed, spilling his drink and pulling Xinh closer to him. "I need comfort, not jokes."

Xinh righted his glass and poured more cognac. She lifted his hand to his mouth. He drank greedily. The amber liquid dribbled from the corners of his lips. Several drops hung poised on the drooping ends of his thin mustache and scraggly goatee.

"My father had three concubines."

"That's not unusual for Vietnamese men," Xinh laughed.

"And three wives, including my mother."

"Was your mother number one wife?"

"Yes. But she had no authority over the other two."

"I can tell you who had the authority." Xinh said.

"Who?"

"The third wife. She was probably the youngest and the prettiest."

"You are right."

"How did your father keep all these women? Three concubines and three wives—that must have been expensive. Was he rich?"

The major was becoming bored with the conversation, and drunker. "Come closer to me my lovely little bamboo shoot. I want to feel your tenderness." He took a long pull from the cognac bottle and fell over backward off the cot. She held his head up and poured more of the French brandy down his open throat.

"Thank you, my darling lotus blossom. You love me don't you?" he mumbled, trying to see Xinh through his swollen red eyes. He reached for her again, but missed and rolled over on his back into a puddle of spilled cognac. He vomited over himself, then passed out.

Xinh kicked him a few times.

"He's out," she said to Thanh standing in the doorway, empty tray in hand.

Thanh set the tray down on the table. She pulled the knife from her calf and walked toward the unconscious NVA commander.

"No. Put it away. The girl might come back." Thanh hesitated for a moment, then obeyed. "Did you feed Steve?"

"Yes," Thanh said, tying the knife back to her leg.

"He couldn't hold much of it down at first, but he's got enough in him now to give him some strength. My God, Xinh, he's in bad shape. He won't be able to travel."

"Yes he will. At least far enough away from here so I can safely nurse him back to where he's out of danger of dying."

"He's nearly dead now. How are we going to get him out?" Thanh asked.

"You'll see. Let's go." She kicked the major again. "He'll be out for hours."

"Poor guy. He was looking forward to having a great time with you tonight," Thanh said with a cynical smile.

"Shhhhh." Xinh stopped dead in her tracks.

"What?"

"Did you hear that?"

"No, what?" Thanh whispered.

"I heard movement outside."

"I heard nothing."

They walked outside and looked around in the graying light. "I suppose it could have been my imagination. Maybe I'm too edgy?"

"Maybe."

"Are you ready?"

"Yes, Xinh."

"You know what to do, don't you?"

"I've already done it. I killed the guard."

"Thanh!"

"Well, I knew we had to, and he made me mad while I was feeding Steve. He called me a dog's whore for giving Steve food, then spit on me. So I killed him."

"What did you do with the body?"

"I hid it under the pier. I tied it under the water. Are you mad?"

"Thanh. You should have waited. Your temper has gotten us into trouble before. I wish you would learn to control it."

"I know. I'm not smart like you."

"Come on." She grabbed her by the hand.

They walked up to the riverbank and looked around. All was quiet. The last light of day persistently held on, reluctant to submit to the encroaching night. Tall coconut palms and swaying bamboo were starkly silhouetted behind the river.

Xinh quickly stepped onto the bamboo pier and gingerly ran along the catwalk, Thanh right behind.

"Start cutting the lashing," she ordered, pulling her knife and slicing at the strong ropes holding Steve's cage to the pier. From inside his prison, Steve watched her feverishly slashing at the ropes.

"Are we going to make it, Xinh?" he asked weakly.

"We make," she said, not looking at him, intent on her work.

"I can't last another day in here. We make, huh Xinh?"

"We make," she said again, chopping relentlessly. "I always say I take care you, GI," she said, looking up for a brief second.

Suddenly there was a rush of noise in the tall grasses along the water. Xinh twisted around in time to see someone bolt out of the cover, leap onto the bank, and then race down a paddy dike. Xinh stood up. It was the Cambodian girl.

"Get her, Thanh! Get her! Don't let her get back to

the village.''

Thanh jumped from the pier and lunged after the girl, knife thrust forward in her right hand. In a flash she was on top of the bank and sprinting down the dike after the girl, her mane of silky hair billowing behind her like a black sail. The Kampuchean was fast but Thanh was faster. Xinh watched the gap between them rapidly close.

The girl looked once over her shoulder, saw that she wasn't going to make it, and began screaming like a banshee.

Thanh was on her like a tigress. Without breaking stride, she leaped high onto the girl's back, digging her heels into her waist and driving her to the ground. The Cambodian writhed like a snake— quick thrusting motions—but Thanh clung tight, wrapped tenaciously around the girl, legs squeezing down along her hips and coiled inside her thighs. With her free left hand and arm, Thanh gripped the girl's head, forcing it forward to expose the back of the neck. The girl, sensing her end and in complete panic, shrieked hysterically. Thanh felt for the separation between the upper vertebrae, thrust quickly with the triangular blade. The Cambodian's head dropped forward, her spinal cord cut.

Thanh, not taking any chances, rolled the body over, planted the knife point beneath the breast bone and leaned on the handle. The body didn't arch as the blade penetrated the heart. She dragged the dead girl by the feet to the edge of the dike and rolled her into the paddy. The corpse made a dull splash, hitting the shallow water. Thanh jumped into the mud beside the body and shoved it down into the rice shoots. She put the AK-47 on semiautomatic, propped it on top of the dike, and leaned her shoulder into the butt plate. She didn't have long to wait.

A few minutes later two NVA poked out from the tree line and looked around, searching for the source of the screaming. A third, then a fourth soldier came out into the open. Thanh sighted down the path. Still just enough light left to bring the iron sights to bear. Don't wait for me, Xinh. Get going. Line up on the lead NVA. *Pow! Pow!* He falls. Quickly shift to the next one. *Pow!* He's down. The other two jump into the paddy. Go, Xinh! Go!

The NVA are returning fire now, Russian rifles chattering. Gray smoke drifts above the paddy, marking their position. The two bodies on top of the dike obstruct their view. Thanh sees that they don't have a clear field of fire. She takes advantage of the situation, steps over the Cambodian girl, and crawls through the young rice to the opposite end of the dike. Crawling over the top, she rolls down the back side and comes up in the paddy adjacent to the NVA, outflanking them. She rapidly crawls another hundred meters to the next dike. Panting, she rests her back against the dirt wall. She can hear them cursing on the other side. Back still against the dike bank, she switches to full automatic, takes a deep breath, and in one motion swings the rifle and leaps to the top of the dike, spread-legged. Fifty meters away the two North Vietnamese desperately try to bring their weapons around. Even before their bodies are half turned, she presses the trigger. *Bam-bam-bam-bam-bam-bam-bam* . . . The impact of the high velocity slugs spins them around, jerking them one way then another.

266

They slump face down into the mud and water, a red ring forming around them.

Ping! Ping! . . . Ping! Small dirt explosions erupt around her feet. *PING! . . . PING! PING!* She jumps back down into the paddy and rolls several times to her right. Bullets crisscross over the area where she'd landed. Using the dike wall as a shield, she runs, crawls, runs. Xinh, go! Go! Don't wait.

Chapter Twenty-two

*ZINGGGGGGGGG . . . ZINGGGGGGGGG . . .
PING . . . PING . . . PING . . . ZINGGGGGGGG.*
The hot rounds poured in. She dodged, zigzagged
across the paddy. She stumbled and fell. Out of
breath she lay panting in the mud. *Thunk . . .
Thunk . . . Thunk.* Shells splattered in the mud
around her. *THUNK . . . ZINGGGGGGGGG.* Got
to keep moving. Get up. Get up. You're dead if
you don't. *Thunk . . . Splat . . . Zinggggggggg.* She
looked up at the darkening sky through mud-caked
eyes.

Try. Got to try. Up and running again. The
rounds tracked her across the gooey paddy. She
collapsed against the wet embankment. Rounds
thudded into the dirt around her, leaving deep
cratered holes in the dike wall. The wet grass felt so
good. The sweet smell of the young rice was heavy in
her nose. I want to stay. Leave me alone!

"*Ma . . . ma oi . . . Ma! Ma!*" The grass feels so
good. I can't go any farther. Mother, I never knew
you. She hugged the bank. Tried to make herself
smaller. Pulled her knees up into her chest. Flattened

into the mud. Xinh, what happened to our youth?

The first slug hit her high in the back. She felt it go in, turn and press downward deep inside. She cried. Her little hands clutched at the rice shoots. *"Ma!"* The second bullet hit her lower, in the side, burning a hot path through her young, firm tissues. She placed a hand over the blood leak and felt her tomorrows draining through her fingers. The tamarind flower fell from her hair. She inched her hand toward it.

Strong arms tugged at her. In the half-light she looked up into Xinh's anguished face. No. She was supposed to go. Oh, Xinh, you should have left. She was on top of the bank now. Bullets continued to pound into the exposed dike and paddy around them. Xinh pulled at her. She tried to help. But her strength was gone. Life was ebbing. Suddenly she was rolling down the opposite side of the dike. Xinh dragged her into the protection of the dirt wall. It was dark now. She felt cold. What are those white spots? Oh, just stars, the night's first stars. I'm so cold, Xinh. Why didn't you go?

Xinh was peering over the edge of the dike. "They won't be coming at us for a while. Too dark. We have a few minutes. I'll carry you."

"No, sister. No. Leave me. It's dark now. You can get away. Please. Take Steve and go."

Eeeeeeeeeeeeeeeeee . . . the whine of a shoulder-fired RPG-7. Xinh threw her body over Thanh. *KAROOOOOOOOM!* Dirt, water, mud sprayed over them. Xinh quickly got up and ran along the paddy, using the dike to limit her exposure to the NVA and VC guns. She popped up forty meters away and

270

scanned the tree line. *Whooooooooosh—BLAM . . . Eeeeeeeeeeeeeeee*. This time she caught the bright flash of the rocket's exhaust blast. She poured a full clip into the fading brilliance. Human screams. Then return fire from the tree line. She ran back another ten meters, popped up again, and laid down a base of fire at the muzzle flashes. More screams. Less return fire. She rolled over on her side, reached into the rucksack on her back and pulled another clip, slammed it home, laid down more fire. She crawled over one dike into the next paddy, being sure she didn't come up at the same spot she had fired from. Then she was running toward the tree line. It was dark. She was only a shadow. Ping . . . ping . . . ping. Down again at the far dike. A right turn away from the tree line. Over the dike. Thirty yards to the tree line. Crawl. Now away. Now into. She knew where they were. But they had lost her. She gasped for breath.

She listened. Nothing. Only the banging of a few rifles. She was thankful that she had studied the village and surrounding terrain when walking through them earlier. It was helping her now. She crawled out of the paddy and ran into the tree line— behind their positions. She waited, letting her eyes adjust. There! She saw them. Three shadowy groups. How many? Can't tell. Too dark. She crawled closer. Felt for the grenades in the rucksack. Close enough. She pulled the pins on two and flung them at the heads. *Boom! Boom!* The screech of flying shrapnel. Yelling. Confusion. Shots. She heaved two more and flattened again. *Boom! . . . Boom!* Metal fragments thudded into the trees and cut through the grass around her. She stood and fired into the smoke and dust. The Chinese assault rifle shivered violently against her cheek. Screams. Another clip. The heavy recoil shook her small body and forced her backward. She kept pulling the trigger. The gun was alive in her hands.

Enough. She was running. Fast. Out of the tree line. Down the dike. Into the paddy. She ran. . . . No return fire . . . The far dike. Still no return fire. She ran. She stayed on the dike until she came to where she had left Thanh. She slid down the bank.

"Thanh . . . can . . . you . . . hear me?" The words were broken by gasps for breath.

Thanh moaned.

"We're getting out. I'm going to carry you."

"I'm so cold, Xinh." She reached up and grabbed Xinh's blouse and pulled her close. "Go Xinh. Go with your man. Don't wait. Go now. While you have a chance. Leave my rifle. I'll give you more time. Go, Xinh! Go!"

"*No!*"

"I'm dying, sister. Go. Please."

"Oh, Thanh. I can't leave you. Don't die." She pulled her little friend close to her and cradled her head to her bosom, rocking her. They lay with their legs in the mud and rice stalks, backs against the dike wall. "I'm sorry, Thanh." She held her closer, kissing her hair, rocking her back and forth. Tears streaked the hardened black mud on her cheeks. She sobbed quietly. "Thanh. Thanh. Oh, Thanh."

"Re . . . mem . . . ber, the tam . . . a . . . rind trees? The beautiful tam . . . a . . . rind trees, sister Xinh?" Thanh said, voice faltering, her life slipping away.

272

"And the riv . . . er Phu . . . Cuong? How . . . pretty the green . . . water."

"Thanh, please—please don't die—please, Thanh," Xinh cried. She picked Thanh's hand up out of the mud and kissed it. She pressed it to her cheek.

"And Duc . . . had to . . . chase . . . your toy bam . . . boo boat when it would . . . get a . . . way from you." Thanh's eyes slowly closed, her hand fell, limp, inside Xinh's.

"Thanh! No! Thanh!" Xinh sobbed.

She opened her pretty eyes one last time. "What hap . . . pen . . . ed to our . . . youth, Xinh? Where . . . did . . . it . . . go? Oh, Xinh, I'm . . . only . . . seven . . . teen. I don't want . . . to . . . die. Hold . . . me, sister. Hold . . . me."

Thanh died in Xinh's arms. For a while she continued rocking the little warrior and stroking her hair. She wiped the paddy mud away from her face with the end of her scarf. She cleaned her hands. She kissed her cheeks and held her to her breast. Thanh's hair had come undone and was hanging loosely in the rice. Xinh carefully gathered it, cleaned the ends that had lain in the mud, then reverently folded the long strands in a neat loop and tied them with her scarf. She kissed Thanh once more. Forgive me. Please, will someone forgive me?

Xinh pulled Thanh into a sitting position, bent over, and hoisted her up over her shoulders. Steadying herself with her left hand she reached down with the right and picked up the two rifles by their slings. Under the cover of darkness and walking stooped over close to the dikes, she slowly struggled through the rice back to the river.

Approaching the bank, she rolled Thanh from her shoulders and crawled to the edge and looked over. Finding it unguarded and the tiger cage still intact with Steve in it, she returned to Thanh, picked her up again and stumbled down to the water where she mounted the catwalk.

Without saying a word to Steve, she laid Thanh's bleeding body on top of the cage. Then she took off the rucksack, reloaded the AK-47, cocked it, and handed it through the bamboo bars to Steve. She stuffed an extra banana clip into his flight suit. He looked back at Xinh, the tears not yet dry on her muddy cheeks. He rested the rifle on a crossbar, aiming it into the tree line.

"O.K., baby, I'm ready. Get us out of here," he said, permanently hunched over.

She managed a weak smile, reached in and touched his face. Taking the lashing she had cut away from the cage, she secured Thanh's body, the rucksack, and her own rifle to the top of the jail. With her knife she cut away the remaining ropes holding the cage to the pier. Pressing with all her might against the back of the cage, she finally broke it loose and slowly slid it to the end of the pier. It stopped. She rested, gathered her strength, and pushed again. It didn't move.

"Come on, honey," Steve said weakly, "you can do it."

She tried again. It wouldn't budge. She sat down breathing hard, looking back toward the rice fields and the tree line. *They'll be here soon. I can feel them sneaking up along the dikes already.* She began gathering the cut rope and tying the pieces into a length. Steve watched her intently.

"What are you doing?"

One end she tied to the front of the cage. The other end she passed over the front piece of the pier and brought it back under the floor of the cage, making a simple pulley system out of the cage, rope, and pier. She handed the loose end to Steve.

"I know you very weak. But you must pull. Pull hard, help Xinh."

"Well, I'll be a . . ." he thought, looking at the rope she had placed in his hand. "This kid is something else." He drew it up tight, prepared to give it everything he had.

Xinh went to her position behind the cage again. Putting her head and shoulder to the bars, she whispered, *"Keo!"* Pull! He pulled, she pushed and the cage moved forward the necessary two feet, teetered on the end of the pier, then plunged the short distance off the end into the river with a soft splash. Xinh quickly jumped in and began maneuvering the floating tiger cage into the current by holding onto the bars with her hands and kicking her legs.

The current caught the cage, now a raft, and the strange conveyance floated into midriver where it picked up speed in its bid for freedom. Steve kept the rifle trained on the shoreline. Xinh paddled with her feet. Thanh lay lifeless on her bed of bamboo. Somewhere a tiger coughed. The stars watched. And they waited, drifting in the silence, the current lapping at the bamboo.

Exhaustion is a funny thing. It can come suddenly and overtake you in the middle of exertion or wait until your ordeal is over and subtly creep through your bones and render you helpless without warning. A delicate, elusive beckoning sucked at Xinh's consciousness. The water was deliciously warm and comforting, soothing her racked body. The river's gentle fragrance reminded her of Grandmother's pleasing body scent and of how she held her, consoling the child Xinh in time of trouble, bringing her relief. The weightlessness of her body in the water eased the grief of losing her loyal companion and her mind no longer struggled against the pain. Numb with fatigue, her surroundings became obscure. She was unaware of where she was—and didn't care. Sleep insidiously seduced her.

All night they floated down the river, enveloped in the blanket of darkness, carried south through the Kampuchean wilderness. It wasn't until past midnight that Xinh drifted back to consciousness and slowly lifted her head from her arms tightly locked around the cage bars. Where were they? She blinked her eyes and looked around. Still in Cambodia. For certain. How long had she slept? Was Steve O.K.? She wiped the water from her eyes.

She swam around to the front of the raft. Steve was half awake, rifle still poised on the crossbar. Seeing Xinh he widened his eyes.

"Where are we, Xinh? Where are we going?"

She looked him over carefully. "How you feel?"

"Not so hot."

"I take care you soon. Take care Thanh."

"She's dead."

"Still must take care. Have ceremony. You call

fun . . . er. . . ."

"Funeral," he said.

"Yes, funeral."

"What happened, Xinh? I heard a lot of shooting."

"Big fight. We kill many NVA and VC. But too many shoot back. Thanh get shot. I try save. But too late." She became quiet for a long time. They drifted on.

"We stop now." She pointed to a stretch of thick overhanging foliage along the bank, and steered the cage into it. She stepped onto the shore and pulled the cage far under the overgrowth until it was well hidden. She untied her rifle and shot away the lock. The prison door swung open.

It took her the better part of an hour to get Steve out of the cage and into the campsite she had set up in a mixed grove of banana plants, shrubs, and coconut palms. He was unable to straighten up, the nerves in his back having been damaged. His broken leg and weakened condition made it impossible for him to walk, forcing Xinh to half-carry, half-drag him to the hammock she had rigged to the palms. Some of the distance he crawled.

Making him as comfortable as she could, she used the heavy jungle knife to whack the top off a green coconut and held the opening to his lips, letting him drink the refreshing sweet milk. When he had finished, she broke off a piece of hull and using it as a spoon, scooped out the soft nutritious endosperm for him to eat.

While feeding him she caressed his head and told him stories of old Vietnam, of when the land was

277

quiet and its people lived in peace. A calm settled over his battered face and he fell asleep, holding her hand. After a few minutes she loosened his hand and opened the rucksack.

She pulled out the U.S. medical bag and examined its contents. As a VC unit leader, she had received combat-medic training and was experienced in treating her wounded guerrillas with captured U.S. medical supplies. She knew the basics. Her quick and alert mind carried her the rest of the way. Morphine . . . antiseptic . . . bandages . . .

Xinh lit the little perfume-bottle kerosene lamp she always carried and hung it from a bush limb over Steve's leg. She cut away the fabric and examined the gangrenous tissues. A Western doctor would have told her his condition was hopeless and that Steve was sure to die from the poisons being poured into his system by his putrefying flesh, that the only way to save him was by cutting off the leg. But Xinh was a Vietnamese country girl, born and raised where doctors were unknown and people survived by their natural instincts and by uncanny practices passed down from generation to generation. She knew the severity of the wound. She also knew what she had to do. Another day—maybe two—and he would be dead. She felt his forehead again. "Very hot," she said to herself. She picked away the maggots.

She loosened the lamp and took it into the jungle. Thirty minutes later she was back with a broad-leafed plant she had pulled up whole by its bulbous roots. She rehung the light and checked Steve. He was deep in sleep. She kissed him and set to work.

She stabbed his leg with a Syrette of morphine then

poured antiseptic over the tissues, her hands, and the scalpel. She made the incision. Under pressure, the sickly gray-brown, greenish fluid spurted and gushed out of the wound, spilling on the ground under the hammock. Xinh was momentarily overwhelmed by the foul odor and had to turn her head.

Recovering, she made two more incisions and massaged the tissues, draining most of the rotten fluid. She poured antiseptic into the incisions. She peeled away the fibrous covering from the medicinal roots of the plant she had dug up and covered the damaged flesh with their pasty contents. Over this she laid crushed leaves of this herb. Finally, she carefully wrapped the leg in bandages.

Xinh wiped the perspiration from her face with the scarf hanging around her neck. She looked at Steve. He hadn't stirred. She walked down to the river and washed her face and hands. She checked Thanh's body still secured to the top of the cage. "I will bury you in the morning. I'm too tired to do it now," she said. "Tomorrow, Thanh. Tomorrow I will take care of you, my loyal friend. Forgive me. I'm just too tired right now."

She walked back to the campsite and blew out the lantern. Crawling into the hammock with her rifle, she looked up at the stars and recited the prayer that Steve had taught her: "Our Father which art in heaven, hallowed be Thy name, Thy kingdom come, Thy will be done. . . ."

Chapter Twenty-three

The siren screeching of black-faced monkeys standing guard in the pendantra trees woke Xinh with a start; an icy chill ran through her fatigued muscles. Her hand moved slowly down her side until it felt the familiar cold steel of the Chinese 56. Grasping the barrel firmly, she silently rolled out of the hammock into the wet, ground fog creeping through the makeshift camp.

Lying on her back she listened. The monkeys with cryptic suddeness stopped their feverish chattering as abruptly as they had started. Silence hung in the white dawn. The insoluble mist drifted over her, coating her skin with a slimy dampness. The thick smell of stagnant water and rotting jungle was heavy in her nostrils. She stretched her ears. Crack! . . . Crack! . . . Snap! What was that? She rolled over onto her stomach and pulled the rifle forward, cradling it in her arms. She cautiously lifted her head above the ground-hugging mantle of fog and looked around. Steve was hanging limply in the hammock. She dropped back down into the dank vapor and belly-crawled toward the sound of breaking twigs.

"Ohhhhhh!" Steve moaned, moving painfully in the hammock. Xinh popped back up through the soup. Not now, Steve. Please, not now. I can't come to you now. She crawled faster. Crack! . . . Snap! . . . Crack! How many are there? In this impenetrable fog I could bump into them before I see them. I'd better slow down and make a plan before I go any farther. She stopped and reached down for the knife, pulling it from the thong and placing it between her teeth. Steve moaned again.

Xinh made a right turn away from the sound and wiggled through the wet undergrowth, biting down hard on the dagger and supporting the rifle between bent elbows. The chill had left her bones, replaced by the hot flush of ambush. How had they found her so fast? She had been so careful. Her heart heaved under the camouflaged parachute blouse.

Thirty minutes later she had completed the flanking. Breaths coming in short gasps, she closed. The penetrating poisonous cloud thickened. Enveloped in the blanket of drift she put her ear to the jungle floor. Thump—thump. Forward again. Again, ear to the ground. Course correction. Crawl. Thump—thump—thump.

Quite suddenly the clinging, deadly vapor began to lift. White wreaths of swirling mist danced across a clearing bordered by flowering acacia. The sweet scent of spice trees drifted through the low grasses sparking Xinh's senses. She sniffed the perfumed air. Grandmother. The strong presence of home. She raised the 56 and sighted into the fog, placing the iron bead on the hazy silhouette of a shrouded form. For an instant, through the shifting veil, her sights rested on a shadowy crucifix. She blinked and pulled the rifle down. As she raised the sights again, fingers of gossamer spread across the clearing, veiling the target once more. Then a gust of air, a swirl, and the fog broke revealing the virgin purity of a muntjac fawn! The doe was feeding a few yards away. Crack ... snap ... crack—the twigs popped and broke as the deer pulled at the branches. The doe pawed at the ground with her front hooves. Thump—thump.

A long, pleading wail split the overbearing silence, scattering the hind and her fawn. Like an apparition rising from the grave, Xinh thrust up through the fog, rifle lifted above her head, knife still tightly clenched in her teeth. The white mist rolled up around her and she staggered forward crying, her voice resounding like the peal of a cathedral bell: "*Ba Ngoai—Ba Ngoai—Xin Ba Ngoai noi em—Tat ca da bien mat?*" Grandmother—Grandmother—please tell me, Grandmother—where did it all go? Sobbing bitterly, she fell to her knees and time was lost in the mist.

Turning back, she pushed through the low-hanging branches and the trailing lianas dripping mist. Will the insanity ever end? The heavy dew felt good on her bare feet—the wriggle of moist, soft grasses between her toes and the swish of leaves on her ankles recalling sensuous memories of play. The fog eddied and curled before her lithe legs. She stopped and glanced back across the clearing. The muntjac peered at her through the wet foliage, their large peaceful eyes innocently trying to comprehend.

*   *   *

Steve tossed back and forth in the hammock, murmuring between puffed lips and trying to focus through half-lidded eyes. Xinh laid the rifle against a tree and stood looking down at him shaking in his sagging jungle bed. She placed her hand on his sweating, fever-hot brow.

"Xinh." His eyes rolled toward her.

"Yes."

"Xinh, is that you?"

"I'm here."

He reached up and felt for her hand.

"Where are we?"

"Cambodia."

"What are we doing in Cambodia, Xinh?"

She didn't answer.

"Xinh."

"Yes, *cung oi.*"

"I'm so cold." He shook uncontrollably.

"Yes, *cung oi.*"

"What happened, Xinh?"

"Nothing. You rest. Xinh here." She held his hand tightly.

"I'm so cold . . . I may not make it."

"Two, maybe three day we know." She slapped a mosquito.

"I'm cold, Xinh." His eyes fell shut.

She removed her jungle shirt and pajamas, wrapping them around Steve. She took the heavy jungle knife from the rucksack and cut a stack of banana leaves, making a thick bed on the ground under the hammock. Then she built a small fire by the bed. Struggling with Steve's weight, she helped him out of the hammock and laid him on the bed of

284

leaves, next to the fire. She wrapped her body around him and pulled a layer of banana leaves over the two of them. Not until the sun was well up and the fog and chill had burned off did she unwrap herself from him.

The sun continued to climb above the horizon and the rain forest once again became a steaming, torrid hell. Xinh fashioned a digging tool from a fallen hardwood and spent the morning preparing Thanh's grave. Roots caused her to abandon several sites but once she located an area free of obstruction the digging went quickly in the soft earth. Several times she went to Thanh's body, still atop the cage, repeatedly splashing it with river water to keep it cool, then returning to the grave site to dig.

The sweet essence of spice and tea trees disappeared with the cool dawn, imprisoned by the odious suffocating fever of the Cambodian wilderness at high noon. Xinh dripped with mud mixed with her own sweat, and Steve lay shivering and baking in the banana leaves.

The grave completed, an exhausted Xinh walked to the river and fell in. She lay in the warm water for a long time until she felt her strength returning, then swam out to deeper water where the cool current ran. She dove to the bottom to get the full benefit of the refreshing springs and languished in the bracing depths before slowly floating to the surface. Then down again, knifing through the clear jade water to the invigorating deep, her long hair twisting about her sleek nude body, embosoming her in soft black ropes. She chased the bright-colored schools of tropical fish and toyed with the streams of silver sunlight diffusing among the lotus roots. She played with the river turtles and entertained the freshwater crustaceans.

Swimming to the surface she floated on her back in the shade of banyan and bamboo, dreaming her dreams. She imagined herself a reigning princess of the Lao Pang dynasty, coming to the river to take her morning bath. She rolled over and swam among the lotus and picked a white blossom, letting it swirl in the tiny pool formed between her young breasts. She grabbed a passing vine and pulled herself up into the spreading, thick branches; surveyed her kingdom from her throne; addressed her subjects; then sprawled out flat like a bronze leopard, her limbs dangling in the water. She slept the sleep of a child who has had her fill of frolic and romp, falling like a stone into the deep well of weariness.

The rejuvenating powers of rest did their work and Xinh woke as the sun was falling from its zenith. Catlike she stretched and crawled down from her bed.

Ceremoniously and with great care she bathed Thanh, untied her from the cage and carried her, as she had from the fire fight, draped over her shoulders, to the grave site.

Steve was delirious, raving about Migs and Kingfish, thrashing about under the banana leaves. Xinh laid Thanh in the hammock and cut more banana leaves. She placed them in the bottom of the grave. The bantering monkeys screamed from the trees, jumping about and clutching each other. Then they fell strangely silent, peering down through the trees.

Xinh hugged Thanh to her breast and kissed her good-bye. Carrying her to the grave she sang to Thanh:

> *Em oi, em oi,*
> *Chi yeu em nhieu lam,*
> *Chu yeu em nhieu lam.*
>
> *Em oi, em oi,*
> *Di voi chu*
> *Em vui bao gio.*
>
> *Em oi, em oi,*
> *Chi yeu em nhieu lam,*
> *Chu yeu em nhieu lam.*

The monkeys held each other and peeped through the pendantra branches, eyes riveted to the sensitive ceremony unfolding below. Baby monkeys were pressed to mothers' bosoms and innocence touched innocence. Somewhere in the jungle a tiger turned away from his kill and coughed; the little stream no longer ran red and the boot with the foot still in it was gone.

Xinh carefully lowered Thanh onto the bed of banana leaves. In the confined grave the fresh soil was cool and damp to Xinh's touch. She took her time, combing Thanh's hair in long strokes and laying the beautiful tresses to rest on her friend's childlike breasts. She folded Thanh's delicate hands over her chest and placed a few grains of rice between her lips. White gauze from the medical bag was wrapped once around her well-formed brow. All the while Xinh sang the enchanting little verse to her friend, touching her, remembering her. Not a tear fell. Her lips quivered but her eyes smiled and a radiant aura filled the dirt tomb.

Digging into the wall Xinh hastily constructed a small altar. She stuck a few long, dry bamboo sticks into the depression so that they stood erect, and ignited them. In front of the burning bamboo she placed a mound of bananas, some rice, and a coconut. Thanh's few personal items—a jeweled comb, a picture of her and Xinh and Duc taken during their childhood days, and her checkered scarf—were placed on the tomb floor beneath the offerings. As the funeral smoke from the smoldering bamboo filled the poor sepulcher, Xinh lamented her loss, trying to fathom the unfathomable. She spoke to Thanh in the melodious strains of her native language:

"When I get back home I'll make you some tamarind candy—not too sour—the way you like it."

She relit a smoking bamboo stick.

"Grandmother and I will burn incense and make offerings for you on this day each year."

She brushed a strand of hair from Thanh's face.

"What is the date today? I don't know the date."

The bamboo went out again.

"It's my fault. I never should have let you come. You should be home in school right now. I should have made you stay in school. Oh, Thanh, remember the tamarind trees and the pretty green river and the toy bamboo boats and Duc and . . ." She stopped. "The flowers—I forgot the flowers."

She quickly clambered out of the vault and frantically searched about the forest. Steve was still mumbling. The banana leaves were scattered and his arms waved aimlessly.

"I found them, Thanh. Pretty yellow- and red-striped ones."

She let herself down again and set a pile of tamarind flowers on Thanh's hands. She selected a particularly fine bloom and with much attention placed it in Thanh's hair.

The last bamboo stick burned out. Xinh covered Thanh with several layers of banana leaves. She filled in the grave and set fruit and rice on top of the burial mound. Additional burning bamboo slivers kept watch.

"Forgive me, someone please forgive me."

Part III

Tamarinds, Rag Dolls, and Little Bamboo Boats

" . . . I feel so clean now."

Chapter Twenty-four

Each morning the deadly mist rolled in from the river and hung suspended over the camp, strangling life. The monkeys climbed high in the trees to escape its suffocating breath. It embraced everything with a cold penetrating dampness, crawling into every dark shadow and hidden crevice, nothing escaping its choking invasion.

The sun rose and drove the fog back into the river. Hot beams of broken light pierced the forest canopy, boiling the land, flower and beast agonizing in the steaming Gehenna. Waves of smothering heat undulated over the tormented terrain leaving the air sweltering.

Xinh sat atop a high igneous outcropping, watching the sacrificial fire burning on Thanh's grave below. The flames leaped up from the combustible heap—cleansing, atoning, twisting with great anguish. A refining furnace, purging, purifying. Deep within Xinh a memory was already evolving; interwoven with the beautiful and the sublime, uncorrupted by evil . . . pure. Time would render Thanh a creation without deception or guile, without spot or blemish—without suffering.

Through the cracks of the burnished, broken rocks new life sprouted, taking root in the crevices made by time. Xinh lovingly stroked the healthy developing shoots. Nearby, several seeds had germinated on the hard surface only to wither and die, having no fertile soil to which to attach their immature roots. Other seeds had fallen among nettles, and the stinging hairs had choked their shoots as soon as they had sprung forth from their mother ovules. Still others had been scattered by the wayside and were eaten by birds before they could get a foothold.

But her seed had fallen in fertile soil and had taken root and would be watered and nurtured. It would flourish and bear fruit and prosper. There had been love, it had matured and blown into a scorching flame. She rested a soft hand on her belly, and as her eyes flooded she was dimly aware of Steve's handsome face floating before her eyes. She was terribly conscious of her mortality and she was struck with reverence, dread, and wonder.

. . . Forgive me, you must.

Oh, Thanh we were so young. Where did it all go? She picked up one of the ungerminated seeds and dropped it into a rock crevice. What happened to Duc? And the little bamboo boats? Will the river ever again flow like it did? She collected water from the hollow midrib of several tapioca leaves and let it fall into the crevice.

She was back in Tay Ninh. The look of the sun, the waving rice, the long curve in the river, the sharp, dry smell of harvest—it all came back. She was a little girl again, a small child frolicking along the grassy river

294

banks, tightly holding hands with Thanh and Duc. And the flowers, I almost forgot the flowers. How lovely the fragile paper blooms of *bong-giay* and the colorful tamarinds.

Look! There's Uncle Dong under the storytelling tree. And here come my barefoot cousins and brothers and sisters. Mama and papa. They were all with me then. No napalm, no artillery. Tay Ninh, Tay Ninh.

Suddenly she could smell Grandmother's husky, comforting scent—feel the security of her protective arms. Hold me close, Grandmother. *Yes, Xinh.* Please . . . close. *Go ahead, little one, cry it out.* Closer . . . hold me tight.

She tried to bury herself in grandmother's breasts and arms, like a little forest animal burrowing into the comfort of its hiding place. *Cry it out, Xinh.*

A violent spasm of fear welled from secret depths, shuddered to the surface, and broke through in a small, plaintive wail. It began weakly, gathered intensity, then burst forth in great convulsive sobs, unrelentingly racking her exhausted body. Oh, please hold me tight.

Tired and weary, hanging just clear of the bottom, Xinh turned away and walked back to the jungle camp. I must get home to Grandmother. We must make the tamarind candy before the seeds dry. Grandmother, Grandmother; I will be home soon.

Chapter Twenty-five

Xinh sat crosslegged on the banana leaves, eyes riveted to the underbrush. She took her finger off the trigger and flicked the sweat from her eyes.

The jungle was deathly still. From time to time a Con Ket, far off in the steaming rain forest, would break the silence with its chilling screech. The sun beat down on the canopy, heating the air insufferably beneath and baking its occupants.

She was tired, very tired, and had lost track of the days. Her clothes were torn, caked with mud, and filled with jungle stink. Her hair was matted with leaves and twigs. She stared into the perimeter of her tiny fortress, her cold, dark eyes unflinching, watching for the slightest movement. Her left hand moved slowly forward, and continuing to scan the foliage, she touched Steve's forehead.

The Con Ket screeched and Steve's eyelids moved. She edged up closer and ran her hand over his face, letting her fingers drift over his nose, mouth, and cheeks, then come to rest on his forehead again. "The fever is going down," she said in Vietnamese. She smiled.

She reached for the coconut shell and placed it between her legs. She dipped her fingers into the water and sprinkled Steve's face. She looked into the nearly empty shell. "I must get more water for him." She had stopped counting the trips she made to the river to fill the shell.

Cradling the rifle she stood and sprinkled the remaining drops on his face. His eyes flickered and his head moved.

"Ah," she sighed.

His eyes slowly opened.

She laid the rifle down and knelt beside him.

"Xinh," he murmured, not yet able to focus clearly.

She bent her head lower, placing her cheek against his.

"Xinh." It was only a whisper.

Leaving her cheek touching his, she talked softly into his ear. "You better now after long rest. Body no longer burn hot." She placed her two hands on him, palms down. "Not so hot."

He raised a weak arm and pulled a leaf from her hair.

"I very dirty. I wash in river now your eyes open."

He held her by the arm.

"I no go yet."

He smiled through scabbed lips.

She pulled a few tiny finger bananas from the stalk lying on the ground. "I make food for you."

"I can't eat much."

"Must eat." Her lips were firmly set. She peeled the bananas and mashed them into a paste at the bottom of the shell.

"I don't have an appetite."

"What that?"

"Appetite?"

"Yes. Ap . . . pe . . . pe . . ."

"I'm not hungry."

"Oh, mean not hungry?"

"Not hungry. No appetite."

"You no eat for many days. Must have food."

He tried to sit up, grimacing from pain. She gently pushed him back down.

"I want to see my leg."

She shook her head and went on mashing the bananas with her fingers.

"It must be pretty bad."

She glanced down at his leg and frowned.

"That bad, huh?"

Xinh set the shell on his belly and picked up the machete. Steve stared in horror at the large, broad-bladed knife. Her knuckles were white around the brown wooden handle. She was looking at his leg.

"What are you going to do with that thing?" He was up on an elbow, pain in his face.

She turned and walked into the forest. "I get coconut."

Steve fell back on the banana leaves. "Whew!"

There was a rustle of leaves as Xinh vanished into the undergrowth, the Chinese 56 slung over her shoulder and the long knife gripped in her hand. Then silence folded in around him and he was alone.

His lungs inhaled deeply, sucking in the hot, wet air. He had a coughing fit, spitting up blood, not so dark this time. He wiped the drool from his mouth with the back of his hand.

Steve raised his arm and carelessly examined the large jungle sores. Mosquitoes and large flies buzzed around his head and his open wounds. Can't think about this. Got to keep going. He closed his eyes to block out the ugliness.

The minutes passed. No Xinh. He began to worry. He raised his head and looked across Thanh's grave to the spot where Xinh had disappeared.

His head dropped back to the ground. He spit a fly out of his mouth and rolled his head back and forth trying to get a bit of relief from the boiling heat. He could feel tiny things crawling over his body.

If he stayed here he would die, he knew that. But he couldn't move. He tried to rise again, to look at his leg. The swelling had lessened and it wasn't nearly as evil to look at, but it hurt like hell. Maybe that was good. It was crooked too, twisted at a strange angle, loose and limp like the leg of a rag doll. Somehow it didn't seem to be a part of him. It was plastered with mashed roots and herbs.

He drifted on the threshold of consciousness passing in and out of sleep, dreaming of flower-swept hillsides back home, of his mother's food-laden table on Sunday afternoons after church, of rain dripping from the roof outside his bedroom window. Sweet childhood memories.

Now and then a troubled figure would pass through the ethereal scenes. She was dressed in black pajamas and was always present, lingering in the background, her beautiful face obscured by shadows and the play of diffused light filtering through high trees. When he reached for her she would vanish into a vapor trail only to reappear in another remote corner of his mind. Her attraction was overwhelming and he was obsessed with the desire to know her. But she was elusive, a gossamer image in the wind, unobtainable and fleeting.

When he awoke from one of these particularly strong visions, Xinh was standing over him with a large coconut encased in its fibrous green husk. She had appeared quite suddenly, and for a moment Steve thought he was seeing an apparition. He blinked his eyes, bringing her into better focus.

"I thought that you left me."

She looked at him curiously. Her lips never moved, but her eyes told him how foolish he was.

"What's that you've got there?"

She dropped the coconut to the ground and held up a crude fish trap woven from strips of bamboo and the midribs of palm fronds.

"Where did you get that?"

"I make." She turned the funnel-shaped trap upside down and three fat blackfish fell out, flopping about on the banana leaves.

He shook his head in amazement. "We just might make it."

She proudly held one of the fish up to him. "You like?"

"I like."

She cut the viscera out of the fish and handed him the liver and heart. She motioned to him to eat them.

He stared at the bloody organs lying limp in the palm of his dirty hand. "I'm not hungry enough."

"No ap . . . pe . . . ti . . . te." She picked up another fish and sliced it open. She quickly ate the fish giblets, expecting him to do the same.

He did.

"You like?"

He swallowed hard. "Can I have some water?"

She pointed to the fresh coconut. "You like better." She shook the big nut next to his ear so he could hear the milk sloshing around.

He touched her hand. "Open it for us and let's have a drink together."

She cut off the top and sat beside him, lifting his head.

"A toast. Make a toast first."

She had a perplexed look on her face.

"Say something in our honor. It's good luck."

She didn't hesitate. She quickly said, "We love together forever."

"To the love between a Vietcong guerrilla leader and a U.S. Air Force officer. I'll drink to that."

She held the coconut back, looking at him earnestly. "Steve really mean that?"

"I really mean that." He squeezed her hand.

She bent over and kissed his blood-caked lips. "Forever," she whispered, tipping the coconut water into his mouth.

He drank long and deep. And then she drank. What was left over she poured into the shell, mixing it with the banana mash and scrapings from the soft, white gelatinous insides; it made a tasty, nutritious meal. She fed him with her fingers.

"You like?"

"I like."

She scooped the mixture into his mouth. He ate heartily, following her movements with his eyes.

After finishing feeding him, Xinh went to the

rucksack and dug around in the bottom. She brought out a pack of Russian cigarettes. Steve's eyes almost fell out of his head.

"Where did you get those?"

"I take from NVA major back at village."

She opened the top of the pack, Steve watching her intently, and slowly pulled out one of the white sticks. Ceremoniously, she placed it between his lips, struck the PX Zippo and flamed the tip of the weed.

He inhaled a couple of times and smiled his satisfaction. He handed her the cigarette. "Here, smoke it with me."

She squatted beside him, placed the cigarette in the center of her puckered lips, and sucked on it like a straw, enveloping her head in a dense cloud of smoke.

"*Ka! Ka! Ka!*" She spit the cigarette out in a fit of coughing. "*Ka! Ka!*"

Steve retrieved the cigarette. He was laughing painfully. "You've never smoked a cigarette before?" He held the weed out to her again.

She shook her head. "*Ka!* . . . bad . . . no good." She made a distasteful face, wrinkling her nose. "I no like."

Steve finished smoking the cigarette, savoring every drag.

"I save them. Give you maybe one every day." She held up the pack for him to see, like a reward given to a child for being good. She tucked it safely back into the rucksack.

Then she got very serious. She bent over his leg and examined it closely, pulling away the sheath of leaves and root extract. Her fingers expertly ex-

303

plored the wound.

"What do you think?" Steve said calmly.

She sat down on her bottom, studying the leg. "It better, but no straight." She bent her arm awkwardly for him to see. "Look like this."

Steve remained quiet, knowing what she had to do.

She looked at him, a pleading but determined look. "Must make straight. Xinh push bones together so leg fix good." She brought her two fists together and twisted them.

Steve flinched.

"Must do."

"Uh-huh," Steve nodded.

Xinh distracted herself by cleaning the fish, deep in thought. She built a small fire and let it burn down to hot coals. She placed the fish, split in half, directly on the coals, turning them often with a pair of twigs which she handled like chopsticks.

"Soon you be well again." She fed him small pieces of the roasted fish.

He ate obligingly, breathing heavily. She fed him slowly.

"Is there time for another cigarette before you . . . before you go to work on me?"

Her eyes wandered over his face. "We do now."

"O.K., kid." His belly tightened.

She placed a stick between his teeth. "You bite hard. It maybe help." There was no more morphine.

Xinh looked over the break one more time. She curled her left leg around his thigh, holding it in a vise grip. Leaning forward she grasped his ankle tightly in her two strong hands. "Ready?"

Steve grunted.

She pushed forward on his ankle taking pressure off the bones.

"Arrrrrrr!" Steve bit down hard on the stick, heavy drops of sweat pouring down his face.

She twisted to the right and watched the leg straighten. Steve howled. The stick fell from his mouth.

She twisted again, this time in the opposite direction and the bulge under the skin disappeared. Steve passed out.

Her leg unlocked from his thigh and she ran her fingers up and down his lower leg, probing deep, following the course of the bones, pushing here and there to bring the break together.

Wiping the perspiration from her eyes, she leaned against a tree to rest, drawing a few deep breaths. The water had come to a boil inside the hard coconut shell.

"You're a strong man," she said in Vietnamese.

Steve lay unconscious, his breathing steady.

"Most men would have died by now."

The Con Ket shrieked somewhere in the rain forest. Xinh elevated Steve's leg on the rucksack and knotted a vine rope around his ankle. Pulling on the vine until there was enough tension to straighten the leg, she tied the other end of the rope around a tree trunk.

Having set the bone and placed his leg in traction, she fashioned a pair of splints from wood, using the machete. After thoroughly cleaning his leg with hot water and root soap, she wrapped it in fresh bandages from the medical bag. Then she secured the splints to his leg with the bandages.

She stood, back rod straight and bathed in sweat, eyes closed and head tilted back. A beam of sunlight broke through the high canopy of trees and focused on her like a theater spotlight. Her lithe body was perfectly still except for an involuntary quiver in a tricep muscle.

In moments like this when she was close to total exhaustion, she pulled an envelope of silence around herself and withdrew into her own private world to regain strength. She stumbled backward into a tree and slowly slid to the ground, limp and worn to the bone.

The jungle was as silent as a tomb. Even the Con Ket had finally been hushed by the energy sapping heat. Xinh cut her mind loose from its moorings and let her thoughts drift on a sea of quiet. She thought of calm rivers and nothing in her ears but the rustle of bamboo in a light breeze.

Her chin nodded against her chest and her magnificent mane of ebony hair cascaded forward in a sudden rush, silky ends touching the leaf-covered ground. Her rose-petal lips were parted and deep labored breathing forced her small breasts to rise and fall beneath her camouflaged-parachute blouse.

Behind the black waterfall covering her face, the long sensuous eyes that gave Steve shivers whenever he looked at them, languished in sleep. Her smooth, honey-skin hands hung loosely at her sides. Her strong, firm legs were stretched out straight. She slept the sleep of the dead.

Chapter Twenty-six

"It's strong enough—but a bit too long." Steve leaned against a tree and handed the crude wooden crutch to Xinh.

She hacked an inch off the end with the machete and gave it back to him.

"That's better. Just about right." He carefully put his weight on it and took a cautious step away from the tree. "Ohhhh." He began toppling over.

Xinh ran up and supported him.

"Looks like I'm going to need some practice on this thing."

Together they hobbled around the camp until Steve was able to handle the crutch on his own.

"Thanks, honey." He looked around him. "How long have we been in this wretched place?" He stepped out, taking two steps this time.

"Maybe two week."

He took another step and rested. His back was still curled forward from the nerve damage. "Do you still have the tiger cage hidden?"

She nodded, pointing to the river.

"I suppose we can use it to float out of here,

can't we?"

She nodded again, turning the fish cooking over the coals.

"Let's take a look at your map again."

She brought it to him. "Our river." She pointed to a blue curving line on the map, then to the river flowing past the camp.

"I went down about here with my plane."

"Yes. Thanh say VC tell her they find your plane that place."

"And there's the village where they kept me."

"That Pak Mek."

"Whew! That's a long walk." He shook his head. "I was unconscious most of the trip." He coughed up blood and spat it to the ground. His broken ribs had punctured a lung.

Steve's severe wounds had responded to Xinh's careful nursing, but he was still a weak man. He was also suffering from a variety of complications, including anemia from loss of blood and jungle rot that Xinh was fighting to keep under control. Her intensive care and his will to live were keeping him alive.

But she knew she would have to get him back to his own people soon. At any time his condition could turn downward again and she might not be able to reverse it this time.

He couldn't stay in the jungle indefinitely. He needed to be in a hospital. Time was running out and she was worried.

"O.K., there's the Mekong, down south here." He held the map close. "We have to make the Mekong,

308

right? We can't make it overland. Got to use the rivers."

"Very dangerous."

"We'll travel at night." He wasn't listening to her.

"Many NVA, Vietcong, and Khmer."

She admired his spirit and his desire to help. He was used to giving orders, but so was she. They both instinctively took charge and she was afraid that he might make her job difficult for her. She decided that she had to exert authority.

"Yeah, the Mekong. If we make the Mekong we've got it knocked," he said confidently. "We'll travel at night in the tiger cage, staying close to the shadows along the banks." He stopped for breath, spit some blood, and continued. "Might take a week or two. What do you think?"

"You crazy."

He almost fell off his crutch. He stared at her, not believing what he heard.

"Communists put you in tiger cage again . . . Xinh with you this time. Catch us both."

He frowned. He wasn't used to being talked to like this.

"You no understand jungle. You no understand Vietcong and NVA. They very smart." She licked her lips and brushed the hair from her eyes. "We last one, maybe two day. You go back tiger cage."

"Look, you don't have all the answers. We've got to—"

"You foolish man; you think communists stupid."

"It's the Mekong. That's the only way."

"We get killed."

"Water, we stay on the water," he demanded. His voice was weak with fatigue.

"Communists kill us easy."

"Are you afraid?" He had become impatient with her.

Her eyes narrowed and she was suddenly very quiet. He quickly realized his mistake. To question her courage was a grave error.

"I'm sorry. That's not true. You didn't deserve that."

She didn't say anything. Her body was very rigid.

"I suppose I still can't admit to myself that you're a Vietcong."

She didn't want to argue the point. She didn't know what she was anymore. Thanh was right. They were children of the damned, with nowhere to go, caught in a free-fire zone.

"Here, take the map." He leaned hard against the crutch.

She took the map from him. "North Vietnamese here, here, here, and here." She pointed to communist strongholds and supply depots along the rivers leading into Vietnam.

"They cover a lot of territory. They seem to hold the whole area between where we are and the Vietnam border."

"Not so many here." She pointed to a rugged corridor of mountains. There was an obvious absence of villages along the corridor. "Communists stay away this place."

"Are you sure?"

She gave him a severe look.

"O.K., O.K." He held up a hand. "Whatever you say."

"Americans here." Her finger moved from Vietnam and crossed the Cambodian border into the corridor.

He gave her a quizzical look. "American troops in Cambodia?"

"They come now. American soldiers cross border when you make raid." She poked him in the chest with a stiff finger. "You start."

"Yeah, I started it all right. I didn't know it at the time, but it's all clear now."

She brought her finger over to their position on the map. "We cross river in tiger cage tonight. Go this way to Pong Lok. Then climb over mountains to Americans here." Her finger came down hard in a remote valley.

Steve looked down at his leg. "It's a long way, Xinh."

"You afraid?" There was a hint of a smile.

"O.K., we're even."

"We can do, *cuong oi*. We make it." She gave him the thumbs-up sign.

"Can do," he smiled.

"Can do, GI."

He looked around the camp. "I've kind of gotten used to this dump."

"No can stay, *cuong oi*."

"You're right. No can stay, broken leg or no broken leg, no can stay."

She touched his face. "We make it. Trust Xinh. I get you home."

Xinh spent the remainder of the day preparing for what she knew was going to be a dangerous and grueling journey through a vast communist-infested wilderness. What she knew and Steve didn't, was that the NVA had built a system of interconnected links in the Ho Chi Minh trail. These terminated in a spider web of supply stations in eastern Cambodia. To reach freedom they had to break through this closely woven net.

She stripped Steve.

"Do we have time for this?" He grinned lewdly.

A playful hand slapped his face. "You need strength. No fool around. Plenty time we do that get home."

She bathed him carefully with hot water, paying close attention to the open sores and wounds that were reluctant to heal. She was worried about his labored breathing caused by the damaged lung.

His leg was redressed and heavy-duty splints were secured around it.

He scratched his head. "Fleas."

She shrugged. That was the least of his problems. She gave him a soft green fruit.

"What's this?"

"Cho-cho."

He took a suspicious small bite, the way he always did when she gave him something new to eat.

"You like?"

He spit it out. "Gaaaaa! That's terrible."

She yanked it from his hand and ate it herself. "You too pa . . . pa . . . pa—"

"Particular," he said for her.

"Yes, that word."

For a long time he quietly watched her cooking fish and making rice balls for their overland trek. She wrapped the food in banana leaves and carefully placed each parcel into the rucksack. He nodded his admiration to her. There are women and then there are women, he mused. He glanced down at the carefully dressed and splinted leg.

"Remember when Thanh and I got you out jail in Bien Hoa?"

Her head remained bent over the cooking fire, but her eyes lifted to him.

"And we took the funny taxi out of town."

"The cyclo," she said, returning her eyes to the roasting fish.

"You led us through the tall elephant grass and we fell off the bamboo bridge into the canal and I made love to you on the bank."

"I remember." Her eyes misted over with happiness.

"It was good, Xinh."

"It always good with you." Her honey-colored skin flushed to copper-red.

"You're not looking at me."

"Must I?"

He could see the red rising into her cheeks. There are women and then there are women, he smiled.

By the time the long shadows of the coconut palms fell across the lazy river, Xinh had erased all signs of their presence. The camp had vanished. She and Steve sat together resting their backs against a tree.

"How about a cigarette?"

She pushed one between his lips. She handed him the lighter.

"Where did you get the Zippo?" He lit up. "They sell these in the PX." He looked it over.

"You really want know?" She took the lighter back.

"Yeah. How did you get it?"

Her eyes narrowed and she looked away from him.

"Well?" he pushed.

"I get it from soldier."

His eyes widened. "A secret love affair you never told me about?"

"He dead when I take from him." She got up and walked down to the river, rifle slung over her shoulder, extra clips stuffed into her waistband. Two grenades hung around her neck.

He grunted. A monkey looked down at him from its limb high in the canopy.

Xinh didn't return until it was very late. She shook Steve awake. "We go now."

He looked out into the inky blackness. "O.K., kid; it's your show."

She helped him to his feet and fitted the crutch under his arm.

He held back a moment, looking around the camp. "Wish I had a camera."

"Come, we go now." She led him down to the river and helped him into the tiger cage. The door had been cut away. "Lay on belly." She put Thanh's AK-47 in his hands and cocked it. His legs hung out the door when he lay on the four feet of bamboo floor.

"You O.K.?"

"Yeah, I'm all right. Push off." He pointed the rifle ahead.

Xinh climbed on top of the cage, next to the rucksack. Using a ten-foot bamboo pole, she pushed the raft away from the bank and into the slow current.

"We need a rudder to steer this thing." He hung his arm over the edge, trying to maneuver the raft.

Xinh straightened them out by resting the long pole over the stern and quickly jerking it back and forth in the water. When she removed the pole, the cage would drift in a wide, lazy circle.

"It's going to take us a long time this way."

She let the raft drift in the starry night. The bank slipped by them, sinister forms protruding over the water, playing on her imagination. She kept one hand on the 56.

"I can't see a thing," he whispered.

"Very black tonight. That good."

"I suppose." He rolled his hip to get more comfortable on the bamboo floor. "How do you know where we're going?"

"Shhh. Better no talk."

They drifted.

"How about another cigarette?"

Silence.

"You very stupid sometimes."

"What!"

"Shhhhh." She lifted the pole quietly from the water and placed it back into the river closer to the bow. She pushed against the bottom and they moved farther out into the current.

"What do you mean I'm stupid?" He was amused with her.

"You fly-boy, never fight in jungle."

"How do you know I've never fought in the jungle?"

"I know."

"How?"

"You smoke cigarette at night."

They drifted.

As the sky began to pale to bullet gray, the raft entered one of the wildest and strangest regions in all Southeast Asia. A region populated by elephants, Bengal tigers, and jungle so dense that one never saw the sun.

"Where are we?" Steve felt the goose bumps rise on his skin.

Phantoms lurked in the trees and an eerie quiet screamed in the torpid dawn.

"We get off here." She poled the raft into an eddy.

A large ogani slid from a sand bar into the murky water.

"This is a weird place, Xinh."

The tiger cage came to rest, bumping against a bank overgrown with thick ferns. Rare black orchids grew in the crotches of rubber trees thick with crawling moss.

He could feel evil eyes watching him. "I don't like this. Not at all."

She stepped onto the bank and scouted the area. In a few minutes she was back, checking her map. She spread it in front of Steve, placing the compass in his hand. "You pilot, you know how read map good. Right?"

Steve looked at the blur in front of him. "I could use more light."

She looked up into the dawning sky. "O.K." She built a shielding screen out of broad leaves and flicked the Zippo.

"That's better." He studied the lines and figures, turning the compass. "Hmmmm."

"What?" She crowded closer.

He pulled her wrist into the light. "What time does your watch read?"

"It say 0530." He studied the map for another minute.

"What time did we leave the camp?"

"2300."

He tore a thread from her blouse and traced the river with it. He stretched it out and measured its length on the scale.

"What's six and one-half times fifteen?"

"Ninety-seven and one-half," she said before his voice died away.

"Subtract twenty-four and one-quarter."

"Seventy-three and one-quarter."

With a sliver of bamboo he pointed to a spot on the map where the river came out of a wide bend. "Right there. That's where we're sitting."

He looked up at her. The Zippo's light was dancing on her pretty face. She was smiling. He looked back down at the map. The splinter was poised on the entrance to the mountain corridor!

"Not bad. Not bad at all." He nodded his approval. She shouldered the rucksack and slung the Chinese 56 over one shoulder and the AK-47 over the other.

"That's a heavy load. Can you carry it all?"

She gave him an exasperated look. "You think Xinh weak child?"

"Why don't you let me carry the Kalashnikov?"

She didn't want to do it.

"I'll need it in a fire fight."

She thought for a moment. "Maybe too much for you." She shook her head. "Gun heavy."

317

"I'll give it back if it becomes too heavy."

She reluctantly unslung it. "We try." She placed it on his shoulder.

Steve tucked the crutch in his armpit. "I'm ready anytime you are."

Xinh checked her compass, lining up with a large rubber tree a hundred yards away, and led off.

Three hours later, Steve was still holding up well. Xinh called a halt each time she checked the compass and let him rest. A familiar uneasy feeling was growing in the pit of her stomach. She began looking around more frequently.

"Man, it's dark in here." He peered into the forest. "I feel like I'm inside a giant, green tomb. The sun's out there somewhere." He glanced into the tightly sealed canopy above him.

Xinh pointed ahead. "We go that way."

"Let's do it." He heaved forward on the crutch.

The farther they penetrated the mysterious interior, the more strange sounds they heard. The cacophony of noise would rise to an unnerving crescendo, then die back to a hush, only to build once again to a din of shrieking, screeching, grunting, and growling.

After another hour of walking, Xinh figured Steve had had enough for the day. She set up camp and took a look at his wounds.

"How you feel, *cuong oi*?"

"I'm making it." He was sweating heavily and his breathing was unsure.

The going was painfully slow through the thick

jungle. Each checkpoint was a monumental achievement for Steve. She fed him cold fish and rice balls, and gave him water she collected from the bole of a tree.

"We'll make it, kid." He gave her the thumbs-up sign.

She nodded and washed his face, then poured water over his shoulders and back to cool him off. His face was drawn with fatigue.

"I think I'll rest a bit now."

She helped him into the hammock and he was instantly out. She pulled the mosquito netting over him, cocked the 56 and slid into the jungle, leaving Steve snoring in his bed.

She moved silently through the foliage, like a vaporous vision, stopping often to become one with the plants—listening, watching. Then moving on.

She sensed danger out there. An ominous presence had been picked up by her highly developed survival instincts. She moved farther off the trail, back into the foliage. Soon, I will know soon.

The assault rifle grew clammy in her hands. With each passing minute the adrenaline entering her bloodstream increased, in preparation for the moment when all her defenses would be needed.

A wet hand reached to her waistband, touching the banana clips, then came back to the rifle's warm steel and rested on the bolt. Soon, very soon. She licked the perspiration from her lips.

Maybe it was the pervading stillness or the squishing of the damp leaves or a change in the chemistry of the air. She never knew what it was that warned her of impending danger. All she knew was that her private DEW line never failed her, that it was as frightfully real as the crack of an AK, or as true as her own breathing and was always on alert whether she was awake or asleep.

The buzzing in her ears was as strong as she had ever heard it. She loosened the grenades hanging around her neck and laid them in the moss next to her sandaled feet. The large stenciled markings, U.S., were facing up.

Steve snored in the hammock, breathing the sinister air, his broad chest heaving in deep, recuperating sleep. The AK rested within reach against a tree. The mosquito net covered the length of his body from head to foot.

There was no noise, nothing happened that would alert an average person to the coming danger. But Xinh knew when it had arrived. Rough bare feet and sinewy legs suddenly visible through breaks in the thick undergrowth were the first evidence that it had come. The primitive Khmer mountain guerrillas moved past her silently and squatted in a circle twenty yards from where she was hidden.

"I get the girl for myself," the leader said in Cambodian.

Xinh smiled to herself, though her flesh crawled as she looked at these grotesque creatures. Their faces were painted white with lime.

"Why must you have her for yourself?" another questioned.

"You must share her," a third demanded.

"You can all have her after I'm done with her," the leader said.

"She won't be worth much then."

320

There were seven of the Khmers. They were naked except for dirty loincloths tied over their crotches. Each wore a red headband around his forehead. Thick, matted black hair, hacked short with knives, stuck out in all directions from their headbands. A white ghostlike lime paste was smeared over their faces and arms. It was the wildest band of creatures Xinh had ever seen.

The leader, a squat stolid man of about thirty-five, spit a gob of betel juice on his foot without noticing. "You will torture the American for information." He pointed to a zombielike Neanderthal sharpening his bone-handled knife on a flat stone.

The zombie smiled through purple-stained teeth. A battered U.S. M-1 was lying beside him. The others carried an assortment of rifles; French, Russian, and Chinese.

The leader spit again. "They will be easy to take. They suspect nothing."

"The girl does not look so easy," the zombie said. "Pah!"

They passed fresh betel around, cutting the soft nut with their knives and chewing it with lime spread on cau leaves. The narcotic heightened their pugnaciousness and several were stabbing the air and dirt with their knives.

The leader began making lewd gestures representative of what he was going to do to Xinh. They all grinned lasciviously and joined in the gesturing with their bodies. Xinh's nostrils flared.

Chapter Twenty-seven

The grenade arched up out of the wet undergrowth just as the Khmer were splitting into two sections. Xinh rolled behind a tree when the explosion ripped apart the silence. Shards of white-hot metal shrieked by her; some tore into the tree trunk. She quickly jumped to her feet. Two of the Khmer lay dead within the spreading blue cloud of smoke. A third stood, looking around, bewildered. She shot him in the spine and he toppled over backward into a jerking heap.

From their cover, the four remaining Khmer began blindly returning fire, forcing Xinh to hunker down behind the tree trunk. For a few minutes they fired wildly at her, but soon settled down to only a few rounds; then the firing stopped completely. The jungle became very still.

Xinh didn't have to think about what they were going to do. She automatically knew that these vicious jungle fighters would start a flanking maneuver to flush her out. One would keep her pinned down with fire from directly in front and the others would split to either side and come after her on their bellies from wide angles on her left and right. They probably would send one around to her rear.

A burst of AK-47 fire came from the direction of the camp. Steve was in the fight. There was another short burst immediately following the first. One of the Khmer to her front screamed.

"Three left now," she whispered to herself.

While Steve kept up his harassing fire, one shot at a time, saving ammo, Xinh slid out from behind the tree and crawled toward the hidden Khmers. She wasn't going to wait for them to come for her.

Knife between her teeth, rifle in one hand, the last grenade in the other, she slithered soaked to the bone and streaked with mud, between the ferns and ficus. She put her head against the wet moss and waited for the shots.

Bam!

She looked to the right, fixing the position in her mind.

Bam!

Almost directly in front of me. She waited for the third rifle to fire.

Bam!

She looked back to the right. Where is the third man?

Bam! The man in front fired again.

Bam! The shot came from the first position on the right.

Maybe there are three men in two positions? She waited.

Bam!

Xinh smiled. Twenty yards to my left.

She doubled back and swung far around to the

324

right. Tiny frogs jumped from her path, knocking drops of water from the edges of the fern fronds.

Biting down hard on the steel in her teeth and brushing wet hair from her eyes, she maneuvered widely and quickly crossed the game trail. She pushed the rifle ahead through the ficus and pulled herself forward by her knees and elbows.

Suddenly she saw dark, hairless legs and thick calloused feet sticking out of the ferns in front of her. The AK-47 popped again. Steve was still on the job.

She edged up a little closer and poked the muzzle of the 56 through the ferns. The Khmer turned his head and looked into the muzzle, uncomprehending. She pulled the trigger and his brains sprayed out the back of his head.

She closed her eyes and rested her head on the moss. Grandmother, will the killing never end? Must I always be fighting?

Opening her eyes, she saw a muntjac through the foliage. I'm sorry. Forgive me. Will someone please forgive me? She crawled through the thick undergrowth.

Steve woke with a start. It took him a few seconds to get his bearings. His mind, fuzzy from exhaustion, struggled to understand. The banging of rifles intensified and he rolled out of the net hammock, grabbed the Kalashnikov, and painfully crawled toward the action. He stopped to collect his wits and to determine where the concentration of fire was coming from. Then he began pumping rounds in that direction.

Xinh was alive and in action, he knew that much from the isolated shots coming from the big teak tree. He aimed to buy her time. Maybe she could work around to him and they could put their firepower together. Several minutes went by. Only a few shots were fired.

He was a sitting duck unable to move about with his broken leg. Xinh, whatever she was planning, would have to act soon. He looked down at the clips. He had three left. He would have to make them last; how long he didn't know.

At first he thought a hot breeze had come up and was moving the leaves in front of him. He blinked his eyes and stared hard. The leaves weren't all that was moving. So were the stems, and then the entire shrub! He watched in amazement while the plant uprooted itself and began walking away. He leveled the sights of the AK onto the center of the bush and slowly squeezed the trigger. The Kalashnikov bucked and the spent shell casing ejected from the breech, flying into the ficus. There was a scream, more of a surprised yell; then the plant wavered for a moment and crumpled to the ground.

For a few minutes sporadic fire came from the three positions in front of him where he figured the enemy, whoever they were, were concentrated, but no shots came from the big teak tree where he thought Xinh was holed up. Could she have been hit? He was confused and didn't know exactly what his options were. I'll sit tight for a while.

The rifle on his left became silent; only two were firing now. Where was Xinh? He waited. Then there were no more shots. The jungle became eerily silent.

A waiting game, he thought to himself. His flesh crawled.

He looked up into the deep green canopy, trying to get a fix on the time. But the sun was completely hidden from him. The black-faced monkeys had disappeared. The silence thundered against his eardrums. *Why aren't they firing? What happened to Xinh?*

His leg hurt like the dickens. He rolled over and looked at it. Blood was oozing through the bandage. *Can't think about that now. Got to get my head straight about what to do next.* His breathing was coming short. He itched to hold the trigger down and pour all his remaining rounds into the jungle. *Better than sitting here waiting for those animals to sneak up on me and cut my throat.* He quickly looked behind him.

They know where I am. Got to get out of here. They've got me zeroed.

But he couldn't move without stabbing pains tearing through his leg.

"*Cuong oi.*"

He froze.

"*Cuong oi.*"

That's Xinh's voice . . . I think . . . must be Xinh.

"Steve," came the urgent whisper.

His heart banged against his ribs. He pointed the AK toward the voice. He gave no reply. He waited. Nothing. The dead air laughed at him.

It's one of them. How do they know my name? Could be the tiger-cage troops found my trail. I'm not going back. Not alive. What did they do with Xinh?

"Steve." The voice was closer now.

Maybe its not that lot. Could be a gang of marauding Cambodian bandits or Khmer guerrillas. They might have tortured Xinh to get my name. I didn't hear any screaming.

He looked nervously around.

She wouldn't scream though. She wouldn't tell them anything, not her; not even my name.

Only Xinh calls me *cuong oi*. Yeah, but these VC broads are smart. They've got some stinking VC woman crawling around out there trying to find me; or a Cambodian that speaks Vietnamese is trying to suck me out.

His mind was jumping around trying to come up with answers. If he could only move. He tried again. "Uhhhhh," he moaned, biting his lip. I'll blow her stinking head off; VC broad, Cambodian broad. I'll blow your head off.

Then it dawned on him that it could easily be a man imitating a woman's voice. His anger flared. Damned if he was going to let them take him easily. I need to know where they are.

"Cuong oi."

The voice sounded more like a man's to him this time.

If I don't answer, he'll know I'm suspicious. I ought to answer. Suck him in, then burn one through his head.

"Pssst, over here. I'm over here."

He pointed the rifle to his left where the counterfeit woman's voice came from. He laid his head flat against the ground so he could see under the foliage and picked a spot to concentrate his fire where the ficus and dripping ferns weren't so thick. He'll come through there; no doubt about it.

"Pssst, pssst, over here, I'm over here."

Suddenly a hand came over his right shoulder and pinned the Kalashnikov to the ground, completely surprising him.

He jerked his head around expecting to see a knife flashing for his throat.

"Shhh."

Xinh's long eyes reprimanded him.

"I thought they got you," he said, relieved.

"No way, GI." She took her hand from the AK-47 and rested her chin on his shoulder.

"How you do?"

"Not so good. Got one—but my leg is killing me."

She looked it over, frowning.

"I fell out of the hammock when the shooting started. Must have banged it up again."

"Can't fix now." She stretched out alongside him.

"How many are there?"

"Two alive—five dead."

"I'm almost out of ammo." He showed her the clips.

She gave him all of her remaining ammo.

His eyebrows shot up. "Won't you need some?"

Xinh shook her head and patted the knife tied to her calf. She pointed to the grenade in her hand.

"What's your plan?" His eyes shut—pain.

She touched his face as she always did when she was concerned about him. "You shoot rifle—no stop. Call, 'Xinh, Xinh!' Khmer come to you."

"I'm the bait."

"Yes, you bait. I catch fish." She untied the knife

from her leg and held it tightly, studying the long sharp blade. "One big fish I catch. I want bad." She turned the blade over and over in her hand. "I catch big fish."

The look in her eyes was frightening. Steve had never seen that terrible look before. It would stop the heart of a lion. "What's the matter, kid?"

"Big fish want do bad things to me. Very bad things. He ugly, dirty man. I make him die slowly." The blade plunged into the ground. She turned it back and forth, pressing it deep into the dirt.

Steve shuddered.

"He look like soldier do bad thing to me when I little girl. He laugh same. Eyes same. Ugly, dirty man." The knife twisted in the soil, her knuckles white on the handle.

Steve set the clips in a neat row in front of him. "You be careful out there, honey. I want you back."

She pulled the knife from the dirt and wiped it clean on her sleeve. "I be back. No worry." Her eyes were cold.

All in a day's work for her. I'm not to worry; ha! Steve checked to see how many rounds he had in the rifle. She'd better come back, he thought. I'll never get out of here without her. The pain shot up his leg.

"You start shooting now," she ordered.

Bossy little thing. He winked at her. "Good luck."

She winked back and crawled away on elbows and knees, knife between her teeth and grenade in her hand.

He pulled the trigger and the rifle banged against his shoulder. "Xinh . . . where are you?" he called. "Xinh." He laid down a steady fire, varying the intervals, and all the time calling out to attract the

Khmers' attention.

Xinh found the tree she wanted and quickly shinnied up to a thick limb. She lay full length on a branch and surveyed the jungle below her like a hungry leopard.

She remembered her childhood days in Tay Ninh when she climbed the tamarind trees and picked the long fruit pods. Thanh and Duc waited below for her to drop the sweet, tasty pods to them. Later they made the sour candy with Grandmother, who would scold them for sneaking pieces. There was always enough candy. Grandmother was very generous.

Xinh's eyes locked onto a section of ficus fifty yards away. The movement was imperceptible, a slight shaking of a few leaves in the middle of a green sea of stillness.

The AK fired behind her. "Xinh!" The leaves shook again, this time changing direction and moving in a line with Steve's location. Farther back, another section of leaves shimmered.

Xinh slid from the tree and vanished molelike under the ground cover.

"Xinh!" . . . Pow! . . . Pow!

In a few minutes she had worked through the ficus and ferns to a fallen mahogany. She raised her head out of the vegetation and peered over the large log. The sea of green was motionless in the dead air. A deep silence lay over everything, heavy like lead. Steve had inexplicably stopped firing. Nor did he call out. It was as if this Kampuchean nether world was holding its breath, anticipating the climax of the strange scenario playing itself out in this steaming jungle.

She dropped behind the log and rolled over on her

back, looking up into the canopy. It had turned a deeper green. The light was fading and the tomb was growing darker. It would soon be night in this wicked crypt—a time when all evil creatures crawled from their hiding places and searched for prey.

Thunk.

Xinh's body went rigid.

Thunk, thunk. A hollow, scraping sound.

Xinh's hand closed around the grenade. Something was moving along the other side of the log.

Thunk.

Her finger found the ring attached to the pin. Sweat was pouring into her eyes, blurring her vision. She blinked away the drops.

With the back of her head resting against the fallen mahogany, she pulled the ring and the pin jerked out. The thumb of her right hand held down the safety handle preventing the fuse from igniting. She took a deep breath and released her thumb.

Hssssss. She watched the fuse burn. She counted two seconds then raised her hand high and gave the bomb a little backward flip over the big hardwood. Xinh closed her eyes tightly and rolled to her side; she shifted the knife to her right hand.

Whoom! The concussion shook the log. Dirt and humus splattered down on top of her.

She raised up and looked over the log, squinting through the choking blue smoke. The Neanderthal lay, torn apart, in a spot cleared by the exploding grenade.

At the same time Xinh came up, her big fish surfaced, an M-16 held in both hands, resting on his hip. He saw her and a ghoulish sneer appeared on his hideously painted face. The acrid smoke drifted over him, and his heavily muscled body glistened with sweat. He stood on a small mound of earth, elevated above the ficus and ferns.

The muzzle of the M-16 lit up and bullets pounded into the log in front of Xinh, ripping splinters out and propelling them high into the air. Through the smoke and flying wood, the Khmer leader saw Xinh's right arm curve behind her head and then quickly snap forward. The heavy blade cut the thick air, flipping end over end, making a whirring sound, before it imbedded itself, with a grisly thud, in his genitals.

"GAAAAAAA!" he shrieked, dropping the rifle and clutching the knife handle with both hands. "GAAAAAAAAA!" His elephantlike bellows were ghastly.

Xinh held her ground, watching him pull at the handle; he screamed like a wild animal. Blood poured through his loincloth. He rocked back and forth, then stumbled forward, eyes flaming coals.

"GAAAAAAAA!" The sepulcher echoed with the Khmer's savage howling.

"How does it feel, dog?" Xinh shouted in Cambodian.

"You filthy swine." He staggered forward on wooden legs. One arm came up groping for her. The knife was buried to the hilt. His left hand tugged at it.

Xinh hadn't moved an inch. "Does it feel good, you offal-eating hyena?"

The whites of his eyes were blood red, his face purple with rage. Rivers of saliva flowed from both corners of his liver lips. She could see the rotted, stained teeth in his wide open mouth.

"Pig!" Her mouth was screwed up in hate.

The Khmer had both hands in the air now, arms extended in a last effort to avenge himself. He was only a few feet from her, the knife protruding grotesquely from his blood-soaked crotch.

And still she didn't move. She spit full in his face. "Your mother was a whoring jackal!"

He pitched forward like a pole, his eyes rolled back in his head, mucous poured from both nostrils. He hit hard on the log, his skull making the sound of a gourd hammered against a wall.

Xinh stared down at his crumpled body. Ticks covered his back and a large leech was stuck to the nape of his thick neck. His black, matted hair was so thick with fleas that they were jumping off his deformed, lopsided head.

A bitter taste rose in the back of her throat and she turned away in revulsion, leaving him to the carrion eaters.

Xinh untied her hair and let it cascade down her back. She threw back her head and screamed a long and wild war cry.

Steve raised up expecting to see a Sioux brave in full battle feathers. Instead he saw Xinh standing on the log, her arms raised to the sky. "Are you all right?" he yelled.

She picked up the Khmer's M-16 and emptied it into the air, shouting at the top of her voice. The echoes came back and roared around her. She threw the rifle down and strode through the foliage, back straight and arms held in the air, her face transfigured.

"No more Khmer." She smiled victoriously at Steve.

"Get me my crutch and we'll get out of here."

She shook her head.

"I can travel."

She was still shaking her head.

"We can't stay here."

"We stay." She brought him his crutch and helped him to camp.

"There could be more of those guys."

"No more," she said, pushing him into the hammock.

"I wouldn't be too sure of that."

She gave him a tired look. "I sure."

He winced while she unbandaged his leg and removed the splints. "No good. We stay here."

"How long?"

"Two—three days."

His head fell back. "Oh, Xinh, is this ever going to end?"

"We make. No worry, *cuong oi*, we make."

"We make," he said, smiling. He took her hand in his. "You did it again, honey. I don't know how you do it. You seem to lead a charmed life."

She had the medical bag open and was building a fire to boil water.

"You know, Xinh, when this is all over I'm going to see to it that you take it easy the rest of your life. You can't go on like this. I mean it."

She stopped looking through the medical bag and stood up. Her exhausted eyes became distant. "How you do that? My life never be peaceful. I never have rest. VC want kill me. Americans want kill me.

Khmer want kill me. Xinh never find rest."

"You'll find rest."

"No, not Xinh." She went back to the medical bag.

"Yes you will, if you'll be my wife."

Her arm froze halfway inside the bag. She was as stiff as stone. She had never in her life expected to hear those words. She had always believed that her life would be over when she got Steve back to the Americans. She would never see him again.

"Xinh, did you hear me?"

She kept her back to him so he wouldn't see the tears.

"You'll find peace. I want you to be my wife. I can't let you go, honey. You mean too much to me. We've been through too much together."

"You make joke."

"Never been more serious in my life. Come here."

She turned around. He saw the tears. "My leg doesn't even hurt so much anymore."

She smiled. It was the first time he had ever seen her look shy. She was wringing her hands together.

"I love you with all my heart, *cuong oi*." Her eyes were on the ground.

This was another woman. Gone was the fierceness in her eyes. Gone was the quick, nervous manner. Gone was the jungle cat prowling the game trails. Standing before him was a sweet, innocent Asian girl betwixt childhood and adulthood, insecure, dependent, and craving love. His heart reached out to her.

"You no make joke, please."

"No, no joke."

She sighed deeply and looked up into the forest canopy. The tears ran down her cheeks in long, curly rivulets.

Steve held his hand out for hers. She gave it to him. He kissed her fingertips.

"I very happy," she whispered.

"We make, huh, kid?"

"We make."

He pulled her close to him and the two dirty, bloodied, tired warriors embraced. She smoothed his hair back and pressed her lips to his eyes, his cheeks, his lips; her salty sweat and tears mingled with her sweet kisses.

He looked into Xinh's long, beautiful eyes, and his bones went soft. "I feel so good, Xinh."

Her hands explored his body and he quivered. She lowered the hammock, slowly, one end at a time and stripped him naked. She stepped out of her torn clothes and let them fall in a heap, revealing her perfectly sculptured, lithe, golden body. Gently, she lay herself down on Steve and made heavenly love to him while the smell of cordite, swamp gas, and rotting leaves swirled around her.

Chapter Twenty-eight

Whap! Steve slapped a mosquito. "These things are as big as airplanes."

"Plenty big, plenty hungry." She tied the splint securely and nodded to him that it was tight enough.

"You do good work," he grinned.

She stood and looked around at the fading light. "Be dark soon. Must find new camp. We look close by."

"You wanted to stay here." His head tilted up at her, a hint of irritation in his eyes. He was in no mood to move.

"No like, too wet. Xinh like high ground. Feel safer, more better for you. We find good camp, rest two—three days; rest leg."

They broke camp and struggled together up the mountain, Steve leaning on Xinh and the crutch. They stopped frequently to rest, then pushed on, Xinh's eyes probing the trees and looking for a dry, defensible campsite.

"We'd better find something soon, we don't have much light left." He pressed forward, leaning heavily on Xinh and the crutch.

Suddenly Xinh stopped.

"What is it?" He followed her eyes.

She pointed to a strange grouping of mounds and rocks rising out of the jungle growth. She changed direction and they limped toward the shadow-covered mystery.

"What in the world is it?" Steve murmured.

As they got closer it was evident that there was an order to the rocks and mounds. They merged together and began to resemble a very large stone structure overgrown with vegetation. An aura, vague and undefined, was drawing them closer.

It soon became apparent that what they were looking at was much larger and more important than what they'd first thought. The obscure stones now became large fitted blocks, joined together and stretching for hundreds of feet in length to form a wall. Rising behind the wall were the ruins of mysterious ornate temples.

"Well, I'll be . . ." Steve leaned on Xinh, mouth agape.

"Kampuchea king live here long time ago." Xinh's voice was filled with awe. "Good camp. Plenty food." She pointed to the heavily laden stalks of bananas hanging from the trees.

She reached up and picked an orange-red mango, and cut it open. Slicing a piece of the yellow meat, she motioned for Steve to open his mouth. He gulped the sweet fruit down.

Xinh pointed the knife at a section of wall that had crumbled and they cautiously stepped through eight hundred years of forgotten time.

"It's like disturbing the dead. Doesn't seem right."

Steve was troubled.

Xinh, however. was unconcerned. "Good protection. Very good camp."

"It's spooky. I don't like it." He could hear dreadful music playing around in his head, warning him away. He reluctantly followed her through the overgrown courtyard to an immense stone temple crawling with thick vines.

Xinh took hold of one of the vines and pulled herself up to the entrance, ledge by ledge. Without looking back at him she unslung the rifle and entered the dark maw of the ancient shrine.

Steve's brow furrowed. He didn't like this at all. Something sinister was grabbing hold of him and he wanted to tear Xinh and himself away from this place. A heavy foreboding atmosphere hung over the decaying stones.

All at once a racket arose inside the temple and a band of angry monkeys sprang from the entrance. They leaped into the trees and scrambled to the tops, screeching and howling their indignation. A minute later Xinh reappeared in the entrance, kicking the last monkey out.

She waved down at Steve. "Belong us now."

"What's it like inside?"

"Strong home. We can stay many days. Many years. Very good home."

"Many years! Don't get any crazy ideas, Xinh."

She grasped a vine and edged down the face sideways until she reached the bottom. She was excited. "Nobody know this place. We first people since Kampuchea king. Make good hideout. We can live jungle long, long time. Be very happy here—

never go back to war." Her eyes danced at him.

"Be serious, kid, I can't live out here. Maybe you can, but me? Forget it."

The sparkle in her eyes died. "Yes, you right." She brushed her hair back. "I think like child sometimes."

The idea fascinated him though. He and Xinh living in an eight-hundred-year-old temple, becoming self-sufficient in the jungle, escapees from the twentieth century, trading the bonds of civilization for the freedom of the wilderness. Why not? It was crazy.

Slowly, ledge by ledge, she helped him up the face of the temple.

"There were steps up here at one time," he said. "They crumbled away, like much of the rest of it."

They rested at the entrance. He turned and looked out over the forest canopy. She turned with him, arm holding tightly to his waist to support him.

"Sky. We're high enough to see the sky." He pointed to the magenta sunset. Below, the jungle had already sunk into darkness.

She led him inside the sanctuary. The light was very dim and it smelled of the grave. It gave him a creepy feeling. Broken pottery was scattered on the stone floor. Idols and animal figures carved from stone were still perched on altars just as they'd been left centuries ago. The rooms were cool, a relief from the baking heat outside.

"An archeologist would go bananas in here. What a find. I wonder what happened to the tenants?"

The musty odor of centuries of neglect hung permanently in the air, and the walls were covered with a slippery blue-green mold that had grown here since the last king had been laid in the vaults under the floor. The sarcophagus smells were heady, driving Steve back to the entrance.

"I feel like I've been buried in a stone coffin. I don't like it. I've got a bad feeling that something ugly is going to happen."

She kissed him. "No worry. We stay short time."

Xinh made a thick bed of leaves for the two of them. She built a fire on the broad step outside the entrance and boiled water in one of the large unbroken clay pots. She bathed Steve clean and doctored his leg and other wounds while he lay stretched out on the bed of leaves.

"This is all so weird, Xinh."

She gave him a curious look that invited him to continue.

"I expect to wake any moment from this strange dream and find myself lying on clean sheets in a soft bed in a curtained bedroom with Fords and Buicks rolling by on the streets outside and children playing on the front lawn." He scratched the fleas crawling through his scalp. "Somehow this pre-Columbian temple, the boiling jungle, and falling in love with a Vietcong chieftain doesn't exactly fit the scenario I had planned for myself."

She smiled to herself and slowly stripped the clothes from her body. "Maybe you wake and no find Xinh there in clean bedroom. What you think?" She dipped a shard of broken pottery into the pot and poured water over her firm, pointed breasts.

His mouth went slack and he inhaled deeply, watching the rivers of water slide over her naked body. "I wouldn't . . . like that."

"You want keep Xinh forever?" She looked at him coyly, her smooth skin glistening in the final rays of daylight shining through the jungle canopy.

"Yeah, that's right." He could barely get the words out. His mouth was as dry as cotton, his tongue thick in his mouth.

She closed her sloe eyes and tilted her head back, letting more water slide down her breasts and flat belly to end in long streams dripping between her legs. "You like Xinh?"

His eyes glazed over. He forgot the pain in his leg, the pain in his body. The narcotic effect of Xinh's sensuous hips rushed through his bloodstream in great spasms of passion. "I like," he mumbled under his breath.

She bent over and dipped another shardful of water, pouring it over her perfectly shaped legs, turning them into two shimmering bronze pieces of art. He wanted to reach for them, but remained transfixed on his mattress of soft leaves.

Her hair fell forward, billowing into a black silky cloud that wrapped around her trim ankles. She wet her hands and slowly massaged her calves. Wetting her hands again, she moved them up to her thighs, caressing them with the cool spring water.

By now, Steve was burning with desire for this girl.

"You want Xinh now?" Her eyes were feverish with desire.

He choked, unable to speak.

"You lay still. I do." She knelt beside him on the leaves and slowly dripped the cool spring water over him.

344

"Mmmmmmm," he sighed.

She placed his hands on her sensitive parts and moved them for him. He watched the skin of her face pull back tightly, and in her baby-smooth voice she said, "Love me, *cuong oi*. Love me, please love me." Her eyes were closed and her face glowed with a peculiar sweetness. Her pointed breasts were stretched taut and her pelvis undulated in great convulsions of pleasure. "I am yours forever, *cuong oi*. Forever . . . forever . . . forever," she repeated over and over, great waves of ecstasy washing over her.

"Xinh . . ."

"Shhhh, Steve. No talk."

"Yes, Xinh, yes."

"No more talk. We love."

She let herself down on him, gently, sweetly, and with such immense feeling that his breath left him.

"Oh, Xinh."

Great tears of joy flooded her face and she cried out, "Steve . . . Steve . . . *em yeu anh nhieu lam*!" Steve . . . Steve . . . I love you so much!

The last beam of light snapped off in the temple and darkness closed in around the two lovers. Xinh made gentle love to Steve through the eight-hundred-year-old night while panthers screamed in the aboriginal forest, tigers prowled the temple grounds, and black-faced monkeys slept in their tree lofts. The lamenting sighs of young Kampuchean princesses seeped from the musty walls to mingle with Xinh's moans of love. The gray, cold stones woke from their long sleep and the old mortar cracked as the currents of her passion touched them.

Xinh gave herself unselfishly and uncondition-

345

ally. Her great need to give love purged the hate in her young life, washing away the killing and pain, and replacing it with the childlike joy of discovering new hope. For this hope she was eternally grateful to Steve and eager to show her appreciation; for by nurturing and caring for him she was experiencing a revival in her pinched soul.

A swarthy tigress lay with her mate in the courtyard, licking his coat. The big male flinched impatiently and moved a few feet away from her, satiated with her lovemaking. Her yellow eyes, dilated in the pitch-black night, looked at him longingly, and a deep, resonant purr rolled from her throat.

The tigress came to him again and, in her heat, bit his ear, snarling her desire and pawing his stiff whiskers. The imperial Bengali snapped irritably, grunted twice, and mounted her. They made violent love and her stentorian roaring announced her great pleasure to the night. The padding on the game trails stopped; the jungle listened and smiled.

"Talk to me."

"Mmmmmm." Xinh soothed Steve's face with her fingers.

"I want to talk."

"Talk." She worked the tips of her fingers under his eyes and brought them around over his eyebrows, stretching the skin.

"That feels good."

"Yes," she said, scratching his beard playfully.

"My leg feels better, a lot better."

"No hurt?"

"It still hurts, but not as much. I can live with it

until we get back."

"We rest. You get strong. Then we go. Xinh take care you forever."

She kissed his healing lips.

"This mattress of leaves is so comfortable. I may never get up."

"I choose big, soft leaves. Make very good sleep." She was bubbling with love.

They chatted together for a long time. She rested her head on the hollow of his shoulder, and her freshly washed hair lay in a spray over his chest. All of a sudden she stopped talking.

"Xinh; what's the matter?"

She didn't answer.

"Is there something wrong, honey?"

"I thinking."

"Oh, you had me worried for a minute. I thought we might have company again."

He turned his head to the temple entrance. Stars dotted the sky behind the tangle of vines hanging over the stone opening. The leaves on the vines began to wave on their petioles and a cooling breeze came out of nowhere, rushing into the temple and refreshing the stale air.

Xinh quietly sighed. "What your God like?" she said without warning.

Steve was surprised. He looked queerly at her in the dark, puzzled by the change in her conversation.

"Remember prayer you teach me?"

"The Lord's Prayer."

"Prayer say God forgive."

"God does forgive."

"Your God forgive Xinh for much killing she do?"

She raised her head from his shoulder."

"If you ask Him."

"Prayer say God take us away from evil." She was sitting up now. Her face and upper body were silhouetted in the temple entrance. "He take me away from killing and war I ask Him?"

"He will. He will forgive your trespasses and deliver you from evil, just like the prayer promises."

"Your God very good. I like Him." She laid her head back down on his shoulder, and began reciting the Lord's Prayer:

> Lay Cha chung toi o tren troi;
> Danh Cha duoc thanh;
> Nuoc Cha duoc den;
> Y Cha duoc nen, o dat nhu troi!
> Xin cho chung toi hom nay do
> an du ngay;
> Xin cho de chung toi bi cam-do
> ma cuu chung toi khoi deu ac!
> Vi nuoc, quyen, vinh-hien deu
> thuoc ve Cha doi doi. A-men.

Her words trailed off to the stars and she fell asleep holding tightly to his hand.

"Move out! Sergeant Jesse Racer kicked his thump gunner in the boot. "Wake up, Brown. Get your weapon out front with Snake. Move it!"

"Yeah, yeah." Brown put his flak jacket on and rubbed his hollow eyes.

"And leave your flak jacket on." Racer threw

Brown his helmet. "Your pot too."

"Yeah, yeah."

Sergeant Racer, his beer gut bouncing under the loose flak jacket, stomped through the foliage, getting his squad on its feet. "O.K., hump it you guys. The blocking force is already in position and the fish are in the trap." He kicked a rifleman to his feet. "The Charlies should be feeling the squeeze. Stay alert—they're going to start popping up everywhere."

"You've been saying that for days."

"What did you say, Brown?" Racer turned on the thump gunner.

"Nothing, Sarge."

"Don't give me any lip." Racer ran a rough hand through his fire-red hair.

Brown, a short stumpy kid with a wandering left eye, found Snake. "Hey, Snake, are we in Cambodia yet?" He took a leak out in the open and zipped up his fly. Some of the dribble got on his leg.

"We've been in Cambodia for two days, Brown."

Brown wasn't too smart.

"What are we doing in Cambodia, Snake?"

Snake, tall and skinny, hitched up his web gear and unslung the M-16 from his shoulder. "Are you working the point with me?"

"That's what Jesse said."

"What's he doing putting a thump gunner on point?"

"I don't know. Maybe he figures you're going to run into lots of Charlies and need 'Old Girl' here." He patted the gun. "Think we're going to get some Charlies, Snake?"

"I hope you use that gun better'n you did back at Loc No." Snake's beady little eyes became pinpoints.

"That weren't my fault."

"Nearly killed me."

"Couldn't be helped." Brown stuck his tongue through a broken front tooth.

Racer waved them out and the squad moved forward lethargically, up the mountainous corridor into the deep-forested jungles of Cambodia.

Sergeant Jesse Racer's men were nervous. Three days before they had been badly mauled by ambushing Vietcong. They had watched many of their buddies die, and they were out for revenge. Trigger fingers were tight and eyes sharp. They moved slowly, quietly, cautiously.

Intelligence had confirmed the presence of a large combined force of North Vietnamese and Vietcong trapped between second battalion's hammer and anvil. Racer's squad was part of the hammer maneuver, the lead element pressing the enemy into the anvil. Major Stinger's blocking force, the anvil, was composed of two companies of infantry waiting to squash the Charlies.

What the Americans didn't know was that the enemy had not continued up the corridor as G-2 had predicted, but had pivoted ninety degrees and swung north, slipping through Major Stinger's net. They were, at this moment, escaping along the Tra Oc.

Snake and Brown were edgy. They imagined a VC behind every bush.

"We haven't seen a slope-head in three days," Snake said.

"They're in here, Snake. I can smell 'em."

"Yeah, that's what I keep hearing from Racer: they're in here—expect them anytime now. Well, I'd like to see just one." His finger tightened inside the trigger guard. "Man it's hot." He looked back. The squad was fanned out behind.

Sergeant Racer called a halt, but word didn't reach Snake and Brown. The rifleman and his thump gunner pushed through the rain forest, intent on their search-and-destroy mission and unaware that the squad had stopped.

Racer picked up the radio and called Lieutenant Betch.

"Zulu-five . . . Hang-fire. Zulu-five this is Hang-fire."

"Hang-fire, Zulu-five."

"Lieutenant, we haven't seen anything for hours. Nothing moving out here."

"They're in there, Racer. They could be all around us for all we know. G-2 says they're here."

"What the hell does G-2 know."

"What's that, Sergeant?"

"Nothing, Lieutenant."

"Keep moving."

"The men are getting freaky with the heat and suspense, sir."

Keep moving, Racer. Before this is over you're going to be in the biggest fight of your career. Zulu-five out."

"*Dinky dau.* This whole operation is crazy." He looked blankly at the radio. "We haven't seen as much as a bug for three days," he mumbled, taking his helmet off and mopping his brow. "*Dinky dau.*"

Meanwhile, Snake and Brown pressed ahead

thinking that the squad was right behind.

"We're going to get some, Brownie."

"Right on, Snake."

"Tired?"

"Naw."

"Can you smell 'em yet, Brownie?"

Brown sniffed the air with his big nose. "I think so." He sniffed again. "I could smell 'coons back home."

"What do they smell like?" Snake shifted the M-16.

"Fish."

They pushed on. Cambodia had become their own private war. Snake picked his nose. Another hour passed.

"What are you stopping for?"

Snake turned around and looked back over their trail. "Where's the rest of the squad?" He'd forgotten Racer in his excitement to find the Charlies.

"Right behind us—I think."

"I don't hear them," Snake said, looking worried.

"You're not supposed to hear them. Racer said to keep it real quiet."

"I don't like it. We can get cut off real easy."

"They're behind us about fifty yards, I tell ya, just like they're supposed to be. Come on, Snake, move out. I want to get some Charlies." He patted the thump gun.

They struggled another two hundred yards through the undergrowth, their eyes quick in the diffused light.

Snake suddenly stopped.

"What now?" Brown was soaked through with sweat.

"Look at that!"

"What?"

"It's a wall," Snake said.

"What's a wall doing out here?"

"I dunno. Let's find out."

They crept closer, weapons ready.

"This bugger's old." Snake felt the stones with his fingers. "Come on, Brownie, let's see what's behind it."

They found the break in the wall and stepped through.

"Jeez, man, will ya look at that?" Brown whispered.

Snake was mesmerized by the ancient city. "Like wow, man." He took off his helmet and wiped the sweat from his red face. His eyes wide, he took in the crumbling ruins hidden behind the invading jungle.

Brown licked his thin lips. "Hey, Snake, think there's any gold in this place? You know, like hidden treasure."

"There's got to be—plenty of it." His eyes glazed over.

"We'll be rich."

"Yeah, rich, man, rich." Snake's jaw went slack and he had a faraway look in his eyes.

"Rubies, diamonds . . ."

Tall Snake reached down and shook Brown by the front of his fatigue shirt until his teeth rattled. "You keep your mouth shut about this."

"Sure, Snake, sure. No need to tell the other guys about it."

"Right." Snake was still shaking Brown whose helmet fell off. "Play our cards right and we're set for life." He released Brown.

"What are we going to do, Snake?"

"We're going to hunt for the gold, that's what we're going to do."

"What about the squad? What about the Charlies?"

"Screw the squad. Screw the Charlies."

"Racer isn't going to like this." Brown was worried.

"Screw Racer too. Come on." Snake led Brown through the square to plunder the royal temples.

Chapter Twenty-nine

Xinh sat at the spring. She washed her face and filled the red clay pot with water. The curious black-faced monkeys looked down at her from the tops of the ruins.

She reached into the waistband of her black pajamas and, removing the jeweled heirloom comb, ran it through her hair with long firm strokes. She hummed quietly, filled with happiness. The dirty war was over for her. She was to be Steve's wife and she would begin a new life in America.

She would miss her grandmother, but maybe she could return to Vietnam from time to time to visit. She would talk to Steve about that. The monkeys began jumping off the ruins and screeching. She looked their way and frowned. Her eyes narrowed, quickly glancing to the 56.

I'm always worried, never a second of relaxation. When I get to America I will never have to worry again. Steve says there is peace in America and we will be happy. She smiled.

Pulling the comb through her hair one last time, she caressed the long silky strands with her fingers and rose. She picked up the water pot and slung the rifle on her shoulder. The monkeys had left the ruins and were climbing into the teak trees.

What could have alerted the monkeys? Suddenly that old feeling of danger rushed through her blood and all her senses were activated. She jerked around and saw Snake and Brown crossing the courtyard at the same time they saw her. The water pot dropped from her hands and smashed on the ground.

"A Charlie! A friggin' Charlie!" Snake's M-16 was already coming to his shoulder.

"It's a broad! Get her, Snake; burn the Charlie broad."

Bam-bam-bam-bam-bam-bam. The puffs of dirt chased Xinh across the square as she raced for the temple.

"You're too low. Raise it up."

"Shut up!"

Bam-bam-bam-bam.

"You're behind her. Give her some lead."

"Shut up, Brownie, or so help me I'll burn one through your eyes!"

Xinh dropped behind a pile of decomposing stones. She cursed under her breath, pulled the sights down onto Snake and held the trigger down. The secure feeling of the 56's hard stock shivering against her cheek calmed her down, and she became coolly calculating.

The ground around Snake and Brown exploded with a long burst of fire, driving them behind the decaying sacrificial altar in the center of the courtyard.

"That broad knows how to shoot," Snake panted.

Brown wiped his face with a grimy hand. "How many do you think there are?"

"How am I supposed to know?" Snake's lips tightened. "The place could be crawling with them." He poked his head around the edge of the altar. Another burst forced him back. "Where's Racer?"

"He'll be coming up in a minute."

"He should be here by now with all this racket." He fired some wild shots in Xinh's direction. "Load that thump gun."

"It's loaded. Do you think I'm stupid, Snake?"

"Just do what I tell you. Lob one in on her."

Brown adjusted the sights then quickly looked up at the temple. "Hey, Snake—look! There's another Charlie." He was pointing to the top of the temple.

Steve was standing in the temple entrance, leaning on his good leg. Holding to the temple stones for support, he waved his arms and yelled. But he was too far away for Snake and Brown to hear him or to see that he was an American. Vines and foliage obscured their view of him.

"Thump him, Brownie."

Brown crawled around to the other end of the wide stone altar to get a better shot through the trees. He aimed carefully and pulled the trigger.

"Get some, thump."

The gun barked and the shell crashed through the trees, missed an overhanging limb, and exploded below the entrance. Steve was knocked back into the temple.

"Get him?"

Brown rolled over on his back and reloaded. "Don't know."

"He's not standing there anymore. Thump him again to make sure."

"Get some, thump." Brown patted the gun and fired.

The shell went wide left and exploded into the wall next to the entrance.

"Can't you shoot any better than that, you hillbilly?"

Xinh suddenly bolted from the rock pile, taking the Americans by surprise. She zigzagged her way to the bottom of the temple, Snake's bullets ripping the air around her.

Heart pounding and lungs bursting, she pulled herself from ledge to ledge. Brown pumped a shell across the courtyard. It arched up and exploded in front of her. The impact threw her back down to the second ledge. Bleeding, she struggled to her feet and started up again.

Firing from the mouth of the temple drove Snake and Brown to the ground. Xinh staggered upward, fell, and crawled to the next ledge.

"That Charlie's back in the fight. You didn't kill him, Brownie." Snake looked toward the wall. "Where's that stupid Racer?" Snake shoved another clip into his M-16.

Steve lay on his belly. "Come on, Xinh, you can make it, honey."

She stopped on another ledge, gasping. She could feel the life draining from her, spilling red on the temple rocks. *I've got to get to him before I die. I've got to reach him, please.*

She crawled on hands and knees. "Steve, Steve."

Snake rose up behind the sacrificial stones. Steve

358

opened up, stitching a line of bullets across the top of the altar. The white lime splattered in the air.

Back down the mountain, Sergeant Racer bent over the radio: "Lieutenant, we've made contact with Charlie. Snake and Brown are in a hell of a fire fight. I can hear a lot of action up ahead."

"What's the enemy's strength?"

"Hard to tell. Could be company strength. It's what we've been waiting for."

"Get up there and give those guys a hand. I'm coming up fast with the rest of the platoon. I'll call battalion and maybe we can get some air support."

Jesse Racer stood to his feet, a big smile on his sweaty face. Those boys are going to get me a medal. "All right you guys, let's get up there pronto and get some Charlies. *Move it!*"

Xinh had crawled to the last ledge. She could see Steve in front of her, only a few yards away, hunched over the Kalashnikov, steadily firing. His face was lined with anxiety and his eyes were white hot with fury.

"Damn them! Damn them! Look what they've done to you, Xinh." He crawled down to help her, dragging his splinted leg over the rough stones. "I'll get them for doing this to you, Xinh. I'll kill them with my bare hands." He pounded the stock of the AK into the stones as he pulled himself over them.

"No, no," she cried, choking on her own blood. "Go back. I make it."

Snake laid the M-16 across the altar. His beady eyes danced with excitement. "Rotten Charlie broad!" He brought the post of the front sight to lie on Xinh's neck. He squinted and his index finger slowly squeezed. "Get some, rifle."

BAM! The high velocity slug whined through the air. There was a sickening crunch and Xinh's body jerked. She felt her shoulder disintegrate.

"Bastards! You rotten bastards!" Steve forgot his own wounds and with a superhuman effort picked Xinh up and carried her into the temple.

"That's it! We got 'em now, Brownie. Let's go finish 'em off."

They leaped from behind the altar and sprinted across the courtyard for the temple.

Steve crumpled into an alcove off to the side of the main room. He held Xinh to his beating chest. He pointed the AK at the entrance.

"*Cuong oi,*" she said weakly, raising her blood-smeared hand to her eyes. She looked at her hand, sadly. "I die."

"Oh, Xinh," he grieved. "I'm so sorry." He stroked her hair.

"No be sorry, *cuong oi.*" She motioned for him to bend closer. Her voice was hoarse and very weak. "I go wait for you in your happy place call h . . . h . . ."

"Heaven?"

"Yes, that place. I ask your God forgive me. He do for me. I feel so clean now." Her voice was only a whisper.

Steve was soaked in her blood, his face twisted in grief.

"I wait for you, Steve. I wait for you in h . . . h . . ."

"Heaven."

"I love you forever."

He raised his head to the sky and felt his heart tearing inside his chest.

"I never forget you, Steve. Xinh never forget her *cuong oi*."

"Oh, Xinh, I love you." He kissed her softly.

"When you see tamarind tree, you remember Xinh."

"Yes, honey. I'll remember." He buried his face in her hair.

"I love tamarind tree. Tamarind candy."

She was going. Steve held her closely, fighting the black angel, not willing to let him have her. "Xinh, don't go; not yet."

"The river," she whispered. "I see river, Steve. Thanh there, Duc there. They waving to me. And I see little bamboo boat. It so big now. They want me get in boat, go for ride." Her eyelids fluttered. "I go now, *cuong oi*. I wait for you. I clean now. God, He forgive me."

Snake and Brown reached the last stones and stood, backs flat against the wall, a few feet from the entrance to the temple. Brown tossed Snake a grenade. He pulled the pin.

"Ready?"

Brown nodded. "Yeah."

Snake tossed the grenade inside.

WHOOM! The blast tore through the temple. Smoke filled the air. Snake rushed in, M-16 jutting forward, swinging it back and forth searching for resistance in the thick, acrid vapors.

Snake didn't see where the bullets came from. He just felt them thud into his belly. He dropped the M-16, his tiny eyes suddenly wide, terrified, and he clutched his intestines. The smoke cleared and he saw Steve sitting in the protection of the alcove, holding Xinh to his chest, a smoking rifle across her body. Snake stumbled backward into Brown, turned and tumbled down the face of the temple, bouncing from ledge to ledge.

Brown threw his hands into the air. "*No! No!*" he begged. Steve emptied the clip into him. The heavy impact of the bullets spun him around and he pitched headlong over the edge. Steve could hear his body crashing over the stones.

Xinh lay dead in his arms. He threw the rifle aside and caressed her hair. She looked as though she were only asleep. There was even a smile on her lips. He kissed her for the last time and held her tightly. "Wait for me, Xinh."

Epilogue

Sergeant Racer testified at the investigation that when he found me in the temple it took five men to break my grip on Xinh. I don't remember much about that or about the helicopter med-evac or my recovery in the hospital. Shrapnel from Brown's hump gun is still working its way out of my arms and legs, and I walk with a slight bend in my back from the nerve damage in the tiger cage. The doctors said that Xinh did a marvelous job setting my leg.

I left the Air Force; my wounds were too extensive to ever allow me to return to flying. I bought a small beach ranch in California and became active in politics. Racer dropped by one hot summer to have a cold beer with me. He was passing through on his way to Fort Ord with orders to report as an instructor with the Infantry Training Regiment. He never got his medal.

Sometimes during the hot months when the pungent smell of humus is strong under the oak trees and the air is torpid, I take a walk through Vietnam and the Cambodian rain forest. Once again I see the diffused light filtering through the jungle canopy

and hear the black-faced monkeys screeching in th[e]
teak trees. The temple ruins loom out of the mist an[d]
I'm back with Xinh in those fateful, bittersweet day[s.]

Knowing Xinh brought out a capacity for feelin[g]
in me that I had thought calloused over. Pathos. [I]
suspect I will never be the same. That was many year[s]
ago but the kaleidoscope of emotions she aroused i[n]
me has indelibly marked my life.

I'll never forget Xinh's eyes. Those beautiful lon[g]
eyes, haunting and sensuous, yet during the heat [of]
battle, cold and empty. They could be so disarming[ly]
innocent.

I promised myself that before I returned to th[e]
States I would ask someone to show me a tamarin[d]
tree. But I never did.

Xinh is pronounced "Sin." This was her story.

THE SAIGON COMMANDOS SERIES
by Jonathan Cain

#2: CODE ZERO: SHOTS FIRED   (1329, $2.50)
When a phantom chopper pounces on Sergeant Mark Stryker and his men of the 716th, bloody havoc follows. And the sight of the carnage nearly breaks Stryker's control. He will make the enemy pay; they will face his SAIGON COMMANDOS!

#3: DINKY-DAU DEATH   (1377, $2.50)
When someone puts a price on the head of a First Cavalry captain, Stryker and his men leave the concrete jungle for the real thing to try and stop the assassin. And when the bullets start flying, Stryker will bet his life — on the SAIGON COMMANDOS!

#4: CHERRY-BOY BODY BAG   (1407, $2.50)
Blood flows in the streets of Saigon when Sergeant Mark Stryker's MPs become targets for a deadly sniper. Surrounded by rookies, Stryker must somehow stop a Cong sympathizer from blowing up a commercial airliner — without being blown away by the crazed sniper!

#5: BOONIE-RAT BODY BURNING   (1441, $2.50)
Someone's torching GIs in a hellhole known as Fire Alley and Sergeant Stryker and his MPs are in on the manhunt. To top it all off, Stryker's got to keep the lid on the hustlers, deserters, and Cong sympathizers who make his beat the toughest in the world!

#6: DI DI MAU OR DIE   (1493, $2.50)
The slaughter of a U.S. payroll convoy means it's up to Sergeant Stryker and his men to take on the Vietnamese mercenaries the only way they know how: with no mercy and with M-16s on full automatic!

#7: SAC MAU, VICTOR CHARLIE   (1574, $2.50)
Stryker's war cops, ordered to provide security for a movie being shot on location in Saigon, are suddenly out in the open and easy targets. From that moment on it's Lights! Camera! Bloodshed!

Available wherever paperbacks are sold, or order direct from the Publisher. Send cover price plus 50¢ per copy for mailing and handling to Zebra Books, Dept. 1591, 475 Park Avenue South, New York, N.Y. 10016. DO NOT SEND CASH.

ASHES
by William W. Johnstone

OUT OF THE ASHES   (1137, $3.50)
Ben Raines hadn't looked forward to the War, but he knew
it was coming. After the balloons went up, Ben was one of
the survivors, fighting his way across the country, searching for his family, and leading a band of new pioneers attempting to bring America OUT OF THE ASHES.

FIRE IN THE ASHES   (1310, $3.50)
It's 1999 and the world as we know it no longer exists. Ben
Raines, leader of the Resistance, must regroup his rebels
and prep them for bloody guerilla war. But are they ready
to face an even fiercer foe—the human mutants threatening to overpower the world!

ANARCHY IN THE ASHES   (1387, $3.50)
Out of the smoldering nuclear wreckage of World War III,
Ben Raines has emerged as the strong leader the Resistance
needs. When Sam Hartline, the mercenary, joins forces
with an invading army of Russians, Ben and his people
raise a bloody banner of defiance to defend earth's last
bastion of freedom.

BLOOD IN THE ASHES   (1537, $3.50)
As Raines and his ragged band of followers search for land
that has escaped radiation, the insidious group known as
The Ninth Order rises up to destroy them. In a savage battle to the death, it is the fate of America itself that hangs in
the balance!

*Available wherever paperbacks are sold, or order direct from the
Publisher. Send cover price plus 50¢ per copy for mailing and
handling to Zebra Books, Dept. 1591, 475 Park Avenue South,
New York, N.Y. 10016. DO NOT SEND CASH.*

THE BEST IN ADVENTURE FROM ZEBRA

WAR DOGS (1474, $3.50)
by Nik-Uhernik

Lt. Justin Ross molded his men into a fearsome fighting unit, but it was their own instincts that kept them out of body bags. Their secret orders would change the destiny of the Vietnam War, and it didn't matter that an entire army stood between them and their objective!

WAR DOGS #2: M-16 JURY (1539, $2.75)
by Nik-Uhernik

The War Dogs, the most cutthroat band of Vietnam warriors ever, face their greatest test yet—from an unlikely source. The traitorous actions of a famous American could lead to the death of thousands of GIs—and the shattering end of the . . . WAR DOGS.

GUNSHIPS #1: THE KILLING ZONE (1130, $2.50)
by Jack Hamilton Teed

Colonel John Hardin of the U.S. Special Forces knew too much about the dirty side of the Vietnam War—he had to be silenced. And a hand-picked squad of mongrels and misfits were destined to die with him in the rotting swamps of . . . THE KILLING ZONE.

GUNSHIPS #2: FIRE FORCE (1159, $2.50)
by Jack Hamilton Teed

A few G.I.s, driven crazy by the war-torn hell of Vietnam, had banded into brutal killing squads who didn't care whom they shot at. Colonel John Hardin, tapped for the job of wiping out these squads, had to first forge his own command of misfits into a fighting FIRE FORCE!

GUNSHIPS #3: COBRA KILL (1462, $2.50)
by Jack Hamilton Teed

Having taken something from the wreckage of the downed Cobra gunship, the Cong force melted back into the jungle. Colonel John Hardin was going to find out what the Cong had taken—even if it killed him!

Available wherever paperbacks are sold, or order direct from the Publisher. Send cover price plus 50¢ per copy for mailing and handling to Zebra Books, Dept. 1591, 475 Park Avenue South, New York, N.Y. 10016. DO NOT SEND CASH.